"Luke."

Ginny's eyes searched the man's face. "Do not get involved."

"Did I say I would?" Luke asked.

"I know that look."

"Then let me help."

"You've done enough." Balancing on one foot, Ginny unlocked the gate. "Which we need to finish here and now. Thank you for everything you've done. But your nights on the couch are done." She gave him a sweet smile. Wrapped her warm hand around his forearm. "We'll be okay, Luke. I promise." She lifted on the toes of her good foot to kiss his jaw.

And just like that his head moved.

The corners of their mouths brushed.

Years fell away. All the loneliness of the past decade vanished. She was his wife again. His heart. His home…

TWICE HER HUSBAND

MARY J. FORBES

SPECIAL EDITION

Published by Silhouette Books

America's Publisher of Contemporary Romance

For Chloe, sister beyond borders

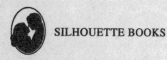

SILHOUETTE BOOKS

ISBN 0-373-24755-9

TWICE HER HUSBAND

Copyright © 2006 by Mary J. Forbes

This edition published by arrangement with Harlequin Books S.A.

® and TM are trademarks of Harlequin Books S.A., used under license. Trademarks indicated with ® are registered in the United States Patent and Trademark Office, the Canadian Trade Marks Office and in other countries.

Visit Silhouette Books at www.eHarlequin.com

Printed in U.S.A.

Books by Mary J. Forbes

Silhouette Special Edition

A Forever Family #1625
A Father, Again #1661
Everything She's Ever Wanted #1702
Twice Her Husband #1755

MARY J. FORBES

grew up on a farm amidst horses, cattle, crisp hay and broad blue skies. As a child, she drew and wrote of her surroundings, and in sixth grade composed her first story about a little lame pony. Years later, she worked as an accountant, then as a reporter-photographer for a small-town newspaper, before attaining an honors degree in education to become a teacher. She has also written and published short fiction stories.

A romantic by nature, Mary loves walking along the ocean shoreline, sitting by the fire on snowy or rainy evenings and two-stepping around the dance floor to a good country song—all with her own real-life hero, of course. Mary would love to hear from her readers at www.maryjforbes.com.

Dear Reader,

I've known Luke since I conceived the "germ" of the Tucker brothers' trilogy. He was always there, hovering in the background, hoping for his day in court, so to speak. And while I understood the reason behind Luke's inner struggle, I had no idea how his story would unfold.

Still, I continued to type something each day, looking to discover the key to the final door that would conclude the trilogy of my beloved Tuckers. Finally, it came to me. Luke and his soul mate, Ginny, needed to face a discord—*side by side*. But what? What would force them to work as a unit?

One day while picking through my junk mail, I saw it: a slip of green paper, a homemade memo announcing the opening of a neighborhood preschool. Staring at that notice, an idea suddenly sprang to the fore like a pop-up on a page.

Would Ginny fulfill her dream? I wasn't sure. But excitement had me hurrying to my computer as images and events leapt to mind. Oh, yes, Luke and Ginny were in for a grand fight. They were about to face down a long-held community myth, but more significantly they needed to find their way through heartache and loss, secrets and forgiveness *together.*

Won't you join me on their healing journey?

Mary J. Forbes

Prologue

She was burying her husband.

Immortalizing him in his beloved Allegheny Mountains of West Virginia, far from where he'd grown up in Oregon. From where he'd known her family but had never known her—until she was divorced and living here in Kanawha County.

Ashes to dust.

Forever goodbye.

Forever goodbye, dear Boone.

God, she wanted to crumple to the ground, bay at the moon, beat her head with stones like the Comanche women of old.

Boone!

Dr. Extraordinaire, saving her when she believed her life done, her soul vanquished. *Oh, Boone. I miss you beyond words.*

Even though they'd lived in the city of Charleston these past eleven years, he'd arranged for her to move back to the Oregon town where they had spent their childhoods—albeit twenty-three years apart. Now the Misty River house would welcome her. So his will conveyed.

"As you know, I've had the house reconstructed." His voice on the TV monitor, so normal. *Alive.* And, he, still able to stand strong and true with a mop of salt-and-pepper hair. *So real.* But not. How had he known it would come to this? How?

"Take our children away from where I no longer am, Ginny. I'll be there. There, with you."

His quirky smile had made her cry all over again.

So. With ten-year-old Alexei at her side, she walked the marshy and remote Lumberjack Trail, sheltered by birch, maple and cherry trees, carrying sixteen-month-old Joselyn on her hip and a tote on her shoulder.

Here and there were the quiet signs of deer: a few bark-chewed willows, a flattened patch of grass. At a junction, she headed up the High Meadows Trail, bound for the sweep of Allegheny Mountain to the west and Mount Porte Canyon to the north where windblown rock cropped from the earth, and shale covered dry southern cliffs.

They'd hiked nearly two miles when the song of the creek drew her into the trees and down a small embankment.

"Careful," she said as Alexei fell in behind her. He carried the precious oak box in his school knapsack. "The underbrush can be tricky."

The creek had been Boone's favorite spot when they'd backpacked and hiked these trails and mountains. Several times they'd lunched here, sharing an hour in quiet conversation. He'd loved the outdoors. Now the children needed to share its peace with their dad this final time before the confusion of relocating took shape.

A few yards from the water they found the spreading maple. Ginny knelt and removed a garden trowel from her tote. Holding out the tool to Alexei, she said, "The earth should be moist. Dig down at least ten inches."

They had arranged their private ceremony at home: Alexei would dig a hole where they would place his father's ashes along with a clump of lilies of the valley, a perennial shade plant that offered sparkling strings of waxy bell flowers to scent the dank creek air. Ginny would collect the stones.

Within a few minutes hole and stones stood ready.

From Alexei's knapsack, she carefully extracted the treasured oak box. Her breath caught when she unlatched the wooden lid. Inside, Boone's ashes nestled in a plastic bag. Mere crumbles of a big man. She bit her lip.

"Da?" Standing between her brother's strong, young arms, little Joselyn pointed as Ginny removed the bag.

"Yes," she said, eyes blurry. "Daddy."

Alexei nuzzled his sister's small cheek. "It's all right, Josie," he murmured. "We're giving Daddy a nice place to stay. He can listen to the water and the birds here, and he'll feel the rain and the sun and see the skies all the time. And when we look up at the stars at night, we'll be able to see him because he told me that's where he'd be when it got too dark. Don't worry."

Joselyn clapped her little hands and stamped her tiny feet on the forest floor. "Gah."

"Oh, Alexei." Ginny brushed a harvest-colored wing of hair from his eyes. "You break my heart with your lovely words."

"I don't mean to, Mama."

With one arm, she hugged the children close. "It's a bittersweet break, honey. The way chocolate sometimes tastes."

"Oh. Okay." Reassured, Alexei smoothed the baby's flyaway curls. "Do you think she understands?"

Ginny opened the ash bag. "Maybe deep in her soul. But we'll tell her again one day."

"I'll tape it for her," Alexei said, and kissed his sister's blond head.

"You're a good and loving brother." *The best son.*

"Even when I don't clean up her toys?"

Ginny smiled. "Let's not push it."

"Hear that, Jo? Mama's backtracking again."

"Ma-ma-ma-mmm!" Out came the finger, pointing at Ginny, who kissed the wet digit, her eyes filling again.

"Let's set in the letters," she said.

Each had written to Boone. Ginny included Joselyn in hers, along with words of grief and love and hope and wishes. *I wish you hadn't died. I wish we could grow old together. I wish I could talk to you, tell you I love you.* Just once more.

Alexei laid his letter in the hole and sprinkled on a bit of dirt. Swiping his nose with the back of his hand, he looked away.

"Oh, sweetheart." Ginny cupped her son's cheek.

"Why did he have to die?"

"You know why, honey."

"Yeah, but why *him?*"

She'd asked the same question endlessly. "Alexei, life is full of fog we don't understand or have control over. The best we can do is face it square on and plow through to the other side."

"Yeah." He sniffed. "I guess."

She kissed his cheek. "Come, let's finish."

Tenderly and together, they held the bag as ashes poured over the letters. Joselyn sat quietly in the crook of Ginny's arm, sucking her thumb. Lastly, they planted the lilies of the valley, then circled the tiny plot with the stones.

She would never come back to this spot. Or to West Virginia.

They were returning to Oregon and her childhood town.

Be at peace, dearest Boone. You'll be in my heart always.

Carrying Joselyn and holding Alexei's hand, Ginny climbed back through the trees, to the trail and her old station wagon.

Chapter One

Misty River, Oregon
Ten days later

In the produce section of Safeway, Luke stared at the woman sizing up a bundle of bananas three bins away.

Ginny?

Blinking, he focused on his ex-wife. It had been over eleven years since he'd seen her last. She had the same profile. Small, straight nose, concave cheeks, dimple in the one facing him. Hair the color of Belize beach sand, though the style looked as if those chin-length curls had frolicked with a breeze.

His heart boxed his ribs. His palms began to sweat. He took a step forward, her name in his throat.

A blond boy sauntered to her side. "Mama, can we make hamburgers in the backyard tonight?"

Adrenaline scooted across Luke's skin as she tousled the kid's hair. "We're having spaghetti with meatballs, remember?"

"Oh, yeah, right. Hey, Miss Jo." The kid pulled a miniature thumb from the mouth of the baby sitting in the cart's basket. "You want rabbit teeth?" Before Miss Jo could whimper, the boy screwed up his face and started gnawing on her neck. "Rawrrr-rawrrr-rawrrr."

The little girl giggled, a sound light as a musical scale. "Ep-say, no." She grabbed his hair and pulled.

"Ow."

"Don't get her started," Ginny warned the boy as she set the bananas in the cart and moved to the oranges.

Luke backed away. He was an outsider, looking in on her family—on a life he'd shunned. Bumping into another shopper, he muttered, "Excuse me," and hurried from the produce section. Near the electronic doors, he dropped his basket on a rack.

She had a family. *A husband.*

What was she doing in Misty River?

They had to be on vacation. It was almost May, after all. Some families took their vacations early, before school finished. They were simply stopping for a few groceries. Probably had a big Winnebago parked around the corner. Husband was likely reading the paper while she shopped with the kids.

Why that bothered Luke, he couldn't determine. Virginia Ellen Keegan hadn't been his wife in damn near a dozen years.

But she could've been.

The thought zapped in. Quick, sharp, leaving a ragged tear.

He strode to his silver Mustang convertible parked on a side street. He couldn't get inside the vehicle fast enough—and when he did, he simply sat staring through the windshield.

Ginny.

Shutting his eyes, he saw her again, heard her voice. A stranger, yet…completely familiar.

He'd never forgotten her.

And if he looked closely, he'd recognize the hole in his heart, where once she had lived and laughed and loved.

At 8:20 Friday morning Ginny pulled in front of Chinook Elementary and turned off the station wagon's ignition.

"What are you gonna talk to Mrs. Chollas about?" Alexei asked, worry between his eyes.

"I want to make sure she understands about dysgraphia, honey. That's all."

"Okay." He stared at three boys chasing a soccer ball. "I don't want her to think I'm special."

"You *are* special, Alexei. The most special boy in the whole world." She leaned over and kissed his hair.

"*Mo-om!* Don't! People might *see.*"

"Oops." She smiled away the tiny prick of hurt; her boy was growing up too fast. "I forgot."

"Okay." He opened the door and hopped down. "Bye."

"Have a good day, ba—" The door slammed. "Baby," she whispered.

"Ep-say." Joselyn squirmed in her car seat behind Ginny. "Ep-say, go."

"That's right, angel. Alexei's going to school." She climbed from the car as her son ran toward the boys chasing the ball. "And we're having a chat with his teacher."

She found Mrs. Chollas waiting for her in the fifth-grade classroom. Immediately Ginny liked the woman's kind eyes and gentle smile.

When they were seated at the teacher's desk—Joselyn on Ginny's lap with a notepad and a crayon supplied by the teacher—Mrs. Chollas said, "Alexei is doing quite well in this first week. He's already made some friends, which really helps ease the transition. He loves math, and is very adept at oral communication in class. But as we discussed on the phone, his writing skills need a great deal of encouragement."

Ginny understood too well. Offering a smile she didn't feel, she said, "Have you ever dealt with dysgraphia, Mrs. Chollas?" Few teachers heard of the word, never mind grasped the tangled process that went on in a child's brain. In Ginny's experience, they recognized the problem, but many passed it on to a colleague specializing in learning disabilities.

The teacher nodded. "In my twenty years of teaching, I've seen almost everything, Mrs. Franklin. Alexei's case isn't entirely unusual. We have a laptop he might want to use—"

"He doesn't want to be labeled," Ginny interrupted. His past teachers had done exactly that by sending him to resource rooms or modifying his workload. Ginny had tried to boost his confidence by saying that holding a pencil differently, *writing* in short backward strokes, was okay. "He prefers to handwrite whenever possible." She looked straight at the teacher. "If you don't mind deciphering what he's written."

Mrs. Chollas smiled. "I'll have Alexei read his material to me if it's too illegible. And I'll work with him after school for a few minutes each day showing him tricks that will make his letters more readable. Would he be willing to do that?"

"Oh," Ginny said. "He will." She hoped. Joselyn on her hip, Ginny stood. "Thank you. For putting both Alexei and me at ease. His other teachers… Well. He hated being singled out."

Mrs. Chollas rose as well. "I understand. Unless it's a dire situation, my students stay with me in my classroom. Why don't we start next Monday, say for fifteen minutes or so after school? Does he catch the bus?"

"I drive him."

"Good. Pick him up at three." She shook Ginny's hand. "I promise you my best, Mrs. Franklin."

Relief washed through Ginny. "Thank you." She offered a small smile. "By the way, would you know of a trustworthy babysitter?"

"Sure. Hallie Tucker. She's wonderful with little ones. Loves babies." The teacher tickled Joselyn under her chin.

"Hallie Tucker?" Ginny watched her baby smile at the older woman.

"She's the police chief's niece. Goes to Misty River High. Want me to write down her number?"

Calling the home of her former brother-in-law and speaking to the child who'd once been her niece had Ginny's belly tailspinning. But she needed a reliable babysitter and Hallie had come with a lofty recommendation.

The delight in the girl's voice at hearing who was calling chased off Ginny's apprehension. Most of all, Hallie met her explanation about Boone's death and the children's needs with adult grace and understanding. Most importantly, Ginny couldn't ignore the love-at-first-sight gazes from her children when the young woman stood on their doorstep a half hour after school.

"Be good," Ginny told Alexei, then kissed Joselyn. Rushing to her green boat of a car—the only vehicle she could find that had cost less than eight hundred dollars—she added, "I should be home by four-thirty, five at the absolute latest."

Her main stop was the grocery store. Everything else could wait until the weekend. Alexei, her all-day grazer, could not.

Forty-five minutes later, the groceries stored in back of her car, she drove down Main Street checking stores she might want to visit in the near future. A small, old-fashioned facade with Waltzin' Paper in quaint, lopsided lettering over the little display window caught her eye.

Why not? she thought, pulling to the curb. Her kitchen cried for wallpaper; she'd give the shop a five-minute boo, then head home.

Boone's chuckle followed her into the store. He'd never been a fan of papering walls. For him nothing compared to the ease and immediacy of paint.

Boone. Today was his birthday. He would have been sixty-three. The more than two decades between them had never been an issue. She'd fallen in love with his kindness. A big gentle man—jogger, kayaker, skier, *daddy*—who loved children and whose eyes misted when her eleven-day-old baby lost the battle against his tiny underdeveloped lungs.

The baby she'd conceived with her first husband, Luke Tucker.

The baby he'd never known existed.

The night Robby had been conceived, she and Luke were in the throes of divorce proceedings. He'd come to the apartment to plead with her, and she'd cried for all their lost hopes. Because Luke had been afraid of failing. In work, in life and, irony of ironies, in his marriage.

And that night, as icing to an already imploding cake, he'd become a father.

Ginny hadn't known of her pregnancy until she'd moved across the country to West Virginia—as far as possible from Luke and the memories they'd made together. For seven months she'd debated telling him about their baby. In the end, eight years of marriage hadn't tempered his ambitions or his fears, and while she understood and absolved all his regrets and excuses, Ginny could not bear hearing them again. Nor could she imagine the guilt her child would shoulder, hearing the reasons for absenteeism or requirement for perfection from a career-driven father.

So she kept her secret—and birthed her son alone.

For almost two agonizing, worrisome weeks, Robby's doctor had been Boone Franklin, the hospital's head pediatrician.

Her solace. Her saving grace.

Today, on Boone's birthday, she would've woken him with a kiss and maybe, if the hour was early enough, unhurried lovemaking. She inhaled long and slow. Sex hadn't happened in a long, long while. Not that she was looking, but someday…when the kids were older, when she had an established income, when there was money in the bank, perhaps then intimacy would be a part of her life again.

The store owner approached. "Anything of interest?"

"These I like." She pointed out bold, yellow sunflowers.

"I have more catalogs in back," the woman offered. "The patterns are last year's, but they include classic sunflower designs that never go out of style."

"Thank you, maybe I'll have a peek." She followed the clerk into a back room which held shelving, a couch and a coffee table.

Fifteen minutes later, she made her purchase. An archetypal country-kitchen border of sunflowers, which she'd hang below the crown molding above her refrigerator, stove and eating area. The walls beneath she'd paint in spring-green.

She wanted her kitchen welcoming and wholesome. The way it had been in West Virginia with Boone. He had loved green. A healing color, he'd said. Although it hadn't healed him.

Outside on the sidewalk, she blinked against the late-afternoon sun and hefted the roll of wallpaper under her arm.

At the big, sprawling homestead house, a mile and a half from where Ginny stood, Hallie would be tossing a garden salad for her and smearing grape jelly over bread for Alexei and Joselyn. Time to get in her clunker station wagon across the street, go home where her children waited—and where her loneliness for Boone wafted from the corners.

From between two pickups, she dashed across the street.

A sound like raptors escaping *Jurassic Park* screeched in her ears. She glimpsed a sleek silver nose.

Not raptors. A car!

The wallpaper roll lurched from her arms as if alive. Her body flung of its own volition through the air, banging onto the pavement. Pain clawed up her spine, shot through her skull.

The last thing she saw was the snarling tread of a tire.

Ginny! Oh, God, Ginny!

Luke leaped from his Mustang and rushed to kneel beside the woman lying on the street inches from his front tire. He hadn't realized he'd shouted until two men materialized at his side.

"Call 911! Oh, jeez. *Ginny!* I didn't see you. *I didn't see you!*"

Her right leg angled crookedly from her thigh. Her eyes were open, sightless. Crouching down, he pressed a finger to her neck, seeking a pulse. *Please.*

There. Faint, rapid under the softness of her skin.

Luke curled her hair behind the delicate shell of her ear, ran a shaky finger down her smooth cheek. *Please be okay. Let her be okay.* Words tumbling into prayer. *Oh, God. Hurry!*

If he hadn't been cruising town looking for her car, she wouldn't be on the pavement. If he hadn't been so anxious to see her again after those moments in Safeway five days ago, she would be okay. If he'd gone home after work, let bygones be bygones… If, if, if.

A small crowd gathered.

"Is she okay?" someone asked.

"What happened?"

"Did she jaywalk?"

"Who is she?"

My wife, Luke wanted to shout. *Get help! She needs a doctor!*

A woman spoke. "That's Ginny Franklin. She was just in my store, buying wallpaper."

"Franklin?" a man said. "Any relation to Deke?"

"Don't know. But she's been living in the old house at Franklin's mill site for the past week or so."

"She'd better watch out then," a gruff-voiced man said. "Place is spooked."

Another woman piped up. "My Allan redid the roof when they were doing all those renovations this spring. Said two guys wouldn't hire on because of what's happened on that land. Likely why the place's been abandoned forty years."

"Wouldn't catch me out there," a third woman squeaked.

"Me, either," Gruff Guy said.

"Is she dead?" asked Squeaky Voice.

"No," Luke snapped. "Did someone call an ambulance?"

"It's coming, Luke." This from Kat, owner of Kat's Kitchen across the street. The granny-aged woman bent on one knee, opposite him. "I called soon as I saw it happen through the window." Her eyes were kind. "You weren't at fault, honey. She just stepped out from between those two trucks. Poor dear. Must have had something powerful on her mind to not pay attention."

Sirens wailed. The crowd shifted as the ambulance arrived. Three paramedics sprang from the vehicle.

Within minutes, Ginny lay on a gurney. The medics hoisted her inside the van, closed the doors.

A hand clapped Luke's shoulder. It was Jon, his brother and police chief of Misty River.

"She just—just— Jon, it's Ginny." Luke ran trembling fingers through his hair.

For a moment the brothers stared at one another. Jon nodded. "Want me to drive you to the hospital?"

The ambulance had left. The crowd dispersed.

"No." Luke sighed. "I'm okay." He headed for his car. "If you need a statement…"

Jon waved him off. "Later."

Later, when she was well again. *If* she got well again.

Why was an IV hanging from the ceiling? Ginny closed her eyes, then opened them again. A motor. Was she in a camper truck? Beside her sat a man—no, a paramedic. She remembered the car…the silver car…

"Hey," the medic said. "You're awake." He smiled.

"You're going to be fine. Just a little bump, but the doctor needs to check it out at the hospital first." He fiddled with the IV. "Got a bit of saline to stabilize you."

"What happened?" she asked.

"Apparently you stepped in front of a car."

Puzzled, she studied the medical paraphernalia around her. "I wouldn't… Why would I…?"

"What's your name?" he asked.

"Ginny Franklin."

He held up his hand, fingers spread. "How many?"

"Five."

"Now?"

"Two."

"What's the name of your town?"

"Misty River. Look, all my faculties are in place. I just—" She attempted to rise. Pain bloomed behind her eyes.

"Take it easy."

"My head—"

"I know." He checked her pupils with a small light. "We're almost there. Doc's waiting."

"My kids…"

"Where are they?"

"With a sitter. Hallie…"

"I'll call her. Got a number?"

She gave it. The ambulance rolled up to the hospital's emergency doors.

"Really," she said, "I'm fine. Can't I just go home?"

"Not yet, Mrs. Franklin. You might have a broken leg."

Because of her concussion, the doctor wanted to keep her for the evening, possibly overnight. She couldn't afford to stay overnight. At First National, her bank account had dwindled to a mere ten thousand. Boone's first wife had drained his savings with her illness just as Boone's cancer had marked every dollar of his health insurance and most of Ginny's account. In the last months, when he'd known he would not return home, she'd sold the house to pay off the remaining debts and moved into a rental duplex. Ironically Boone had the Oregon house repaired—unbeknownst to her—with a fund they'd saved for Alexei's college.

Their worst—and final—argument.

I want you safe and secure, he'd said.

From what? she'd asked.

From whatever happens.

Premonition? Who knew.

But he hadn't counted on her jaywalking.

Stupid, stupid, stupid.

Tonight her kids could be alone for the first time in their lives, without mother or father. Sure, they'd have Hallie. But they'd just met, and she wasn't mommy. Ginny imagined Joselyn's cries, saw her rosy mouth pucker, the tiny tears.

And Alexei. Would he hide in his bedroom with his music, the way he had while cancer ate Boone's brain?

She studied the cast on her right foot, tractioned and swinging above the bed to keep the blood from pooling the first hours. A nice, clean break, the doctor had told her. How are broken bones nice or clean? Was it the same as having a nice, clean brain tumor? Nice and clean didn't warrant painkillers. Didn't warrant a young boy's horror.

The door to her room opened. A bouquet entered—an immense fireworks-like display of deep gold sunflowers. Then the door closed and a face peered around the ribboned, blue vase.

Her heart jolted. "Luke," she whispered as if she saw a phantom instead of the man who had once been her husband.

"Hey, Ginny. How are you?"

"I'm…" *Amazed.* Her mouth worked without words. "What—what are you doing here?"

"Seeing you." He walked to the window where a high-rolling table stood, and placed his summer bouquet upon it before scooting the table near her bed.

As he moved about, she stared openly. If possible, his shoulders had grown broader under the cloth of his expensive teal shirt, and at his temples silver reeled into his clipped, pecan-brown hair.

Tucking his hands into the pockets of tailored black slacks, he looked down at her with the same somber gray eyes she had fallen in love with at seventeen.

She struggled past the fumble of her brain. "How did you know I was here?" she managed.

He studied her leg. "I live in Misty River. Have a law office just down the street from where you…from where I… Ginny, it was my car."

That had struck her. That *she'd* walked into, mindlessly. They hadn't told her who, and she hadn't asked.

She closed her eyes against the grim lines around his mouth. "I'm sorry."

"No." His warm hand covered her cool one on the light-weight blue blanket. "It was my fault. I should've been paying attention."

A laugh escaped, short and bitter. She slipped her hand free, curling it into the palm of its twin. "Okay, so we agree to disagree. Like always."

"Ginny."

She opened her eyes, studied him while he studied the

casted leg. His Adam's apple worked. His hand found its pocket again.

"Sorry," she whispered. "That wasn't called for. I'm being a shrew."

"You have the right." For the first time his mouth shifted and she caught a half smile before it vanished.

She said, "The doctor figures it'll be healed in six weeks. Only a hairline fracture in the tibia, just above the ankle."

He swallowed. "Only. Right."

"It's not as bad as it looks, Luke." She forced a smile. "I'm not dying."

"Huh." He surveyed the room.

"I'll be released tonight," she said, aspiring toward the positive.

His eyes wove to her. "Who's with your kids?"

He knew she had children? "They're with a sitter. Your niece, actually."

"Hallie?"

"Yes."

Relief loosened his shoulders. "Good kid. You won't find anyone more responsible. I'll check on her. Or... where's your husband? Shouldn't he be here? I asked at the desk, but no one's come to see you. It's like no one knows you in this town."

Her chest hurt at his offhand remark. "We moved here eleven days ago. Hard to make friends when you're uncrating boxes and setting up a home."

Those gray eyes remained sober. "Is there a Mr. Franklin?" he repeated.

She glanced at the flowers, lustrous and cheerful in the window's light. "My husband passed away."

Luke tugged at his thick, short hair. "I'm sorry. I mean… Hell, I don't know what I mean."

"It happened three months ago."

"Sudden?"

"I suppose six months of cancer is sudden by some standards."

His eyes held hers. Seconds ticked away. "I won't say a bunch of banal words for something I don't understand and never experienced. But I will say you and your family have my deepest sympathy. If there's anything I can do…"

"Thank you."

Silence. A food trolley rattled past her door. He said, "Heard you're living on the old Franklin property."

"We are."

"Why?"

Because Boone wanted me there. "Because it's my husband's land—*was* his land."

"I meant why did you come back to Misty River?"

"Boone wanted our kids to know their heritage." At least that was what he'd told her. "Both of us have roots here. Why are *you* here and not in Seattle?" Where rewards had knocked on his office door more than on the door of their marriage.

He stroked a finger along the petals of a sunflower. "I left Seattle after we divorced. Things weren't… Well." He dropped his hand. "They feed you yet?"

"Just the saline and some painkillers."

He turned for the door. "I'll get you something from Kat's Kitchen. She's got the best food in town. Anything in particular?"

Ginny couldn't help but laugh. Luke was still Luke, ready to rudder the barge of discomfort toward happy land.

He'd been an excellent lawyer because of the trait. "Would she have a spinach salad with focaccia bread?"

He gave her a thumbs-up. "Still your favorite lunch, huh?" Then he was gone.

Ginny leaned back against the pillows, her eyes settling on the bouquet. She hadn't thanked him for brightening her room. A dozen years, and still he remembered—remembered her favorite flower, her favorite lunch.

Ah, Luke. What haven't you forgotten?

Recalling the expression on his face when he first walked into the room, she was afraid to contemplate the answer.

Chapter Two

Luke pulled Ginny's rattling old station wagon off Franklin Road onto a single-track dirt lane that wound through a thicket of birch and Douglas fir. The track was worn smooth from the crews he'd seen coming and going throughout the spring.

"I suppose six months of cancer is sudden by some standards." No doubt the diagnosis prompted Boone Franklin to renovate his parents' homestead. The work had begun four months ago, in January.

He'd heard a family named Franklin was reopening the sprawling house and wondered which of the far-flung kin decided to return. He never would have guessed Ginny.

Breaking through the trees, he saw the aged house—or what used to be an aged house. Now it sported vinyl siding that sparkled like snow in sunshine. He noted other changes: windows, fascia and door painted in burgundy; a new cedar-shake roof; the reconstructed surrounding porch.

Only a coat of paint was required on the replaced pillar posts and railings. Were the tins of mint-green paint in back of her station wagon meant for the job?

Luke swung in front of the porch steps and stopped beside his youngest brother's '92 blue Honda hatchback. Hard to believe Seth's daughter, Hallie, was old enough to drive.

Hands gripping the wheel, he stared at the house. Now what?

You're here for Ginny's kids.

Because you owe her.

And he'd promised to help Hallie with them, which meant meals, baths, story time—everything that set worry in Ginny's eyes. It meant *him* helping with the jobs she'd outlined. It meant staying the night if she wasn't released.

It meant acting like a parent.

Sweat streamed from his pores.

God, why had he volunteered? Why hadn't he told her he'd hire a dependable woman to replace Hallie when his niece went home for the night? He wasn't cut out to play nursemaid or daddy or babysitter, or whatever else looking after kids entailed. Hell, Ginny divorced him for the very reason he now sat in front of her home. Well, not exactly for that reason, but close.

The bottom line was he hadn't wanted kids. And she was the mothering kind.

The door of the house opened. A boy stood gawking at him. Her son. What was his name? Allan? Alex? Yeah, like Alex, but more…Russian. Wasn't there a hockey player with the name? Alexei. Yeah, that was it. Except she'd pronounced it Ah-lek-say.

Luke stepped from the car. He raised a hand in greeting. "Hey, Alexei."

The kid walked to the top of the steps. A big-pawed, black Lab-cross pup bounded through the door and plopped beside him. "Who're you? Why are you driving my mom's car?"

Because the thought of driving the Mustang right after it had crashed into Ginny sat like a dirty stone in Luke's gut. "Your mom asked me to bring home her groceries and to talk with you— Hey, Hallie."

Luke's sixteen-year-old niece came through the door, carrying the same curly-haired toddler he'd seen in Ginny's cart at Safeway last Saturday. "Hi, Uncle Luke. How's Ginny?"

He came around the hood of the car. "Doing pretty good. She'll be home in a few hours." If she convinced the doctor.

"Why can't she come home now?" Alexei grumbled.

"Well, she's—"

Hallie set a hand on the boy's shoulder. "We talked about that, buddy," she said easily. "Your mom had a little bump on the head and the doctor wants to make sure she's okay."

"She will be, right?" Alexei's eyes rounded on Hallie and for a second Luke tasted the kid's fear.

"You bet," Hallie confirmed.

"No doubt about it," Luke added, hoping on top of hope.

The boy swung around. Accusation sharpened his eyes. "Then why didn't you leave her car at the hospital?"

"She can't drive," Luke said amiably. "And her groceries need a refrigerator. Want to help carry them in?"

"Daee?" The baby pointed a wet finger at Luke.

"No." Alexei grabbed her hand. "That is *not* Daddy."

The toddler squirmed in Hallie's arms, reaching for Luke. "Daee!"

"No, Josie," Alexei repeated. "*No-ot* Daddy."

Joselyn's face scrunched. "*Daee*," she cried. "*Daa-eee!*" Her little legs kicked as she held her arms toward Luke, almost unbalancing Hallie. Fat tears plumped in the baby's eyes.

Luke's heart beat behind his tongue. *The kid's going to fall.* Before he could think, he lifted her from Hallie's straining arms. "Hey, there," he said.

Joselyn latched on to him, a tenacious koala cub. Tiny hands gripped the first part they touched: his hair and neck.

"Easy does it." Her sharp little nails would leave their mark. She was heavier than he'd expected. A warm, sweaty bundle. "I'm not your daddy, Josie-Lyn," he soothed, patting her back awkwardly, "but if you'll be quiet now, I'll hold you, okay?"

Alexei scowled. "It's Joselyn."

"Oh." Luke felt like a fifth-grader unable to wrap his tongue around *aluminum.*

The child cuddled her head on his shoulder. Her fingers eased on his flesh and scalp.

She smelled of sweetness, of innocence. God, what if he dropped her? Or squeezed too hard? He knew zilch about babies. Had never wanted to find out. *Ah, Ginny.*

Hallie laughed. "Relax, Uncle Luke." She stroked Joselyn's soft curls and smiled up at him. "Looks like you've got a friend for life."

"No, he doesn't." Alexei's eyes dared defiance. He stomped into the house, the pup galloping behind. Seconds later an inside door slammed.

"What's got into him?" Luke asked as he jiggled Joselyn in his arms.

"Oh, don't mind Alexei. He's worried about his mom. Guess I would be, too, if my dad just died."

Luke and Hallie carried ten bags of groceries into Ginny's kitchen. The melted ice cream had to be tossed down the sink. The milk and yogurt still smelled and tasted okay, but a frozen chicken had partially thawed: tomorrow's supper. If he had time tonight, he'd buy her several new packs of frozen vegetables.

Joselyn dogged Luke. She clung to his legs when he stood still, and toddled after him with tears in her eyes when he moved around the kitchen island helping Hallie store the groceries. He was terrified he would step on the baby.

Alexei holed up in his room.

After setting the table, Luke walked down the hall, Joselyn at his heels. Nerves tight—what did he know about ten-year-old boys?—he knocked on the door Hallie had pointed out. "Alexei?"

No answer.

Luke cracked open the door. The kid sat at a computer. Under his chair lay the pup, gnawing on an old shoe.

"Supper's ready."

"Go away."

Joselyn pushed past Luke's legs. "Ep-say. Um!"

Alexei swiveled in his chair. "Who asked you, huh?"

Halfway across the floor, the little girl stopped. She looked back at Luke. Her bottom lip poked out. His heart took a slow revolution.

"I don't care if you dislike me, boy," he said mildly. "Just don't take it out on your sister."

The kid scowled. "Leave me alone. You're not my father."

The words struck. Hard. If he and Ginny hadn't... "No," Luke said and inhaled an unfamiliar regret. "Nor am I trying to be. But I'm sure *your* father taught you some manners. You forgot them already?"

Alexei blinked. His cheeks flushed. He faced the computer screen. "I'm busy."

Sometimes it was easier to simply do, rather than discuss. That much he'd learned from watching his brothers with their kids. Luke walked to the computer and punched Power.

"Hey! That's not how you shut off a computer."

"Pretend an electrical storm hit a line. Now, come to supper. It's not polite to let Hallie wait." He strode out of the room.

Joselyn toddled after him. *"Daee!"*

Damn. How could he convince this tyke he wasn't her father, didn't want to *be* her father, or anyone *else's* father?

Waiting in the hallway, he watched her rush toward him in a waddling run, arms upheld. Resigned, he picked her up and headed to the kitchen. "There, there." He patted her little spine. "No one's going to leave you behind."

"Alexei coming?" Hallie asked. She had prepared a quick meal of ravioli, toasted garlic bread, salad and corn on the cob.

"Dunno." At the moment, Luke didn't much care. Well, he did, but he had no clue on how to handle a prepubescent's attitude. Thing was, Alexei reminded Luke of himself at that age—lugging a monstrous chip on his shoulder and a snarl on his lips.

A thread of kinship with the boy tugged Luke's heart.

He lowered Joselyn to the floor as he sat down at the

table. The baby immediately climbed his knees, wanting his lap. Lifting her, Luke let her settle, her dumpling weight suddenly welcome.

Hallie mashed the ravioli for the baby, then spooned a few kernels of corn onto her plate. "Mix those in." His niece handed Luke a minuscule, round-tined fork.

He stared at the foreign utensil between his big, clumsy fingers. How the hell did you feed a sixteen-month-old baby with something so ridiculously dwarf-sized?

Before he could maneuver the instrument, Joselyn grabbed it from his hand and stabbed the mixture on her plate.

Okay. That's how.

Luke watched the child feed herself. A corn kernel plopped onto her bib and she carefully picked it off with elfin fingers. The scent of the simple meal made his stomach growl. He looked around. Toys were scattered across the floor. A pair of women's ice-blue shoes waited near the back door. *This is how a home should be,* he thought and sat in stunned awe.

Minutes ago, the idea would have been lost on him. Growing up under the rule of Maxine Tucker's sharp tongue, he'd learned early that family did not mean *Mayberry* reruns. Going to bed at night didn't ensure tuck-ins or children's Bible stories. If his toys had ventured more than ten feet from their toy box on a day his father wasn't home, Maxine might have slapped him upside the head while she railed all his inadequacies in her drunken slur.

And she damn well never let him sit on her lap—not that he could recall.

Hail to home, sour home.

Then he'd met Ginny. Sweet, loving Ginny, who would have given her right arm to have a family.

Luke surveyed the clutter on the floor. *Looks like you got your wish, Gin.*

But not with him. No, he'd been too set on beating Maxine's taunts out of his head. *"You'll never amount to a hill of beans."* Ha. He'd proven her wrong, hadn't he? Not that she even knew. Hell, seeing each other across the street every five years was about as much of a family reunion as it would get between them.

Alexei shuffled into the kitchen. The pup gamboled at his heels. The boy slid onto the chair a table length from Luke, and looked only at his plate.

Something about the kid's sullen face annoyed Luke. He might have been looking at himself at ten. *Hold your head up,* he wanted to demand. *Don't take a backseat to anyone.*

But he said nothing. Alexei wasn't his responsibility.

Except for Joselyn sucking her tiny forefinger with each bite and humming her food away, they ate in silence.

That evening, a nurse helped Ginny gather her belongings, and pull on the blue skirt Luke had brought in a bag from home. The jeans she'd worn into town would not fit over her cast.

Dr. Stearns had been reluctant to release her unless another adult stayed at home with her throughout the night. She'd had a mild concussion, after all. Ginny promised the good man there would be someone. Who, she wasn't sure. She'd find an off-duty nurse, *anyone,* just so she could be with her children.

Outside the room's window, a heliotrope sunset animated the landscape. A robin sought worms in the patch of grass between the twenty-bed hospital and its parking lot. On the topmost branch of a walnut tree, two crows squabbled.

Life, plodding on.

She'd phoned the children; their excitement wet her eyes.

She'd called a cab—and argued with Luke over her decision.

Two hours ago he'd slipped into her room carrying a bag stuffed with French onion soup and a sumptuous vegetarian concoction that tasted of Mexico—again from Kat's Kitchen. Afterward, the nurse had shooed him out with the excuse Ginny needed an hour's sleep. She'd lain awake wondering what on earth he'd wanted. To assuage his guilt over hitting her with his car? To talk over old times? Be friends? Once he'd been her closest friend, her soul mate.

Since then she'd come to realize that in a world of billions, a soul mate wasn't necessarily your one true love. Soul mates could be sisters, mothers, friends or a husband you loved simply because he was who he was.

Like Boone.

The nurse pushed a wheelchair to the side of the bed, checking Ginny's train of thought. "Let's get you in this."

"It's okay. I can walk. I just need my purse and crutches."

"Hospital policy, honey. We don't want you fainting before you get out of here."

Ginny laughed and it felt good. "I'm not the fainting type."

Determined, the older woman nodded to the chair. "Indulge us and enjoy the ride."

Ginny sighed. The nurse helped her into the wheelchair, arranged her purse and crutches then lifted the sunflowers from the windowsill.

"Oh," Ginny said with a twinge of regret. "Could you leave them at the nurses' station?"

The woman's eyes widened. "You don't like them?"

I do. But I'm not comfortable accepting a gift from my

ex-husband. "Let them brighten the hospital." She softened her objection with a smile.

"All right." Reluctantly, the woman replaced the vase. "Do you mind if I give them to Mrs. Arken instead? She'll be in here for another couple of weeks."

"That would be nice."

They wheeled from the room and down the Lysol-scrubbed corridor.

"Looks like your ride's waiting." The nurse chuckled. "Got another batch of flowers for you."

Ginny could see that. Luke stood waiting in the hospital's admittance center, a wicker basket of ferns, ivy and African violets balanced on one big palm. Her pulse leaped—though she couldn't determine if it was due to the cut and shape of his chinos and green polo shirt, or her irritation that she'd need to cancel her taxi.

"Don't you have some files to review?" she grumbled.

His grin faltered as he fell in beside her. "All caught up."

They broke through the electronic doors and he pointed to Hallie's hatchback parked twenty feet down the sidewalk.

"Where's your car?" she asked.

"I wasn't sure if you'd want to ride in the Mustang after… Well, you know."

Her prickliness evaporated. He'd always been sensitive to her needs. *Except one.*

"Luke, your car doesn't scare me." *You do.*

He opened the door, folded back the seat, set in the planter basket and her purse, and arranged her crutches on the floor.

"Where are the sunflowers?" he asked.

"They're making Mrs. Arken smile."

He blinked. "You gave them away?"

She should have considered her actions. She hadn't meant to hurt him. "Luke, I'm sorry. I thought it would be nice—"

"Forget it." Gently, he lifted her from the chair into the passenger seat and helped her with the seat belt. When he finally slid behind the wheel, he asked, "Straight home?"

Ginny clasped her hands in her lap. "Yes."

Luke started the ignition, pulled toward the exit. "It's okay, you know. About the flowers."

"It's not okay. I should've given your gift more thought."

He shrugged. "You're right. They'll make Mrs. Arken happy."

They rode in silence until they reached the road out of town. Ginny asked, "How are the kids?" How had he reacted to them and they to him?

"Fine. The boy's a bit of a handful. Baby looks like you."

Suddenly she wanted to know. "Do you have children?"

"Nope."

So in twelve years his mind hadn't changed. Relief, disappointment, regret. Each emotion struck her separately and made her heart ache harder. "Married?" She hadn't seen a ring.

"Double nope." A grin flashed strong white teeth. "And no significant other, in case you're wondering."

"I wasn't." Of course she was.

She stared out the side window. They passed a small farm with lambs hopscotching at their mothers' sides.

Her property lay south of town. The ride was quick, quiet. Luke signaled and turned into the fir-shaded lane leading to the clearing and the house Orville Franklin had constructed for his family almost eighty-five years ago.

As Luke pulled up beside Ginny's car in front of the welcoming arms of the porch, Alexei stood in the doorway with

Bargain, the six-month-old Lab-pointer cross she'd found at the SPCA before their move to Oregon. Ginny waved.

And just like that boy and dog bounded across the deck and down the steps. He hauled open her door, great grin on his face. "Mama! You're back! Are you okay? How's your leg? Where's it broken? Can I write on your cast?"

She laughed. "Hey, sweetie. Hold the questions until we're inside. Help your mom out, will you?"

"Hold on a sec." Luke strode around the hood. "I'll help your mother."

Her son's grin curled into a frown. "I can do it."

"You don't have the strength. Watch it, little dog," he said to Bargain, nosing her way between Ginny and the door. Catching Ginny under the arms, Luke eased her from the seat until she stood gripping the open door of the car.

Alexei glared at Luke. Mouth tight, he ran up the steps and into the house. Whining, Bargain clambered after him.

"Alexei," Ginny called. To Luke she said, "You should've allowed him to help."

"I couldn't take the chance you'd fall." At her stern look, he said, "I'll apologize to him."

"Fine. But Luke, Alexei is my son. He takes precedence over anything or anyone outside of our family." A family that did not include him.

His mouth thinned and he reached inside the car for her crutches. "Right."

She had hurt him again, she saw. Guilt nudged her heart until she remembered the choice of having no family had been his alone.

"Ma-ma-ma!"

Ginny swung toward her daughter's voice. Hallie carried the baby down the steps, then set her on the ground.

Arms outstretched, Joselyn waddled as fast as her tiny legs would allow toward the car.

"Hey, pookie." Holding the door, favoring her bulky casted leg, Ginny bent toward her daughter—and found herself dizzy. She set a hand to her forehead.

Luke was instantly at her side. "You okay?"

"I'm fine."

Hallie lifted the baby out of the way.

"Mam. Daee. Hoe." Joselyn waved at Ginny and Luke.

"Yes, pooch, Mom's home."

Luke slipped an arm around her waist. His warmth nudged aside her vertigo.

"Let's get you to bed." Heedful of the porch steps, he slowly guided her toward the lighted doorway where her son had disappeared.

She wanted to see Alexei first. A crutch under each arm, she hobbled down the hallway to her "office" where she'd hooked up a computer within two days of their move. Her boy was a computer nut, pure and simple. She knocked on the door.

"Can I come in?"

"Yeah."

He sat staring at some homework assignment on the screen. A small banker's lamp chased off shadows. Bargain, tail windmilling, rose to sniff her cast. "Hey, girl," she said softly to the dog. Stepping beside Alexei, she stroked his gangly arm braced on the chair. "Luke didn't mean you couldn't help me, honey. He was afraid I might be too heavy for you to support."

Her son's regard of the screen didn't waver. "Yeah, I heard."

Alexei's snooty tone distressed her. Luke might not have wanted children while he was married to her, but his motives had evolved out of an obsession to overcome failure, not a dislike of kids. In all their years together, she'd never seen him treat a child unkindly. Not his niece, not the children of friends.

She strove for another tactic. "Luke isn't used to children, Alexei."

"Figures. He didn't know how to carry Joselyn when she wanted him to pick her up. He held her like she was a wet, smelly dog or something."

"Maybe she was—wet and smelly, that is."

A small smile threatened. "Would've served him right."

Ginny toyed with her wedding ring and decided to go with honesty. "A long time ago I was married to him."

Eyes round as CDs, Alexei stared. "You were?"

"We used to live on the same street when I was growing up." *And I fell in love with him then.* "But we didn't really get to know each other until my sophomore year. Then we started dating and when we were in college we…got married."

Puzzlement rushed her son's brow. "How come you got a divorce?"

"A lot of reasons." She traced his hairline with her thumb. "Which I will not go into, so don't ask."

She shifted her crutches to leave. Alexei scrambled out of the chair to assist. "Does that mean you still…you know, like him?"

Already he stood taller than her five-five. The moment she'd seen Alexei she'd loved his classic Russian features: thin, straight nose, high cheekbones, delft-blue eyes. And long dark eyelashes that paid homage to the sky.

"Yes," she said cautiously. "I like Luke. But as a friend, no more." Which was as truthful as she'd allow. Luke held a sorrow in her heart no one could touch. "Now, come read Joselyn a story before she goes to bed." She hobbled toward the door.

Alexei rushed forward and stamped a hand against the wood. The pup barked excitedly. "Shush, Bargain," the boy whispered. He looked at Ginny. "Is he, you know, gonna be around a lot?"

She considered. Between her and Luke lay an expanse of unresolved history, most of which Alexei had no inkling of, however, it was something she was ethically obligated to disclose if she meant to make Misty River home.

And her lost baby, Luke's child, was not her son's affair. Or even Boone's, when he lived.

She tried another angle. "Son, we've barely been here two weeks. And then I break my leg by running into Luke's car. Right now, he's feeling very guilty about that." *And so am I.*

"He should've watched where he was driving."

"Honey, *I* shouldn't have jaywalked."

"He thinks he knows everything and everybody."

She pushed the hair out of her son's eyes. "In a town the size of Misty River, it's not unusual for everyone to know everyone else. Most have grown up together. Some families have lived here for several generations."

"Great, now they'll all know our business. I don't want people knowing our business."

People, as in Luke. She studied Alexei's frown. "When we lived in Charleston, our whole block knew each other, son. Remember the parties we used to have at Thanksgiving and Christmas?"

"That was different. People were friendly there."

More so than Luke, she imagined, usurping Alexei's right to assist her into the house. "Give him time," she said gently. "He's not a bad man." She glanced at her casted leg. "So far, he's the only one who's come to our aid, driving the car home with the groceries and helping Hallie. And—" she gave Alexei a stern eye "—helping you and Joselyn."

The boy's mouth turned down. "I don't like him. Or this town or the school. Stinks."

Ginny's internal antennae rose. "What's going on at school, honey?" Was he being teased about his handwriting? It had happened in Charleston. Another reason she'd been glad to leave.

"Nuthin'."

"Kids not friendly?"

"Some are. Some are snots. Why'd Dad want us to live here, anyway? Why can't we move back to Charleston?"

"Are you saying we should let folks scare us off?"

As she anticipated, his eyes flinted. "No way."

Leaning in, she kissed his ear. "Thought so."

On Ginny's porch, Luke stared up at the night and its spangle of ten trillion stars.

He'd survived bath time with Miss Josie-Lyn.

Large wet spots mottled his shirt and chinos, soap had caught in his eye and his hands smelled of baby. She'd damned near drowned him, *and* scared the bejesus out of him with her water-wing fish antics in that slick tub.

When he'd left the bathroom thirty minutes later—a giggling Joselyn running naked ahead of him, the pup ahead of her—he'd nearly slipped and cracked his nose on the door. *Next time, dumb ass, don't forget to mop up the floor with the bathmat after drying the squirming, shrieking mite.*

Next time. Right.

It hadn't endeared him to Alexei when he'd growled at the boy to do the mopping while Luke chased the kid's streaking sister through the house.

Huh. And Ginny figured she could care for the kids alone, on crutches. Hell, with two legs—which endured a daily six-mile run—he'd discovered a man had to exert ten times the effort bathing a slippery, squiggly baby over catching a greased piglet at the local August fair.

Tomorrow he'd find Ginny a nanny. No way was he going through another of Miss Jo's waterworks.

He looked back at the living room window. The drapes hung open. A small reading lamp beside the cushiony sofa called to him. He pictured himself seated there, looking over files. Ginny beside him, head on his shoulder. Like years ago.

Jeez, what was he thinking? Shaking his head, he turned back to the stars. Night air chilled his skin under the damp fabric of his clothes. He enjoyed his life. He enjoyed the liberty it allowed, when he wanted, with whom he wanted.

Right. And what had it gotten him? An empty house, empty friends and a lot of empty years.

Again, he glanced over his shoulder at the window.

You owe Ginny, man.

Busting up her leg like that.

Busting up their marriage.

Yeah, he'd been a real big-shot lawyer then, hadn't he? Gotten exactly what he'd wanted. Big name, big firm, big partnership. All for what? To prove his drunk of a mother wrong? That he had brains, had guts, had what it took to be *somebody?*

Ah, hell.

He should call his brother and ask if Hallie could return, stay the night with Ginny. She'd never manage those stairs.

Not fair to the teenager. Tomorrow was a school day.

Okay. So *he'd* stay. For tonight. In case of…of…in case of fire. Not because he wanted to see Ginny in her nightie.

Not because he wanted to see her in the morning with those sleepy eyes and grumpy smile and mussed hair….

Idiot. That was then. *She's a mother now.*

Who said mothers couldn't be sexy?

She's got a broken leg, for Pete's sake!

Behind him the door opened.

"Thought I'd find you out here." Her soft voice geared his heart rate into fifth.

A silhouette in the muted light, she stood with one crutch positioned under her left arm.

"Where's the other crutch?" he asked, coming forward.

"It's easier to maneuver around the furniture with one." She limped toward the railing, the crutch's rubber tip thudding softly on the wood.

He felt helpless in the face of her pain. Pain he'd caused. He wanted to pick her up, hold her close to his heart.

She wasn't his to protect anymore.

Stepping beside her with a cool distance of a foot between them, he asked, "How're you feeling? Did you take your meds?"

She turned, leaned against the wood. "I'm feeling fine and yes, Doctor, the meds are digesting. Scout's honor."

He grunted.

"Seems Joselyn got more water on you than herself. If you want, I can dig out a shirt for you."

Luke had no intention of wearing her dead husband's

clothes. Truth be told, he didn't want to think about her with Boone Franklin's wardrobe hanging in her closet.

"Nah, these will dry, but thanks."

They were silent for several long seconds.

She said, "I love Oregon nights. It's so quiet here you could hear a butterfly's wings. I remember how we used to…"

"Try counting the stars," he finished for her.

She scanned the night. Venus courted the treetops. Somewhere near the water, three hundred yards hence, a mosquito hawk cried. Closer by, bullfrogs blew tuba notes to their lovers.

She said, "We'd count to eighty then get confused and have to start again. I haven't tried since…"

The divorce.

His heart pounded. "Me, either. Ginny—"

A sigh. "You need to go home, Luke."

"No." He turned his head and looked directly into her green eyes. "I'm sleeping on the couch."

She shook her head. "That isn't necessary—"

From his mental hat, he pulled the worst scenario. "What if there's a fire?"

"A fire?" she asked, amused.

"This is an old house. Everyone in this town knows the Franklin place was built in 1921. Sure, you got a new roof and siding, but the structure is old."

"The structure is sound," she argued. "Boone had four inspectors in here before he decided to renovate. They listed everything that needed work. They also said the foundation is as good as when it was built." She held up a hand to stop his protest. "It has new insulation, wiring, plumbing, furnace and a forty-gallon water tank." Her fingers ticked off the additions. "*As well as* new fire barriers and smoke and carbon monoxide alarms. This house is probably safer than yours."

He blew a long breath. "Even new ones can burn to the ground," he said quietly. "I'm staying, Virginia. What if one of the kids gets sick in the night? Starts throwing up all over the bed or something?"

He had no idea if kids did that sort of thing. Kids weren't part of his life, unless they came as a package in a family dispute before a court of law or because of an accident or some other traumatic legalese, and he might see them in his office while he talked to their parents or guardians.

His condo wasn't kid-centered.

His home with Ginny hadn't been kid-centered.

He pressed on. "What if *you* get sick or dizzy?"

Suddenly she ran a palm across her forehead. "All right." A weary sigh. "Come inside. I'll get you some blankets."

He held open the door. "Show me where they are and I'll get them myself."

Her eyes were cool as moonlight. "This *will* stop. Tomorrow."

This. His desire to be with her. She knew him well— even with all the years between. *Focus on your responsibilities, Luke.*

He simply nodded and followed her inside.

Deep in the night, he awoke to voices murmuring and little feet pattering above him.

Ginny. *Sick.*

The thought drove him from the blankets. A chilly moon in the window outlined his pants draped over the coffee table. He struggled into them. The pup growled softly from the kitchen.

"Go back to sleep," he mumbled to the dog. "It's just me." As he stumbled his way in the dark, his bare foot crushed a sharp object, and he grunted in pain. "Son of a—"

A toy, no doubt. That Alexei hadn't picked up. The kid needed a lesson in organization, as well as personality.

His arch throbbing like a piston, Luke headed for the stairs, checking the time on his illuminated wristwatch en route: 3:43. Lucky him. He'd gotten about three hours sleep. Too many memories. The worst, no, the sweetest, happened when he'd carried Ginny up these stairs to bed six hours ago.

She'd argued—stubborn woman—then finally agreed to let him pick her up, do his duty.

See, he'd told her. *I do have a reason for staying over.*

Hmph was all she'd replied. But her arms had been around his neck, her mouth inches away, her scent in his nostrils.

Upstairs in Alexei's room a lamp glowed on the night table. Bedsheets tossed aside. Boy gone.

Except for a Mickey Mouse night-light, the baby's room remained dark. Luke crept to her crib. She slept on her back, face turned his way. Little mouth agape, thumb tipped to her tiny bottom lip.

Something bittersweet—regret?—streamed over his heart. Shoving it aside, he turned for the hallway.

Ginny's door stood open; filtered moonlight shrouded the room. Two lumps under the quilt.

Luke walked to her side. Alexei lay curled in a fetal position away from her, snuffling little snores.

Like her daughter, Ginny lay on her back. Staring up at him.

"What are you doing?" she whispered. Her eyes scanned his torso, and he realized he stood there without a shirt.

"Somebody have a bad dream?" he whispered back.

"Yes. We're okay now."

When he continued to look down at her—God, she was lovely—she said, "Go back to bed."

He would. In a minute. Bending on one knee, he hunkered on the floor. "Ginny…" *I'm sorry for breaking your heart. But I couldn't resist the lure of status in the firm.*

God help me, it meant everything.

More than you.

"I'm sorry."

"For what?"

"For breaking your leg. Upsetting your life."

"It's not your fault."

"It's all my fault."

The night rang with silence.

"Luke," she warned quietly. "It's been more than a decade."

"I never forgot."

"Yeah, well." Voice flat, she sliced him with her cat eyes. "I haven't either. I remember every second of every day Boone lived. Now please. Go back to bed."

Bowing his head, he rose. "I'll make things right between us, Ginny," he said softly. "I promise."

"So you said twelve years ago and look what happened. Now *go*," she said.

He did. But on the sofa below, he lay awake wishing back the years until dawn licked the window.

Chapter Three

Luke threw back the blanket and grabbed his chinos. Daybreak painted the living room in sepia. He located his shirt, slipped it on. Bargain trotted in from the kitchen, tail wagging. She plopped her butt on the mat by the front door.

"Gotta go, too, huh?" Luke opened the door a foot. The pup bounded outside.

In the washroom off the mudroom he found five new toothbrushes. If his head wasn't stuffed with fog, he might have smiled. Ginny hadn't lost her bent for stocking up on necessities. When they were married, he used to joke about her habit. *We expecting Armageddon?* he'd tease.

Nope, just opening a store, she'd quip back.

Splashing water over his face and hair, he wondered if she thought of those moments.

If Boone Franklin had teased her.

Or had known she'd fall asleep in minutes if he scratched her scalp with his fingertips.

Luke scowled in the mirror. *Live with your choices, man.*

Outside, he stood on the porch steps, shoved his hands in his pockets and inhaled deeply. Wilderness, river, earth. Hypnotic scents for peace and calm.

Above the dark stand of fir, birch and alders lay a finger-smear of pink. A robin trilled its love lyrics across the clearing.

He was an urban man. So he told himself. He worked in town, lived in a condo, socialized in restaurants or the homes of friends and relatives. A subdued scale to what he'd had with Ginny, but the same nonetheless. He saw that now.

Twelve years ago he'd returned to Misty River to lick the wounds of his divorce, vowing to change. And he had—in small ways. He no longer craved the prized rung on the law ladder. He no longer vied for the best cases. Nor hungered for a judgeship. Those days had ended when Ginny walked out. Losing her had taught him the essence of the old cliché that happiness couldn't be bought.

So why hadn't he married again? Why hadn't he found a woman, settled down, had the two-point-five kids?

A thousand stones he'd skipped to those questions at the river's edge just beyond the clearing.

The answer remained steadfast. Ginny. None of those women had been Ginny.

Ginny of the loving heart.

Ginny who'd battered his own heart when she'd left, who now slept in the house behind him. Who he'd finally learned to forget.

So he'd believed.

Guilt rose like a claw. Their divorce had been for the best. While his acclaim for ruthlessness in a courtroom was high, winning cases without effort, his skill as a husband had been dismal. The only lot in his life where his grade notched a D.

A deserving D.

Calling softly to the pup sniffing an overgrown honeysuckle bush, he coaxed the animal up the steps and into the house. "See you tonight, little girl," he said and closed the door.

Settling into the leather seat of his Mustang, he thought of his brother. Luckily Jon had been up when Luke called at eleven o'clock last night or he might have been hoofing it back to town this morning. Luke's mouth curved at the thought of his brother driving the car to Ginny's. His brother hadn't wanted to leave his warm house, but he'd damn well enjoyed the power behind the wheel of Luke's car.

Checking the dash clock—6:02—Luke dialed Eva Asher's number on his cell, hoping she wouldn't have a cardiac arrest when her phone shrilled beside her bed. Ginny required a helper and he'd find one if it took him all day. In his opinion, Eva was the perfect match. She knew kids, had a kind heart and she'd known his family forever.

He hoped she was available. If not, he'd hunt around until he found *someone*. Grade D or not, he would not let Ginny down, not in this or anything else. *Far past time you do what's right, Luke.*

"H'lo." The woman's voice sounded like a gravel crusher.

"Eva, it's Luke Tucker."

Silence. And then she replied, "Ah. Gotcha. Head's a bit muzzy in the morning."

And a tad deaf, he figured, from all the kiddie yelling over the years. He swung the car onto Franklin's Road. "Eva, I'm real sorry to call so early, but I need a favor."

"You realize it's six o'clock and dawn's barely broke, boy?"

He grinned. Eva was only fifteen years older than Luke, but she'd once been his babysitter; in her eyes he was still a "boy." "Yeah," he said. "But I know you're always up with the birds."

"Don't mean I wanna talk to 'em," she grumbled, though he heard the underlying affection.

"Sorry. Did I take you away from something?"

"Nah. Just doing some baking for my son's wife. She had a new baby, y'know?"

"Yeah, I heard. Congratulations. Listen, Eva. I was wondering if you'd like a job for about six weeks."

Whatever it took he'd square away some of his wrongs with Ginny. Hiring a nanny was just a start.

Her skin tingling from the warmth and strength of Luke's arms when he'd carried her downstairs and to the kitchen table moments ago, Ginny eyed the woman making pancakes on her stove.

Eva Asher. A nanny.

He'd hired the kids a nanny and her a housekeeper.

She pinched her lips together. She didn't need a nanny. Yes, she had a broken leg. Yes, she'd be forced to wear flowing skirts like the green one she had on. But if he'd give her one darn chance, she'd prove the stairs and the children weren't obstacles. Besides, who wanted a stranger in their house?

Damn the man. Okay. She'd wait until they drove Alexei to school. And Mrs. Asher went home. Then she and Luke would get down to the nitty-gritty of this nanny business.

Joselyn banged her spoon on the tray of her high chair.

Ginny picked up the child's juice mug and held it to the baby's rosy mouth.

"Daee." Joselyn pointed her spoon at Luke, still dressed in yesterday's clothes, pouring coffee into two cups at the counter.

"Luke," Ginny corrected.

"Daee!" Joselyn insisted and dug up a spoonful of cream of wheat. Again, she held the utensil toward Luke. Porridge dripped onto the floor.

Luke set the cups on the table. "Hey, button nose. You're making a mess."

"I'll get it later," Ginny told him.

He grabbed a paper towel and came around to her side.

"I said I'd get it," she growled in his ear as he squatted between the two chairs. He looked up, winked. "Uh-huh."

Alexei and Bargain bounded into the kitchen. "I smell pancakes, Mama." As if noticing a wall too late, boy and pup slid to a halt. "Who's that?"

Luke threw the paper toweling into the trash under the sink. Mrs. Asher carried a stacked plate to the table. "Eva. And you're Alexei, right?"

"Yeah," he said cautiously.

"Good." Her face was an atlas for laughter. "I heard blueberry pancakes are your favorite."

"I could eat a thousand," he avowed shyly and slid onto a chair.

"A thousand it is, then." She turned to the stove. Right there, Ginny's admiration for the woman rose.

"Well, maybe not that many," Alexei admitted.

"No? Too bad. I was hoping for a spot in the *Guinness World Records.*"

"Yeah, right," he muttered, but a smile tugged his mouth.

Luke snatched a pancake off the plate. "Gotta run."

"Wait," Ginny called as he strode from the kitchen.

"Daee!" Joselyn banged her spoon and kicked her heels.
He popped his head around the corner.

"You and I," Ginny said, curbing her frustration at having
to push to her feet with a crutch *and* dealing with Luke in
front of her children and a stranger. "We need to talk."

"Can it wait?" He checked his watch. "I'm due in court
in an hour."

"Now." Damn it, he might have heavy-handed her with
the nanny gig, but he would not run out on her until the
issue was settled in her favor.

"Daaa!"

"He's not Dad!" Alexei snapped. The dog cowered under the table at the pitch of the boy's voice. "How many
times do we have to tell you that?"

The baby began to cry. Tears spilled over her cheeks.

"Hey, now, little princess." Eva plucked the child from
the high chair. "Luke's gonna come back. Don't you worry."

No, he's not, Ginny thought.

Joselyn held out her arms to Luke.

He shook his head. "I can't take her with me."

Ginny almost felt sorry for him. "She wants a kiss."

"What?"

"Boone used to kiss her goodbye."

"Daee!" Joselyn still clutched her spoon.

Eva walked toward him with a gentle smile.

"A kiss?" He stared at the baby. Cream of wheat
smeared her rose-petal cheeks and lips.

Ginny curbed a laugh. *Oh, Luke, if you had a mirror.*

A look of utter helplessness lined his mouth. His gaze
darted to her, to Eva, to Joselyn, back to Ginny.

He bent his stubbled cheek close to her daughter—and yelped when she grabbed his ear and nose for an open-mouthed smacker just below his eye. A sweet cream-of-wheat kiss.

Ginny giggled.

He flared her a look. "Somebody needs to cut that child's nails," he groused, and stalked from the house.

Ginny couldn't help it. She burst out laughing. "You're too funny, pookie."

Not until the door closed behind Luke did she remember she'd wanted to inform him his services as protector were done and his debt for hitting her with his car was paid.

"It isn't necessary for you to be here, Eva."

Braced on her crutches, Ginny stood beside the woman and dried the few breakfast dishes. Eva had driven Alexei to school, then returned to find Ginny busy at the sink and Joselyn playing peekaboo on the floor with Bargain and several small packing boxes. Squeals, laughter and happy growls. The essence of her day. "I can handle things on my own."

"I'm sure you can, Ms. Franklin, but Luke hired me for six weeks, and six weeks is what I'm giving you."

"It's Ginny. Please." She set a plate in the cupboard. "I understand what he's trying to do. Except I'm not bedridden. I *can* climb the stairs, as you saw, and for most of the day until Alexei gets home, I'll be on the main floor, quite capable of watching Josie."

"I'm sure. But who's going to do the laundry? Strip the beds upstairs? *Vacuum* upstairs? Take the trash to the roadside? Change the baby's diapers? Take her for a walk in the sunshine? Chase after her if she runs down the road?

Ah." The older woman patted Ginny's hand. "See, there is a point to my being here."

"But I…" *Don't want to be obligated to Luke.* She laid the second crutch on the kitchen's island, out of reach of tiny fingers, and hobbled to a chair. "Okay. Fine. But I want you to go to your own home at night."

Eva wiped down the counter. "Impossible. Night can be difficult if there's an emergency."

The woman and Luke had a one-track mind-set. "If there's a true emergency, I'll call 911."

"Luke's paid me—"

"You can reimburse him. Look. I do appreciate your help, Eva. Don't get me wrong, but I'll be okay. Honest."

The older woman rinsed the last two glasses before pulling the drain plug. "How do you propose to make a living here?"

Ginny sighed. Okay, her business was her own. She wasn't about to discuss her plans—or finances—with a stranger. Even a kind stranger. "What's that got to do with your employment here?"

Eva leaned against the counter. She folded the damp dishcloth over the sink's tap. "Once your leg heals, are you planning to get a job in Misty River? If so, you'll need a babysitter for the little one. I'd be happy to be that sitter."

"I wasn't… I mean, what I'm planning…" She pressed a finger to her temple where a headache tingled. "I'd like to open a preschool." *I need an income and can't afford a sitter.*

Eva's brows lifted. A great grin broke. "A preschool? Oh, honey, you're talking right up my alley."

"I am?"

"You bet. I operated Misty River's only preschool for twenty years. When I retired two years ago, people had to transport their kids to Clatskanie, eight miles up the road. You're going to hit a jackpot."

Ginny stared at the woman across the kitchen, then let out a half laugh. "Guess I will."

While Ginny strapped on a fanny pack containing a flashlight, Eva bundled Joselyn in her little yellow wool-lined jacket, tied on her yellow cap and set her wee feet into diminutive white sneakers. "There you go, princess. All ready."

In a lopsided puppy gallop, Bargain rushed forward.

"Go!" Joselyn toddled to the door. "Bug. Go!"

"Yes, pooch," Ginny said. "All of us are going for a walk."

Holding Joselyn's hand, Eva walked onto the porch. She closed the door behind Ginny. Slowly, they maneuvered the steps, Ginny hobbling one to the other in much the same manner as her daughter; Bargain taking a nose-dive off the last step. Her long black pointer's ears swept the dirt.

"Uh-oh." Joselyn gestured. "Bug, uh-oh."

"Yes, angel." Ginny watched as the pup romped after a wily crow. "Bargain bit the dust for a second, didn't she?"

Eva let go of the child's hand once they were on solid ground. The toddler ran after dog and bird.

"Not so fast, little girl." Eva trotted after the baby.

"Ma, go!"

Ginny laughed. The sun warmed the air. Clouds feathered an azure sky. A sweet two-pitched whistle announced a song sparrow in the nearby trees.

A perfect day to inspect the small cottage butting the forest between the house and the old mill site. Boone's great-grandfather had built the house and the mill, in hopes of beginning a lucrative logging business. The venture petered out with the approach of the Depression years.

As they walked, Eva said, "I remember when Deke Franklin built those cabins along the river's edge." She nodded to where the trees secreted away three small buildings. "They were hoping to begin a small resort. But then…"

Ginny knew the story. Tragedy had taken a life as well as his parents' dreams.

"Did anyone ever live in the cottage?" Ginny pointed with her chin to the fourth building—a small Cape Cod—which she hoped to change into her preschool. The dwelling stood a short distance west of the house and three hundred yards from the water. According to Boone, it was to have housed the resort's caretaker…or Boone, had he elected to shoulder the business once his father retired.

Eva shook her head. "Probably transients. When the Franklins built it in the sixties, they had this grand opening for what they called a 'getaway on the water.' The whole town showed up. People danced and laughed and had a great old time. I was thirteen then, but went with the older teens to swim in the river. Franklin's swimming hole was a well-known hangout in those days." She sighed audibly. "Never expected tragedy that day."

Ginny navigated the crutches past a bump in the path. "Maggie Stuart's drowning." In the Misty River not twenty feet from the resort cabins. Her body had never been found.

"For days police dragged the river." Eva fixed Joselyn's little cap so it shaded the child's face. "Then three weeks later the hauntings began. Someone saw Maggie kneeling on the riverbank, sobbing. Crazy if you ask me."

Ginny agreed. As the tale went, **spectral sightings**

sprang up every other month for almost two years, before the novelty wore thin and the story turned legend.

And while the Franklin's resort dream floundered in a haze of tragedy and ghostly gossip, Boone's father committed suicide. A year later, Boone moved to Boston to study medicine. He never returned to Misty River.

As a child Ginny heard the stories from her own family—and later, in the privacy of their marriage, from Boone.

While she limped toward the cottage to inspect it as a possible place for her own dream, a sadness hung in the air. Forty-five years ago, Boone had loved Maggie Stuart's twin sister, Maxine.

Luke's mother.

The door of the cottage was locked, the windows boarded.

"It needs a ton of work," Ginny told Eva. "I'm not sure if it's even hygienically safe. Probably got mice and bugs."

"Maybe." Carrying Joselyn, Eva walked along the outside of the house. "Foundation is cement. Must have a basement."

"That's what—" *Boone said in his will.* "I figured."

Eva returned to the stoop where Ginny stood. "No structural damage to the outside. Been inside yet?"

"Nope." Ginny set aside her left crutch and removed the flashlight from her fanny pack. "First time for everything." She took the key from her pocket and turned the lock. The door stuck. Shoving a shoulder to the wood, she pried the door open on a chord of squeaks. A rustling noise sounded in the shadows. Flicking on the flashlight, she stepped across the threshold.

Joselyn pulled her thumb from her mouth. "Ma?"

"Mom's right here, hon. Stay with Eva, okay?"

Ginny shone the light around what appeared to be a surprisingly spacious living room for such a small house. Faded posy wallpaper dragged in long curly strips from the ceiling's crown molding. A corner harbored a kitchenette, all inclusive with sink, L-shaped counter and cupboards.

Had it not been boarded, a tall, broad window would have looked south, across the meadow to the river. Behind her, near the door, a staircase descended into the basement. Dust and dirt overlaid all surfaces. Cobwebs stitched corners and angles.

Her crutches thumped the wood as she hobbled across the room to the first of two doors. Smaller than the main area, but still expansive, the second room was a bedroom; the third a bathroom—toilet, sink, claw-foot tub. And a tiger-eyed tabby cat hissing from a nest of moth-eaten cloths.

"Now, where did you come from?"

The cat hissed again, before streaking past Ginny and out the front door. Bargain let out an *awrrr, awrrr!* and took off on a gangly gallop across the grassy clearing. The cat scurried up a thick-limbed poplar; the befuddled pup plunked her fanny in the dirt, looked back at the trio then set to howling.

"Kee," Joselyn cried from Eva's arms. "Ma, kee! Bug! Kee!"

"Right, honey. Bargain treed a kitty." Baffled, Ginny asked Eva, "Wonder how it got inside?"

Eva peeked into the house. "Basement likely has a vent somewhere."

"But wouldn't it be closed?"

"After forty years? Hey, anything's possible."

Outside again, Ginny breathed deep of the clean morning air. "One thing's certain. That cat's kept the mice horde away." She studied the cottage and its kinship with vines and brambles. "It's going to take some work, Eva, but I do think I have a place for my Small Wonders."

"Small wonders?"

"The name of my preschool."

Eva nodded. "I like it."

Ginny locked up and they headed for the house. She whistled for Bargain. Under the tree, floppy black ears pricked their way. Afraid to be left behind, the pup raced back.

Eva said, "You'll need a strategy to draw people in."

"The fact I'll be the only preschool in town won't do the trick?"

"No, honey, it won't. Not when you're on cursed land."

A chill scored Ginny's arms. "Cursed?"

"All started with the drowning and your late father-in-law committing suicide in that house of yours."

Luke arrived at five after eight that night, just as Eva walked down the porch steps heading for her Chevy Malibu.

"She's setting up to argue with you," the housekeeper told him as he climbed from his car. She tossed a purse the size of a storage shed onto the front passenger seat. "Just thought you'd like to know."

"Thanks." Luke grinned. Sometime during the afternoon, they'd come to terms: Eva would work a twelve-hour day shift; he'd take the nights. "Maybe these will change her mind." He reached into the vehicle's rear seat and pulled out a dozen yellow rosebuds. Yellow for friendship, the florist at Faith's Flowers told him.

Friends. A good place to start.

"Hell's bells, boy. If they don't do the trick you can drop 'em off at my place."

Laughing, Luke trotted up the steps. "See you tomorrow, Eva."

"Good luck," she called and drove off.

God willing. He raised his hand to knock.

Alexei flung open the door, pup at his side. "You again."

"Me again."

"We don't need tucking in."

"Especially not by a Tucker, huh?"

The boy didn't laugh. Not even a twitch.

"Well," Luke said. "Least it'll save me a trip up the stairs."

"Alexei?" Ginny's voice sifted through the house.

The kid stepped aside as she hobbled on her crutch around the corner of the hallway and into the foyer. "Luke. What are—oh, my," she breathed when he held out the bouquet. Her green eyes searched his. "These are for...?"

"You." His ribs hurt under the hammer of his heart.

Alexei snorted and disappeared into the kitchen, dog in tow.

Ginny came forward to cup a vivid, half-opened bud. "They're lovely." She studied him a moment. "If this is about tonight—"

"It is." He stepped inside, closed the door. "I'm sleeping on the couch again, Ginny, whether you want me to or not. You need someone here until that walking cast comes off. Now, where's a bucket or vase?" He strode to the kitchen.

Alexei sat at the table, notebook and text spread out before him. Bargain sprawled across his feet.

"Homework?" Luke asked, opening a cupboard.

The kid grunted and eyed him suspiciously. "What're you doing?"

"Looking for something to put the flowers in."

"Up there." From under the kitchen's archway, Ginny

pointed to the cupboard above the refrigerator. "You'll find a tall green vase somewhere."

He hauled down the slender vase and she carried it to the sink to turn on the tap. From a small pot, she sprinkled a teaspoon of sugar into the container. She'd always used sugar, warm water and sunshine to sweet-talk rosebuds into opening.

Okay, so he hadn't forgotten everything.

Hands in his pockets, he wandered to the table where the boy was working on some writing assignment.

The instant Luke pulled out a chair, Alexei stopped. Slowly, the boy lifted his head. Blue eyes, nippy as ice cubes. If the boy had been a man he would have told Luke to get lost.

Well, tough. Luke planned to spend a few nights here—until he was certain Ginny could handle the stairs and her family—so the kid had better get used to his presence.

"What're you working on?" he asked, hoping to change whatever topic about them the boy might have in his head.

"Does it matter? I don't need *your* help."

"Alexei." Ginny turned from the sink. Beside her, on the counter, the roses streamed from the slim vase like a cluster of miniature balloons on the Fourth of July. "Rudeness is not permitted in our family."

The boy lowered his eyes to his work. "Sorry," he mumbled.

"Forget it," Luke told him. "I'll stay out of your way. How's that?"

Alexei shrugged. "Whatever." He stared at the page in his notebook, made a mark with his pencil, holding the instrument in a death grip, fingers curled at a peculiar angle. The words on the page resembled a type of Asiatic writing:

all strokes and slashes. Upside down as the page was to Luke, he couldn't make out one detail. Was the kid learning Chinese or Japanese?

Luke scanned the top print of the handout in Alexei's notebook. The first instruction—in English—read:

Independent Novel Study
Chapter Four: Answer the following questions
in complete and concise sentences.

Concise? Luke thought, studying Alexei's answers. Hen scratching was more like it. How the teacher gleaned a grade for the boy was beyond Luke. He glanced at the novel—*The Old Man and The Sea.* The kid was reading Hemingway? How old *was* he?

Ginny touched Luke's shoulder, crutch under her right arm. "Would you carry the roses into the living room?"

"Oh. Sure." He walked to the counter, picked up the vase. "Whereabouts?" Yesterday, she had placed the planter basket on the dining room table.

"Near the south window."

He carried the bouquet into the living room. Plastic teacups and a ragamuffin doll littered the floor and the coffee table. A children's storybook lay open on the couch.

Luke ignored the mess and headed for the small end table. Flowers in place, he was struck at how much they reminded him of Ginny with their golden heads and sleek thornless stems.

"Thank you. Can we talk for a minute?" She turned and limped to the front door.

Night shrouded the porch. A scent of rain swung in the breeze. Ginny shut the door behind them.

"What's wrong with Alexei?" Luke asked when she came to stand beside him at the top of the porch steps.

Her gaze jerked toward him. "Wrong?"

He saw he'd caught her off guard. They weren't here to discuss her son. "His writing. How's his teacher read it?"

Her spine stiffened. She looked out across the meadow. "Officially it's called dysgraphia. Public schools rarely use the term because there's virtually no criteria that squarely defines the problem." She turned to him. "Ever heard of the word?"

"No, can't say I have."

"It's a fine-motor-skill dysfunction. Most children out-grow it. Meantime, they compensate through various meth-ods. Did you notice the lump of clay beside his book?"

"Yeah."

"He uses it for manipulative therapy to warm up his muscles before he begins writing."

Made sense to Luke. "Does he take special classes?"

"No. Boone and I thought it wrong to remove him from the classroom. We didn't want him singled out. It's been a struggle with teachers who favor sending students to the resource room. Thank God his teacher here agrees."

Luke did as well. He knew firsthand what it felt like to be blacklisted. "What causes dysgraphia?"

Ginny shrugged. "A number of things. Sequencing problems, dyslexia, ADD. We've had Alexei go through myriad tests. The last one indicated a twelfth-grade reading level. Which didn't surprise us because he loves reading. Spends hours engrossed in a book." She smiled. "He's read *The Grapes of Wrath* and *Macbeth*."

Luke's brows jumped. "Impressive." Hemingway was easy reading in comparison.

"Very. So you see dyslexia is out—and he's not hyper-active. He's the opposite. Quiet and rather serious."

"You think?" he teased. "I haven't seen the kid smile once."

Her mouth remained solemn; she wasn't in the mood for teasing and he wished his words back.

The night held its stillness.

She said, "He wasn't always like that. Before Boone died, Alexei used to tell jokes and giggle and...his eyes had this sweet sort of impishness in them. Different than when he first came to us."

Come again? Was she saying the kid wasn't...hers?

"Alexei is a Russian orphan," she continued as if inter-preting his thoughts. "I adopted him as a single mother when he was two. Three months later Boone and I married and Alexei became a Franklin then."

"Alexei's not your biological child?" The news stunned Luke. "But I thought..." What? That she'd be-come pregnant the year following their divorce? Some-thing she'd begged of him for eight years, she who desperately wanted a family, who wanted children shout-ing and laughing through their house? He recalled her grief that last night, when he'd held her in his arms until she slept.

No. She wouldn't have gone to another man so quickly.

Yet...

"Boone had a low sperm count," she went on, sadness toning her voice. "His first wife never had children because of it and she didn't want to adopt. I met Boone five years after her death. We married four years after you and I..."

"Divorced."

"Yes."

And while Luke had wallowed in his sorrow—for years!—she'd found someone new.

A family man.

Burying his foolish pride, he stared into the darkness. "How did you meet?"

Her answer came slowly. "He was my doctor."

"That must have been cozy."

Her head turned. Eyes cold. "It was hell."

"And still you married him? Interesting."

She flinched. "He was the kindest man I've ever known."

Kinder than him. Kinder because Boone Franklin had wanted kids, whereas Luke— "Is Joselyn adopted?"

"No," Ginny said softly, looking up at the ragged clouds filtering the moon. "She's ours. And a miracle."

No doubt. He couldn't imagine the angst of struggling to procreate all your life and then suddenly have it happen. He had seen the same heartache with parents he'd represented in surrogate and adoption cases; handed tissues to teary mothers in his office when the case finalized happily.

But Boone had died. He would never see his only child, a gift to him late in life, mature into a beautiful young woman.

Luke's choices had been his own. No kids. Ever.

It had cost him Ginny.

The irony of their lives caught him square in the chest. Alexei disliked him because he thought Luke stood between Ginny and the memory of Boone Franklin. Exactly the way Luke himself had felt when, as a kid, he stood between his father and his mother.

He shoved his hands into his pockets, sighed. Better to get it in the open. "Your son thinks I'm stealing his dad's spot."

"You're not."

The exactness of her words dinted his heart. And a little of his ego. He touched her cheek. "I know how he feels. When I saw you for the first time a week ago, with *kids,* no less…well, hell. It was like I'd stepped off a cliff. Then aw, damn it… You ran out into the street and my car… Ginny, my life stopped. Just like that, I was back twelve years and you were—I was losing you all over again."

Torment in her eyes. She evaded his reach. "I should check on Alexei."

He caught her shoulder. "I want, I need— *Ginny,* can't we at least be friends?"

"I don't know. Can we?"

"I think so." *If you can forgive me.* "It'd be a start."

"As in starting over?"

He shrugged. Was he was ready to take that step with her?

"I have kids now, Luke," she said, settling the issue. "As I recall, you didn't—"

"Want children." He drew back. "That was a long time ago. Maybe I've changed." What was he saying? *Had* he changed? Did he want to get involved with a woman who had kids?

But this is Ginny.

Uh-huh. With someone else's kids.

Before he could think it through, he said, "Maybe I'm not the man you knew. Did you ever think of that?"

Her eyes doubted him, told him he remained the man she remembered.

His skin prickled.

At last she said, "When it involves my kids I consider only what's best for them." Crutch under her arm, she limped to the door. Slanting a look over her shoulder, she said, "You know where to find the blankets. And Luke? It would be easier on Joselyn and Alexei if you left before they got up."

And her, he knew. It would be easier on her, as well. As the door closed between them, he had to agree.

Chapter Four

Luke wanted to fix Alexei's problem.

All day while he discussed procedures with his clients, pleaded their cases before the judge, he thought of the small boy at Ginny's kitchen table struggling with a blunt-tipped pencil. He saw, again, the tennis ball and Play-Doh. He could not fathom the tangled process going on in Alexei's brain that would not transmit the correct motor skills to his fingers.

There had to be an easier way for the kid to manipulate one small, skinny piece of wood over a page.

During lunch, he searched dysgraphia on the Net and came away with a small horde of information. What he learned was the disability often deceived teachers into believing the child was lazy or stubborn. Many kids with dysgraphia, Luke read, were bright stars. They could verbalize and read at high levels, just as Ginny had said.

He wondered what Alexei's former teachers had told her. What they'd *done* to Alexei. He wondered what the teacher at Chinook Elementary had recommended and whether she understood the degree of Alexei's problem.

One of Jon's girls attended fifth grade. Luke would phone his brother and find out what he could about the school and, in particular, Alexei's teacher.

At four o'clock, intent on heading down the sidewalk to the Misty River Public Library, Luke locked the door to his law office. He'd scout the musty old shelves for whatever they contained on learning disabilities.

He didn't expect to run into his mother shelving books from a trolley in the very aisle he needed to research. So focused was she on deciding where in the Dewey decimal system the book she held should be placed, that he simply stared at the woman dressed in a neat pink blouse and black slacks. He couldn't recall the last time he'd seen her without her shabby polyester clothes, bent like an ancient woman.

"Ma?"

Her head jerked around. Her wire-rimmed glasses slipped down her long, thin nose. The nose he'd inherited.

"Luke." His name was an expelled breath.

As if her actions weren't apparent, he asked, "What're you doing here?"

Her gaze darted away, then back. "I'm shelving the returns."

He shifted on his feet. "I can see that. But why? You working here now?"

Far as he knew, she hadn't worked since he relocated to Misty River eleven years ago. But then he'd seen her no more than a dozen times over those years. Mainly at Christmas, with his brother Seth and niece Hallie present at the dinner table. A cozy mother-son relationship wasn't in the cards for Luke and Maxine Tucker. Not since his toddler days—when he'd endured the first scream in her drunken voice, the first swat of the wooden spoon.

"Part-time," she said in answer to his question. "Every Tuesday and Thursday afternoon. For the past year." She smiled, her lips quivering slightly. Nerves, he suspected. His own jangled under his skin. "Are you looking for something in particular?"

Can I help you? was what she really meant. He saw it in her pale gray eyes—another gene he'd inherited—that anxious eagerness to come to his rescue.

Where were you when I really needed you, Ma? He stepped back. "No. I see you're busy here. I'll come back another time. See you." He turned for the exit.

"Luke," she called softly.

He stopped.

"You don't come here often, do you?"

"Is that a crime?"

"Not at all. The Internet's more convenient these days."

That she would know about computers surprised him. While he was growing up, she'd worked as a cashier at Whole Hardware during the day and watched sitcoms or smoked cigarettes on the back porch in the evening with her beer. She hadn't been a particularly educated woman, or so he assumed. And the booze had annihilated whatever brain cells were left. So he'd thought.

Again that wavering little smile. "Amazing, huh? That I'm not completely pickled?"

"I didn't say you were."

"But you were thinking it. I don't blame you." She

walked toward him. Removed her glasses. "It's been a long time since we talked. I'm glad you came in, son."

Son. Whenever had she called him son? Bastard. That had been her favorite, years ago.

"Look," he said, itching in his skin. Itching to escape. He'd return when she wasn't here. "See you around, okay?"

"Sure." Her hand lifted. Gnarled fingers reaching. Wanting to touch him. She set back her glasses, magnifying her eyes. Magnifying regret.

He left her standing in the musty, old library, clutching the outdated book to her heart.

He would not look back. Would not *feel.*

But her eyes burned into his scalp just the same.

Ginny walked Seth Tucker around the cottage.

"Think it's worth saving?" she asked the tall construction man who was Hallie's father and Luke's younger brother. A man she'd once sat behind in tenth-grade math. A man who'd once been her brother-in-law.

So many years!

Now Seth owned and operated Tucker Contracting. His expertise consisted mainly of stonework and landscaping, but Eva claimed he was a marvel with renovations, as well. To Ginny, Eva's pride in the new bathroom he'd constructed for her last winter during his "downtime" was résumé enough.

"No cracks in the foundation," he said, toeing the cement beneath the wood. "Roof needs replacing. Clapboard's got rot. Steps are hatched. Yeah…" He lifted his Mariners cap, shoved back shaggy hair. "It'll last another fifty years."

"Even the inside?"

While they'd toured the interior, she rediscovered Seth still remained, after all these years, the quiet Tucker. He said not a word until she asked a question.

Finally at the door, he rubbed his cheek, contemplated. "Wiring needs to be brought to code. Plumbing needs replacing. Hot water tank's fairly new."

"How new?"

"Fifteen years."

Amusement crept into her voice. "What's old?"

"Twenty-five, thirty. Boiler's another story, though."

Ginny shifted on her crutches. "The boiler?"

"For your radiant heating. Boiler's twenty-eight years old, on its last leg."

He must have caught her frown because he added, "I can get you one wholesale."

"Thanks, Seth."

"You're welcome." His eyes were summer-blue; his smile sweet, shy. Like Luke, he had dark hair and the frame of an NFL running back, with tough shoulders and long bones.

He studied the cottage. "You serious about making this into a preschool?"

"I am. Think it might be a problem way out here?"

"Hell, it's closer than driving to Clatskanie."

"Eva thinks people may reconsider since a ghost apparently walks the river sand three hundred yards away."

Seth snorted. "If that's what they think then they're idiots."

"That may be, but it won't get me customers."

A corner of Seth's mouth lifted. "Jon's wife had a boy a few months back. Another couple years she'll probably need a preschool. And Breena's—" He couldn't hide the grin. "My wife's in her first trimester."

"Congratulations!"

"Yeah," he said, palming his nape. "Whole family's pretty much over the moon about it."

Whole family. Including his brothers. An ache rose from a deep corner of her soul. Had she and Luke stayed married, she'd know all the trivia, the details.

She'd be giving Seth a sisterly hug.

So many things different.

Alexei wouldn't be here, nor Joselyn. Impossible, impossible thoughts!

And Robby wouldn't have existed. Unthinkable. Whatever the past held, those few days she had cradled Luke's tiny son in her arms would be hers to keep. *Forever.*

They headed back toward the house where Joselyn served Eva make-believe tea in a sketch of sunshine on the veranda.

By Friday, Ginny had reached the end of her patience with Luke's insistence to sleep on her sofa. Okay, so he didn't arrive until 8:00 p.m. and, yes, he left before her family awoke, but still. She did not need his tall, trim body sleeping on her couch. She did not require him carrying her up the stairs each night, the warmth of her flesh pressing his, that man smell inebriating her senses.

She did not need him encroaching on her dreams.

When he drove up that evening in his silver Mustang, she was waiting with Eva on the porch.

"Hey," he called cheerfully, climbing from the car. As always when he arrived at her house, he'd changed from his daily lawyering clothes—suit, tie—to casual. Tonight he wore black cargos and a white polo.

Mammoth purse hooked on her shoulder, Eva trotted down the steps to her Malibu. "Take it easy," she said and grinned. As if she knew a spit fight was in store.

In the next minute, the trees swallowed her car, its motor fading quickly. With the ensuing quiet, Ginny looked down at Luke where he'd halted at the foot of the steps. A small amount of his joy ebbed from his eyes. "Something wrong?"

"We need to get a few things straight."

He hesitated. "And they are?"

"I'll be paying Eva from now on."

"Now, Virginia—" He placed a foot on the first stair.

"No." Hanging on to the pillar, balancing on her left foot, she swung up the crutch and set its rubber tip against his chest. "You will listen and you won't take another step until you do."

"Huh. You gonna brain me with that thing?"

"Don't think I won't."

Their eyes locked.

Slowly, he pushed the crutch from his body. "All right. You have my attention."

"Thank you. You always were a stubborn man."

He took a step forward. "If this is a bash-Luke day, forget the listening part."

Again she hauled up the crutch. "It's not an insult, but an observation." She offered a smile. "Come on, Luke, admit it. You can be stubborn."

His mouth twitched. "No less than you."

Inclining her head, she lowered the crutch. "Agreed. Now, about Eva's payment—I've discovered I like her. She's also a tremendous help with Joselyn, so thank you for finding her. However, I have enough money to cover her salary and—"

"So do I."

"I'm thinking she can assist with my preschool once the cottage is fixed." Ginny glanced through the gloaming, at the tiny building snuggled in dark trees, where Seth Tucker had reshingled the roof today.

"Ginny," Luke said quietly. "Let me pay the six weeks." When she opened her mouth to cut him off, he continued. "I was behind the wheel, remember."

How could she argue against the truth? Against the ruefulness in his eyes?

She bowed her head, stared at the walking cast where Alexei had scratched with a Magic Marker, "Mom has a foot fetish!" across her toes that first day. Her funny little son. Trying so hard to make her see another side to her dilemma.

Like Luke.

His lashes were black, straight, thick…a woman's fantasy. The slumbering sun glazed their tips, burnished his linear eyebrows, shadowed his obstinate jaw. Once, long ago, she'd kissed them all.

She drew in a breath. "Fine. Only the six weeks. That's it."

"Thank you."

When he started up the steps, she said, "Another thing. This is the last night you're sleeping here. As you can see with me standing here, I managed the stairs quite well in the morning after you left. And Alexei takes Joselyn down. I've gone up the stairs during the day while Eva's in the house, and I've walked the ones you're standing on, as well. So. There's no reason for you to be here. Tomorrow night you can go to your own home and get a decent night's rest in your own bed."

"You about done?"

"Not yet. I need a lawyer to file the deed of the land and house. Boone kept all the records with a guy in Charleston, but I'd like you to have those transferred to your office. I'll give you his name and pay whatever the costs. And I want to register for a license to run my preschool. Any tips on how to go about that would be helpful." How staid she sounded. How brisk, how *efficient*. As if she were laying ground rules to an employee instead of the man whose baby she'd once carried. Her heart pounded while he studied her.

He nodded. "I'll see to it Monday."

"I also want to write up a will. Just the usual," she said when he blinked. "But with a video included."

He swallowed. "We can do that Monday, too."

"Thank you." After they'd buried Boone's ashes in West Virginian soil, she had mulled over this last detail, the will, extensively. Her children needed security to the nth degree. One never knew the instant life slammed its door shut.

"That it?" Luke asked.

She tipped her chin. "That's it."

He came up the steps, stood less than a foot away. The heat in those few inches had nothing to do with the lingering warmth of the day. "I have something to say, as well. I'd like to take you for coffee. Tonight."

"I can put on a pot—"

"Away from here."

"I can't leave the kids."

"I've asked Hallie to babysit. It's Friday. She can stay as long as we want."

Her pulse bounced. "Luke, I'm not dressed."

"What you have on is perfect."

Her black tear-away joggers? The only item besides floating skirts she could wear these days with her unwieldy cast? Her yellow tank? Nike sneakers? Maybe if he'd planned a hiking jaunt.

His palm cupped her cheek. "You worry too much," he said softly. "It's only coffee."

"Why?" She stood entranced by his touch—and when it disappeared, felt the shiver of a cool breeze.

"Because you haven't been away from the house in a week." A motor hummed into the clearing. "There's Hallie now. Will you come, Ginny, come with me just for an hour?"

Her heart galloped. She'd be with him, *alone*.

The first time in a dozen years.

She glanced at the door of the house, behind which one child slept and the other played a video game. Hallie got out of her hatchback, called a friendly greeting. Luke waited.

"Fine. But I need to tell Alexei." She hobbled toward the door and turned. Backlit with the sun's dying rays, he hadn't moved from the top step. Hallie came up beside her uncle. "Sixty minutes," Ginny said. "Not one second more."

Soberly, he gave her a thumbs-up. *Don't worry,* his eyes said. *I'll keep my word.* If nothing else, she knew Luke Tucker believed in principles.

He drove eight miles north to Clatskanie. They spoke little en route, but her presence sang along his skin.

By the time they arrived, night induced home lights and thinned traffic on Highway 30 through the downtown core. At Bailey's Restaurant and Lounge along the tiny Clatskanie River, he came around the hood to help her out of the car.

"I can do it," she said, even as her hand caught his shoulder. "Just give me a minute."

"Not when you've given me only sixty to get you back home." He plucked her crutches from behind the seat, propped them against the Mustang's side.

"Okay, maybe I was a bit rigid."

"A bit?" he teased, catching her under the knees.

"Let's just see how it goes."

He held her against his chest. Their noses were inches apart. Her lips held the slightest lift. A nudge of his chin, and he'd be on them.

Her eyes darkened.

"No," he said, more as a warning to himself than an explanation to her. "I made a deal." He carried her to the sidewalk where he lowered her gently next to a corner of the building. Then he retrieved her crutches.

It had been years since he'd stepped inside the old restaurant, but the sights had altered little. Wood-hewn signs telling the story of the town hung on every wall.

They sat at a table beside a window overlooking the Clatskanie River. Night-lights shimmered on its murky waters. A waitress came by and took their orders. Luke needed coffee, Ginny wanted peppermint tea.

"And bring us each a slice of apple pie à la mode," he said.

When the waitress disappeared, Ginny laughed. "You know what dessert at this time of night does to the body?"

"Your body is perfect."

"Ha. You haven't seen it naked in a long time."

For two heartbeats he couldn't breathe, the memory erotic and sharp. Then a grin tugged his mouth. "From what I see, it's exactly how it should be."

"Such a diplomatic answer." But laughter gleamed in her eyes.

He had missed this easy camaraderie between them, this lack of shyness.

Long seconds passed and their grins faded. Still neither looked away. Her eyes, green as budding leaves, enthralled him. He could lie down and die in the soul of her eyes. Years ago, when she left, he nearly *had* died. Drinking himself to sleep every night. Praying never to wake. Without her nothing had existed. Nothing had mattered.

She said, "Why are we doing this, Luke?"

"Doing what?" he asked, feigning incomprehension, feigning they weren't in sync. "Having coffee in a restaurant?"

She frowned.

The waitress arrived, coffee, tea and pies on a tray.

When they were alone again, Ginny stared at her dessert. Her fork rested untouched beside her plate. "Having a date," she whispered. She lifted her head. "That's what this is, isn't it?"

He set his arms on either side of his pie. His fingers spread toward her. Ten digits begging to connect. "I want to be with you, Ginny. Without the commotion of life. Just for a little while. Give us the chance to, I don't know, catch up, get to know each other again."

Her eyes sparked. "That commotion of life as you call it is who I am now, Luke."

She'd missed his point. "I realize that."

"Do you? My kids are my whole world. Nothing beyond them exists for me. It just…" Her voice wobbled. "It just can't."

A man and woman at a table across the room rose and headed for the entranceway. A dish clattered somewhere out of sight. In another part of the restaurant a vacuum ran. Closing time approached. Soon they'd leave.

"And Boone?" Luke asked softly, though his blood thumped. "How did he fit into the picture?"

"That's not fair. Boone was my husband, the father of my children. We were a family."

"And now he's gone you don't have room for anyone

else, not even a friend?" He wanted to shake her. He wanted to kiss her.

Calmly, she removed the tea bag from the metal pot of hot water; poured a cup. "I refuse to get into this with you."

Meaning, back off, none of your business. Trouble was, Luke had never been good at backing off. Not in court. Not in his personal life. Hadn't he drilled his logic—or illogic as she'd once called it—into their marriage?

And now?

Now, strange as it was even to him, he wanted a chance. He wanted to be that man she could count on, that better man. He wanted the respect she gave to her beloved Boone.

She'll never believe you.

He had to try. "I won't give up, Ginny. We were a pair once, we can be again."

Her eyes hardened. "We didn't have kids."

"That was then. This is now."

She studied him as he bit into his pie. "How old are you, Luke? Forty-four? All those years you believed one thing, and in a week you change your mind? Sorry, that doesn't wash with me."

"It hasn't been a week. It's been…" A month? A year? Since Jon married Rianne? Since Seth married Breena? Since Luke witnessed how family had healed his brothers? Maybe. Or maybe it was Ginny *and* Alexei *and* little Miss Jo.

"I don't know," he said. "But I do know I'd like the opportunity to show you this is a more mature Luke you're looking at." He wrapped his fingers around hers; smiled. "I'm no longer the selfish bastard you knew."

"You were never selfish."

Only when it concerned her dream of family. What an

ass he'd been! "We had something once, Ginny. Was it so easy to forget?"

She rolled her lips inward, and gently withdrew her hand. "Oh, Luke. You ask too much."

He did. And when he drove her home back to her children, back to sleep on her couch, he damned himself for permitting the hollowness of their divorce to creep back into his soul.

Maxine Tucker loved Saturday mornings. Most of all, she loved reading to her little people, as she called them.

Maxine opened a copy of *The Very Hungry Caterpillar* and looked out over the twelve preschoolers crowded on the library's carpet at her feet. Sometimes she had to pinch herself; a year ago she would have been home, hiding in her shabby clothes and watching the *Ellen DeGeneres Show, Regis and Kelly, Dr. Phil, Oprah.* Daytime TV to kill the daytime blues.

Her daughters-in-law, Rianne and Breena, had encouraged her to volunteer at the Misty River Public Library. Maxine had always loved books and reading, though for too many years her vision had been hampered by beer and whiskey. Not until her granddaughter Hallie was five had Maxine finally given up her dates with Jim Beam. A granddaughter shouldn't have a drunk for a granny—the way her sons had a drunk for a mother.

She scanned her miniature audience, smiled. A couple of parents sat on chairs behind the group. At a nearby computer a young boy worked. Maxine offered him a little nod and received a shy smile in return. This was his second Saturday morning in the library. Why wasn't he out playing with other boys on such a bright day?

She held up the reader. "What do you think this story is about?" she asked her little charges.

"A caterpillar!" twelve voices shouted.

Maxine laughed softly. "What a clever bunch you are." She opened the first page. The group shifted closer. The boy at the computer leaned his arms over the back of his chair, listening.

She read three stories. Closing the last page, she said, "All right, princes and princesses, that's it for today."

"Aw, Miss Tucker." Heads shook, ponytails flipped, pigtails batted. "One of your stories. Please."

Her stories. Those she created in her head. The boy at the computer inched closer.

"Hmm," she said, pretending to give the suggestion a measure of thought. "There once was a little seashell who lived on a lonely beach…"

When she finished and the children scattered to their waiting mothers, Maxine noticed the computer boy had disappeared. Shaking out the sweater she'd folded in her lap, she rose slowly from her chair.

"Miss Tucker?"

He stood a couple feet away. "Oh," she said, "I thought you'd gone."

"Are you a retired teacher or something?"

She smiled. "Just a grandmother." He was a tall boy with a sweet face.

"I like the stories you tell best," he said.

"Thank you. What's your name?"

"Alexei. We moved here three weeks ago."

"Ah." She looked around. "You like books, Alexei?"

"I love books. Mama read to me when I was littler than my sister. She still reads to m—" He blushed.

Maxine said gently. "My boys used to beg me for bed-time stories." When she wasn't drunk.

"Is one of your kids Luke?"

She nodded, but her smile faltered. She saw them. Seth and Jon beside her on the pillows…. Luke, at her feet…. Always at a distance…. *Never good enough, sweet enough, loveable enough.* Buttoning her sweater, her fingers shook. "How do you know Luke?"

The boy looked away. "He, um… He's helping my mother."

"Who's your mother?"

"Ginny. She used to live here and they were married once—a long time ago," he added hurriedly. "But then they got divorced. Why did they get divorced?"

Maxine shook her head. Ginny Keegan was back? "I don't know." She picked up her purse and moved past the boy. *Luke and Ginny together again?*

Suddenly Maxine stopped. For a moment, she studied the boy. "Are you Luke's son?"

Had she dropped her day's garbage on his head, the boy couldn't have pulled a more sour face. "*No-o*. My dad was Boone Franklin. He used to live here just like Mama."

Boone? The Boone Maxine had grown up with? The Boone she and Maggie and Travis had chummed with since they were six? The Boone Maxine was going to marry—before Maggie drowned…?

"You must be mistaken, lad. Boone Franklin is old enough to be…" *Your grandfather.* Boone was married to Luke's Ginny?

"I'm not mistaken," Alexei insisted. "He is—*was* my dad. And now he's dead." Tears amplified the boy's eyes. "Can you tell Luke to leave my mom alone? We were fine until he showed up and started bossing everybody around and making everything into a—a stupid mess!" Biting his lip, he backed away. Another second and he rushed from the library.

A sharp, knife-edged pain sliced through Maxine's stomach. *Boone, dead?* She stared at the big oak doors. Alexei was his son?

Oh, Lord. Luke and Ginny.

Please, she half prayed. *Don't let my mistakes come full circle with this boy.*

On Sunday night, Luke leaned against Ginny's kitchen counter and watched Alexei labor over another written assignment. Since their "date" Friday night, Luke had convinced Ginny to let him stay the weekend. Well, *convinced* was a mild way of saying *bulldozed,* but he just couldn't watch her wrestle with those crutches, see the flashes of pain on her face and walk away.

Thus here he was, observing another stubborn struggle. Initially, he had wanted to expound on the benefits of doing homework Saturdays rather than leaving it until the last minute. He'd always faced his battles head-on. *Get it over with* was a motto he lived by. He'd learned early from his mother.

But Alexei was a child whose biological family had been extinguished. A child Luke saw as single-minded rather than belligerent. The same as Luke had been at ten.

"Ever used a tape recorder?" he asked in the near silence. Ginny sat in the front room reading Joselyn a bedtime story. The soft murmur of her voice drifted into the kitchen.

Alexei raised his head. "What for?"

"To get your ideas down first. To compose your sentences the way you want before you write them."

The boy surveyed what he'd written. Another exposé on Hemingway. He looked back at Luke. "No."

"Want to try it? I have a Dictaphone in my truck. Use it all the time when I need to do a court brief or report on a case."

"While you're driving?"

"Yep. Never get anything finished if I didn't."

"Cool." The word sprang into the warm kitchen before the boy realized. His cheeks pinked.

Luke smiled. "I'll get it."

A minute later, he set the instrument on the table and pulled up a chair. "I've put in a new tape. Here's where you record, stop, rewind, play." He demonstrated, clicking the buttons along the machine's edge. "Tape's double sided."

"Thanks."

"No problem. Give it a whirl."

Alexei clicked Record. "Testing, one, two, three. This is Alexei Franklin working on his novel study." He flashed a grin at Luke. "I feel like a CEO or something."

"You are a CEO. Of your homework."

"Yeah," the kid said. "Guess so."

Luke pulled up his chair beside Alexei. "Let me show you how to hold your pencil."

The boy drew back. "Why?"

"You're not holding it right."

"So?"

"Well, if you placed your fingers like this…" He took Alexei's hand, maneuvered the boy's forefinger into place along the pencil, his thumb beside the tool. "There. Try it now."

Alexei tossed down the pencil. "I've done it that way. Takes too long."

"To write?"

"Duh. Yeah, to write."

Luke picked up the pencil. The Net info encouraged kids to practice—a lot. "Nothing's perfect at first."

The boy scraped back his chair, gathered his books. "I don't wanna be perfect."

"No one's asking you to be, Alexei."

"Coulda fooled me. Here," he shoved the Dictaphone toward Luke. "Keep your stupid old tape recorder. I don't need it."

"What's going on?" Ginny asked. She stood leaning on one crutch in the doorway.

Alexei barged past her. "Nothing."

Seeing Luke, Joselyn bubbled out her lyrical little laugh and ran toward the kitchen table. "Daee!"

"Luke?" Ginny hobbled a step.

Carefully, he set the Dictaphone on the table. "Nothing." He rose and walked past her. "I'll be back in a while."

"Daee?" Joselyn queried.

"Come here, angel." Ginny held out a hand. "We'll finish the story."

"No!" She rushed after Luke, tears in her voice. *"Daeee!"*

He stepped onto the porch and closed the front door before the baby reached it. Her wails followed him into the night.

Chapter Five

What the *hell* was he thinking, screwing up that way? Just because he'd read a bunch of Internet research didn't make him an expert in knowing what was best for a kid he'd met a handful of days ago. And not just any kid, Ginny's son.

Luke strode across the clearing, heedless of the dark or the bumps and mounds left by construction trucks, and a logging era of decades past. He knew the path instinctively. He'd come a thousand times to the river with its soothing chuckle, skipped a thousand stones, thinking of the turmoil in his heart.

As a boy it had been his mother.

As a young man it had been Ginny.

Tonight it was her boy.

He wanted the kid's friendship. Or at least an ease between them. They'd nearly reached that ease minutes ago, but Luke had blown it. Figured he knew best. Just the way his mother had known "best" in his childhood: *"Don't make meat sandwiches for lunch. They grow bacteria." "Don't slouch. You'll get round shoulders." "Slant your book to write neater."*

Hell. How often had he come here, wishing away her criticism with every stone he skimmed across the water?

The short slope to the rocky section of beach loomed ahead between the trees. He halted at the bank's top. Shame and guilt might gnaw a hole in his gut, but he wasn't crazy enough to access the darkened trail to the water without a flashlight.

He tilted back his head, breathed deep of the crisp moist air. No moon floated in the sky. Instead the night spread like spilled ink over the earth. A rush of wings beat the air several feet to the left and, flinching at the cold draft, he strained to peer through the obscurity. But the bird—an owl?—had vanished.

"Place is spooked." Frowning, he recalled the woman's words while he knelt beside an unconscious Ginny on the street. Except for an assortment of birds and wildlife, including deer, not once had Luke encountered a ghost in thirty-five years of visiting this clearing or the river's rocky shoreline. Not the legendary Maggie Stuart sobbing at the water's edge. Nor the plagued Deke Franklin toting a winchester.

He wasn't about to imagine one now.

Still, the hair on his nape remained firm.

"All BS," he muttered.

He started back to the house where tonight the lit windows and porch offered a welcome the river ignored. And where Ginny, leaning on her crutch, searched the dark.

* * *

She watched Luke walk out of the night and enter the pool of porch light. Thank God. She'd called his name and he hadn't answered. But then, not wanting to distract Alexei or wake Joselyn, she'd called only once and not too loudly. Yet, images of holes and slippery rocks, and him cracking bones while she stood impotent, skittered through her mind.

She released the breath she'd held as he walked past their vehicles, straight toward her.

"Where did you go?" she asked when he stopped at the steps.

"The river. It's too dark to go down to the water. Baby okay?"

"Yes. Alexei's reading to her."

A corner of his mouth tugged. "Worried about me?"

Yes. She shook her head. "You're a big boy."

He came up the steps, stopping one below where she stood, his eyes level with hers. "That I am."

A whisper of breath on her cheek. She felt herself leaning toward him, toward the kiss she knew was there. In the dusk of the porch, his eyes were charcoal. Steady on her. Reeling her in to their mystery.

She pulled back, blinked. Levered her crutch. Spruced her spine. And remembered why she had come looking for him. "What happened between you and Alexei?"

A shutter closed over his face. "I offered my Dictaphone so he could tape what he wanted to say before writing it down."

"And?"

"He thought it was a neat idea. At first."

She waited, remembering her son's unhappy eyes.

Luke's chest rose in a deep breath, his discomfort corporeal. "I've done a little research. Once I explained the tape recorder, I thought I could show him how to hold his pencil. He, uh, took it the wrong way."

She could almost forgive him. He didn't know kids.

But he had been a kid himself. He'd known, *known,* how an adult's authoritative manner could crush the most fragile confidence.

And she'd told him about Alexei, what her son was up against. And still he'd interfered. She told herself his desire to help was that simple, but their years together had taught her Luke Tucker was a man geared to perfection. A trait that had evolved in his childhood while he tried desperately to please a mother who hated imperfection in her eldest son. In their marriage, Ginny had understood—and accepted—that everything required its place.

But that ended with their divorce. And with Robby, Alexei, Boone. Life was not perfect. Life was a series of bumps and bruises and *imperfect* conduits. Pups shredded shoes. Beds weren't always made. Children made messes.

And some had learning disabilities.

"You had no right to barge in and decide what is best for Alexei," she said, temper grazing the surface of her outward calm. "None at all. He is not your son." Crutch under her arm, she hobbled a step back. "I will ask you to remember you are a guest of your own choosing in my house, Luke. Do not muscle your way into the lives of my children—or me. Is that clear?"

His cheeks darkened, his nostrils flared. "As rainwater."

Ginny limped across the deck.

He said, "I was trying to help."

She turned. "Help? Did you not think we've gone through those physical maneuvers—how to hold a pencil, how to slant the page, how to form letters? Or did you think we simply let that slide by all these years until now? I told you we had him tested. Dozens of times. Buckets of frustrated tears have been shed, and not just by Alexei. He's an incredibly intelligent child. I will not have him humiliated over a tape recorder."

Luke stepped onto the deck, bewilderment sharpening the edges of his face. "Ginny, I wasn't doing it to humiliate him. I honestly thought I could help."

"He has help. From me and from his teacher after school."

"Please accept my apology. I'm no good at...this."

This. Raising a family. The anger in her ebbed. Luke might be stubborn, often misguided and cold in a court of law, but he did not have a cruel cell in his body when he saw defenselessness. The trait was the reason he was an outstanding lawyer.

She saw him glance toward the big bay window where, behind the drapes, Alexei and Joselyn sat on the sofa, playing with her dolly and tea set. Nearby, Bargain lay like a sausage, hind legs extended, gnawing Alexei's old sneaker.

"Think he'll talk to me?" Luke glanced at the window.

"I can ask."

"Thank you. And, Ginny?" A half smile. "I learn fast."

"Sometimes." Her eyes pinned his. He understood. It had taken him eight years to learn she could not survive without a family of her own.

"Come in," she said. "I'll get Alexei."

The boy shuffled into the kitchen where Luke waited at the table. God help him, but he had to do this right. For Ginny. For him, too, if he was ever to have her look at him again the way she had on the porch five minutes ago. When she'd almost leaned into the kiss he had wanted to give.

"Hey, Alexei," he said. "Pull up a chair."

The boy remained by the island. "Mom said you wanted to talk." *But I don't want to.*

The words slung between them.

"That's right," Luke said and smiled.

No return smile.

He continued, "I wanted to apologize for the pencil thing. I was wrong. There's a lot I don't know, including what you've experienced, and I was out of line thinking I knew better."

Alexei shrugged. "'S okay."

Luke relaxed in the chair, one arm hooked over the back, one resting on the table. Open body language, he knew, was key in discussions. "Actually, I was thinking if you showed me some stuff maybe I'd understand better."

"Like what?"

"I don't know. Maybe tell me what you're thinking when you're writing, that sort of thing."

Alexei's eyebrows slammed together. "So you can laugh?"

"Laugh?" Luke sat forward. "Alexei, the last thing I'd do is laugh at you. I may be a lot of things, but I'm not someone who finds his thrills in another's hardship."

He'd taken the boy aback. A mask dropped from his face.

"Okay," Alexei said after a long moment. He walked to the table, sat across from Luke. Bargain trotted into the kitchen; the boy patted his thigh, encouraging the dog closer. "What do you want to know?"

"How do you feel when you're writing?"

"What are you, a shrink?"

"I'm a guy who hasn't a clue what you go through."

Alexei narrowed his blue eyes. "Why?"

"Why what?"

"Why do you want to know so bad?"

Because I want to show your mother I'm not the ogre she believes. And I want to help you. "I've never run across your situation, and in my profession I see a lot of families who are in an unhappy state. Sometimes I find them alternative solutions. Sometimes these involve schools and teachers. I want to ensure the kids have proper school support—especially with a uniqueness like yours."

"Oh."

Luke smiled again. "Want to give it a whirl?"

The pup rested her head on Alexei's knee; he stroked her silky black ears. "Sometimes, I hate writing."

"Because it takes so long?"

"Because I can't get details down. They fly out of my head before I'm there, y'know?"

"Did you try the tape recorder tonight?"

"No." He shot Luke a side look. "I was mad."

"Don't blame you. I would be too if I had an arrogant idiot trying to tell me how to do something."

A small, sheepish grin unfolded. "Yeah."

Luke held out a hand. "Truce?"

Alexei took the offering. The child's hand was small, warm and a little damp. Like he'd been sweating. Luke's heart pitched.

"Does this mean I have to be your friend?" the boy asked when Luke gave his hand a good pump.

"It means we don't growl at each other."

"Oh. Well. See ya." Alexei jumped off the chair and with Bargain at his heels, bounded from the room. Two seconds later, the stairs rattled with pounding feet.

Beside the fridge, the kitchen clock, a gaudy sunflower, ticktocked. Luke looked around the big square room where already she had put her stamp. The sunny windowsill above the sink reminded him of their home in Seattle with its assortment of potted herbs. She'd loved raising her own spices then, too. White lacy curtains covered the window and the one in the back door. A frilly, pumpkin-hued apron hung on a hook near the pantry. Oven mitts of the same color lay on a narrow strip of counter beside the stove. On the island, bananas hung from a wooden hanger and apples and oranges filled a two-tiered wire basket.

A ragged cloth doll lay on the floor near the pantry and crumbles of dry dog biscuits scattered the newsprint around two metal bowls at the back door.

Luke rose to pick up the doll. At its soft, worn feel, something shifted inside his chest.

Home. A little love-frayed and so damned *real*.

Tilting back his head, he stared at the ceiling. Above him, Ginny was putting Alexei to bed. She'd climbed the stairs herself tonight. Slowly, arduously. Determined to prove her ambulatory capability remained. Determined to show him he wasn't needed.

Except…he needed her. And the children. The doll between his hands, the kitchen's warmth, the boy and his pup. The baby. He needed them all.

He'd lived twelve years alone and done fine. But he no longer looked forward to returning to his condo. To soundless nights and stark rooms.

Her husband hadn't yet grown cold in his grave.

Luke set the tattered doll on the island. *You damaged her leg. You owe her. Hell, you owe her a lifetime of help-me-outs.*

From the hall closet, he retrieved the sheet, pillow and blankets. At least for tonight he wouldn't be alone.

Two days later, with a midmorning sun streaming across the meadow, Ginny and Eva packed Joselyn into the station wagon and drove into town, Eva at the wheel.

As they headed down Main Street, Ginny asked, "Where should we start?"

"Wherever there are young mothers. The pool, the elementary school, the grocery store, post office, Toddler Trends."

"A clothing store won't put up my poster."

"Why not? They're in the business of preschoolers. That's the motto of Misty River. 'Businesses, support your people. People, support your businesses.' The banner hangs at the chamber of commerce." Eva ducked her head and looked at Ginny above the rim of her sunglasses. "I put it up when I was a member."

Ginny relaxed slightly. During the past week, she and Alexei had spent several hours on the computer composing just the right information and attractiveness for a dozen bright yellow posters announcing the grand opening of her preschool September 8.

Eva pulled up beside the curb of the post office and Ginny reached into the backseat for a poster. She reread its contents, just to make sure.

SMALL WONDERS PRESCHOOL
34 Franklin Road
Ginny Franklin, Early Childhood Educator
Caring, Creative, Experienced

She scrutinized *experienced*. Should she have included the eight years she worked at the Charleston preschool? Would a number have looked more official, more professional?

It's done, Ginny. Get on with it.

Skimming down, she reread the heart of her school.

Boys and Girls 2–4 Learning:

Arts/Crafts	ABC's	Language /Literature
Music/Song	Weather Watch	Dramatic Play
Reader's Corner	Circle Time	Snacks
Nature Walks	Math/Science	Nap Time
Woodworking	Creative Motion	Parent Hour

Register early for your chance to be a Small Wonder!

Against her throat the bump of emotion was huge. Her preschool. In West Virginia she'd been an employee. Here she'd be sole owner. Heady, that feeling.

Fanning the twenty tiny tags listing their phone number along the bottom of the page, she saw again Alexei's painstaking effort to form each digit. *Feel the shape, son.* Boone's words not more than six months ago.

"You'll be full up by the end of the week."

Ginny glanced at the woman beside her. "Oh, Eva. I hope so. But…" She sighed. Misty River was her heritage, the town where she'd grown up, fallen in love. The town she no longer knew.

"Uh-uh. No negative thinking. Remember, people have been crying for a preschool since I retired."

"Why didn't someone buy yours?"

Eva laughed. "That old double-wide? Thing needed a

ton of work. Besides, I sold it to a young couple who needed a home." She smiled. "Boy's in construction. He'll fix it up."

Ginny glanced back at Joselyn in her car seat. The baby had fallen asleep.

"I'll hang them up," Eva said.

Ginny opened her door. "I can handle it." She eased herself down to the curb. From the backseat, she tugged her crutch.

Inside the post office, the bulletin board was a paper rainbow. Dozens of sheets, advertising everything from kittens to piano parts to motorcycles. Her poster didn't stand a chance.

She tacked it to the wall beside the board.

"You Ginny Franklin?" A tall, thin woman with a toddler on her hip stood reading the poster.

"I am."

"Nobody's gonna bring their kids out there, y'know."

"Why not?"

"'Cause it's cursed."

She blinked. "Beg your pardon?"

"Your place. Haven't you heard of the legend? Don't know how you stand it. And with little kids, too."

Ginny laughed softly. "You mean the ghost legend? Hasn't that run its course? It's been forty years."

"Ghosts can hang around hundreds of years. Especially bad ones."

"Well, I can assure you. There's no ghost at my house."

The woman had skeptical eyes. "Don't say I didn't warn you." She turned and walked out the door.

The next stop was the public pool, then Chinook Elementary, where the principal headed Eva off with the excuse the school wasn't a commercial zone. They hit several more spots, including the grocery store before stopping at Toddler Trends.

"Franklin's is bad land," the proprietor, a thin blond woman about forty, said. "People die there and get burned and kinfolk go missing. Heck, just last year the police busted a marijuana crop."

Ginny fought the urge to roll her eyes.

At the car, she hoisted herself into the passenger seat. "This town is unbelievable. I don't get it. Half a century and people still act like Maggie Stuart drowned yesterday." She shifted, held out a hand to Joselyn who grabbed her fingers. "How you doing, punkin?"

"Mam. Go?"

"Home, baby. We're going home. We'll try again tomorrow."

Today, three out of twelve. Dismal odds.

"Let's see if Kat's Kitchen will take a poster," Eva suggested. "And grab a coffee while we're at it." She glanced in the rearview mirror. "Maybe Kat will make a yummy cracker with jam or have some fruit yogurt. Would you like that, Miss Muffett?"

"Bab." The baby kicked her feet, clapped her tiny hands.

Ginny laughed. "Not patty-cake, angel. Cracker."

She was in a booth along the street-side windows with Eva across the table and Joselyn in a high chair munching a piece of toast and jam when she spotted Luke.

His back was toward her. Seeing those big shoulders enveloped in a cobalt-blue shirt and that crisp, dark hair—and his companion's enraptured face...Ginny's pulse stumbled.

Of course he knew other women. Young women. With willowy bodies and fresh faces. Without kids.

So had she read him wrong then? Those long-eyed looks? That almost kiss on the porch? Those subtle innuendoes?

Can't we at least be friends? he'd asked.

They had been once. He'd been her mate for life. She had imagined them returning to each other in different lifetimes.

But that was before. Before she'd realized how in-grained were his fears. Before the divorce. *Before Robby.*

The woman's pretty eyes went dreamy. She flashed a coy smile. Ginny jerked her gaze back to Eva, to Joselyn.

"More coffee, ladies?" Kat paused beside them.

"If you'll bring us each one of your to-die-for apple muffins, Kat." Eva held up her hand to Ginny. "This is my round."

"And you, little miss cutie-pie?" Kat bent and smiled at Joselyn. The little girl offered her a chunk of toast. Kat grinned. "Thank you, sweetums, but it'll do better in your tummy than mine." She kissed the baby's unruly blond curls. "Mmm. I could just about gobble you up. You ladies want those muffins warmed?"

"Absolutely," Eva said. "And Kat?" She held out the poster. "We're wondering if you wouldn't mind display-ing this where people will read it?"

The grandmotherly waitress set down her carafe and took the bright yellow sheet. Her sharp, blue eyes scanned the print. She looked at Ginny. Smiled. "After what you went through out front of my restaurant…you bet. I'll set it right beside the till. And I'll even point it out to those I figure could use your facilities. But I will warn you." Leaning down, she lowered her voice. "There are folk in this town who still remember what old Deke Franklin did."

Not that again. Ginny fiddled with her napkin. "You mean that he killed himself? But that was decades ago."

"Trouble is, people here have long memories." She poured the coffee. "Ask me, it's time this thing was put to bed."

When she'd left, poster and carafe in hand, Ginny wiped Joselyn's dumpling cheeks, nibbled on her little fingers.

Luke rose from his chair. His black trousers fell in a clean line to glossy black shoes.

Sorrow scraped her heart. At twelve would Robby have resembled his father? So tall and strong and darkly handsome?

En route through the restaurant, the woman at his heels, Luke greeted fellow diners. A nod, a word, a touch to the shoulder.

"Da." Turned in the high chair, Joselyn extended sticky fingers. "Daeee!"

Luke's head swung around, silver eyes searching, finding.

Electricity shot along Ginny's skin.

"Mam. Daee!" Several patrons twisted in their seats. Luke grinned—and headed for their table.

"Hey," he said. "Didn't expect to see you all here."

"Daee." Joselyn wanted up. In Luke's arms.

"We're distributing posters for my preschool." Ginny wiped the baby's fingers as the tot struggled to stand. The last thing she needed was Luke's pristine shirt mottled with jam prints.

"Great. I'll take a couple, put them up at my office."

Relief rushed into her smile. "Thanks. There, muffin," she said to Joselyn. "All clean."

"Up." The baby held her arms to Luke. "Daee. Up."

Kat arrived with the two steaming muffins.

"Luke." His companion touched his arm.

He turned. "Ah, Kim. Right. Contact my secretary. She'll set up a time."

Joselyn began to fuss.

"Sure." The woman flashed Ginny an ice-cold look. "Whenever."

"Daee. Up. *Up.*"

"Let's go with Friday." He lifted Joselyn from the chair. "Otherwise it's next Wednesday."

Ginny stared at Luke. She doubted he realized how daddylike his actions appeared.

The woman nodded. Her gaze flicking from Luke to Joselyn, whose head was resting on his shoulder, and back. "Bye, Luke."

But he was looking at Ginny. "Mind if I join you?"

She moved across the bench, pulling her casted leg out of the way. He settled in, close. Their thighs touched. Warmth fed Ginny's cheeks.

Eva nodded at the baby sucking her thumb on Luke's shoulder. "She's certainly taken with you, buddy."

"Don't know why," he muttered.

Ginny said, "She thinks you're Boone."

"Well, I'm not Boone." Irritation sparked.

Their eyes held. "No." Ginny offered a piece of muffin to her daughter; the baby turned her face into Luke's neck. "You're not. But it's—"

"Ginny Franklin?" A tall, angular man and mousy-haired woman paused by the booth. The woman held a poster tag. "How much you gonna charge? For your preschool?"

Hope raised an antenna. "You interested in registering?"

"Maybe."

Maybe, depending on her costs. She quoted a price. The man nodded. "We'll be in touch."

Eva's face bloomed creases. "You'll end up with a waiting list before the week's out."

Joselyn suddenly lifted her head. "Ma. Poo."

"Uh-oh."

"What?" Luke asked.

"She's ready for a number two."

His eyebrows pitched. "She is?"

"Yes, and *now.*"

Eva scrambled from the bench, diaper tote in hand. "I'll take her." She reached for the baby, but Joselyn locked on Luke's neck like an Australian joey.

"Daee, *go.*"

"No way." Eyes wild, he looked at Ginny. "I can't take her. I know nothing about changing diapers."

She sat back and crossed her arms. "Guess you'll learn."

"Ginny."

"Daee! Pooo!"

Eva waited at his shoulder. "Luke Tucker, you're coming with us whether you want to or not. *Now.*"

Joselyn howled.

Restaurant patrons stared.

Ginny couldn't help it. She giggled. Then laughed.

"You owe me, lady." Luke glowered and slipped from the bench, a red-faced Joselyn choking his neck.

Yes, she thought, watching his tall frame stride away. *I do owe you.* Because she could no longer deny that in the eleven days of their son's life Luke would have worried as much as she. And possibly cried as many tears.

Clueless. That was how he was with babies. And ones sporting a stinky diaper…forget it. Joselyn, determined not to go with Eva into the ladies' washroom, shrieked until Luke feared she'd rupture a tonsil. The harder he tried to tell the baby he couldn't go with her, the harder she screamed. And the smellier the little washroom corridor became.

"Damn it, Eva. Take her. I'll wait here."

Digging little fingers into Luke's neck, Joselyn kicked her miniature hard-soled sneakers out at the older woman, and spurred his ribs. *"No-no-no-no! Daee!"* Tiny pearl tears fell from her leaf-green eyes.

Eva shoved the diaper bag into his free hand. "She wants *you,* bright boy. Now take her in the mens' before Kat's customers stampede out the door with all this ruckus."

"Come on, Eva—"

"She isn't really potty trained yet, so find a clean spot to lie her down. The wet wipes are in the bag."

"Eva—"

"Boone would've done it."

Luke glared. "Wait here."

"Oh, I will." Eva smirked. "Wouldn't miss it for the world."

Slapping a palm against the door, he strode into the washroom. Joselyn hiccuped against his neck. "Miss Josie-Lyn, you are one ornery gal. I don't know why you're so enthralled with me. I don't look anything like your dad."

"Da." A sweet smile exhibited a dozen tiny, perfect teeth.

"Okay, the defense rests, Your Honor. We won't argue case in point for fear the witness will shriek in my ears again."

Luke looked around the empty washroom. Two stalls. Three urinals. A couple sinks—with counter surface between, which appeared semi-sanitary, but he wasn't taking any chances. Hooking the diaper bag over his shoulder, he stepped to the paper towel dispenser and tugged free a batch of sheets.

After arranging the toweling on the counter, he laid Joselyn on them. The baby stared up with solemn eyes. Crying had spiked her dark lashes. A last wee tear rested on her pillowy cheek.

Luke's heart split in two. And lay humbled at the awesome innocence, the *dependence* in those Ginny eyes.

"Sure wish I knew what you wanted, little lady," he whispered. He plunked the bag beside the baby. Zipping the bag open, he looked inside. "Clean one of these, maybe?" He held up a diaper.

The baby remained silent, motionless. She'd fisted her hands in a prayer-lock under her chin.

"Yeah, I'd be praying, too, sweetheart," he muttered.

Her eyes moved in sync with his gestures. He opened the new diaper, spread it out on the bag. Studied it. He should have paid attention to those ads on TV. "This is the bottom," he finally determined. "Where you'll sit." But how did it stick to the kid? He searched the bag for pins. Looked back at the diaper. "Never mind. We'll check the old one." He took a breath and nearly choked. "Jeez, kid. What'd you unload in there? A Dumpster?"

Slowly he began pulling off her pink tyke jeans. Trouble was, *everything* was coming with them. "Oh, shi— Sorry. I meant shoot. *Shoot,* this is *not* working. Okay, let's see. Take pants off, Luke. Pants first, *then* underwear. Diaper, I mean."

Five tries and he'd accomplished the first step. Or almost. The pants hung inside out from her dwarf sneakers. Luke closed his eyes. How the hell did Ginny deal with this every day, all day long? *"Boone would've done it."*

His eyes snapped open. Joselyn still stared at him. Waiting.

Determined to outdo the ghost of Boone Franklin, Luke ripped open the diaper. "Holy...*smokes*. All that from such a little woman? Incredible." He searched the bag for the wet wipes. "You, Miss Josie-Lyn, are going to learn about toilets. They're the most fascinating, most enjoyable, most technology-inclined pieces of equipment ever invented by mankind. You would not believe how intelligent it makes people when they use 'em. You can read the news, do crossword puzzles, check the stock market."

He talked and cleaned and finally it was done. Joselyn stood on the counter, smelling fresh as a newly picked rose. Carrying tote and baby, Luke left the washroom.

Eva's eyebrows lifted.

"Piece of cake." He strode through the restaurant to where Ginny greeted him with a smile that lifted his lonely heart.

Chapter Six

"Alexei?" Ginny knocked on the door of her son's bedroom. Three minutes ago—it had taken her the speed of a fast snail to climb to the second floor, damn her broken leg—Alexei had stormed through the front door, heading straight for the stairs.

"He wouldn't even say hi when I picked him up from school," a worried Eva whispered. She stood at the top landing. "Not a word all the way home."

Ginny knocked again. Beside her, Bargain whined.

"Alexei. I'm coming in."

The door swung open. "Mom, I don't wanna talk right now."

Puffy red eyes, mottled cheeks. He'd been crying. *Oh, baby.* Her mother's protective instincts reared; she debated forcing the issue, slaying the dragon directly. "All right. I'll give you time to calm down." *She'd* need time to calm down. Crutch thumping, she started for the stairs and Eva.

"Mama?"

Ginny swung around. His eyes were misery. "They call me Casper."

Casper the friendly ghost. A sixty-year-old cartoon character as familiar to today's youth as previous generations of children. Legends and curses and unkind names. Passed from father to son, grandmother to grandchild.

Ginny limped to where Alexei stood in the doorway, Bargain leaning against his leg. "Who's calling you Casper, honey?"

He shrugged. "Doesn't matter."

She stroked the hair from his eyes. "It all matters when it concerns you or Joselyn. Did you speak to Mrs. Chollas?"

Panic. It flooded his face. "No! Mom, do *not* tell Mrs. C., okay? I can handle this on my own. Don't tell, *please.*"

Ginny studied his anguished eyes. She would do anything for her child. Anything. Including removing the posters. Forgetting the preschool. Boone's funds and pension would get them through several more years. Once her leg was healed, she would get a job in town. Face the gossipmongers on their own turf.

"Okay." She lifted his chin so there would be no mistaking her words. "But, honey? If it goes further than name-calling I won't be sitting idle."

Eagerly, he nodded. "I know and it won't, Mama. I have friends there. Ian, he's the class genius and is really respected, and this popular girl, Brittany. I think she's related to Luke 'cause her last name's Tucker. They're cool. And Jones—that's his last name, but he likes being called Jones—we always team up in math projects and computers. And there's this really cute girl, Nina. I think she likes me." Pink swept his skin at this last disclosure. "Anyway," he said, staring at the floor. "We all hang out at recess and lunch. They… They help."

Ginny breathed relief. And guilt. Three weeks he'd been at Chinook Elementary. She hadn't known of his budding friendships, its growing pains. *Too busy dreaming of your preschool, Ginny.* And a certain persistent man.

She asked, "How'd your session with Mrs. Chollas go after school?"

"Good. Now can I do my homework?"

"Sure. Want a snack first?"

"I'll get one in a bit."

"Okay." She gave him a smile and turned for the stairs.

Eva met her at the bottom in front of the childproof gate. "When he came out of the school his friends weren't there."

"After tutoring?"

"I had the car windows down. There were three boys and two girls playing at one of the basketball hoops."

"Do you know who they were?"

Eva unlatched the gate. "I've taught them all at my preschool. They're not bad kids, Ginny."

"But misguided by their parents."

"And their grandparents."

"I'm taking my posters down."

The older woman stared, then rehooked the gate. "You're not doing any such thing."

Ginny hobbled to the kitchen. Alexei liked yogurt with grapes and strawberries. "I won't have my kids threatened by my job." She looked over her shoulder. "And that's all it is, Eva. A job."

"It's your dream."

"Yeah, well, dreams don't always work out." A truth in three faces: Luke, Robby, Boone. She turned on the tap, rinsed the fruit. "I don't want to talk about it anymore."

"Fine," Eva said, her mouth mulish. "Give up then."

"I call it compromise. You know, life's survival tool."

"Hmph. We'll see about that."

The phone rang. Eva picked up the receiver. "Franklin residence." For a long moment she was silent. Ginny lifted her eyebrows. "Yes," Eva said, "she's right here." Holding out the phone, she said, "For you. The man from the restaurant. He wants to enroll his four-year-old in your preschool."

Luke hadn't shut off the engine of his car at Ginny's before Eva opened the driver's door and grumped, "Tell her she's crazy to let a bunch of gossip hounds ruin her chances." Wheeling around, the woman he'd hired as nanny and housekeeper marched to her car, tossed in her purse and drove away.

Ruin her chances? What the hell...?

Dragging his briefcase with him, he climbed from the Mustang. Tonight he needed to review a custody case, two divorces and an estate dispute. But first, Ginny. Every day he looked forward to the instant she opened the door—he still knocked—and their eyes met. Hers full of wonder, as if his presence wavered like a distant mirage. His full of feelings he had stashed under the heel of time.

At the door his knock went unanswered for a third time. Pushing open the door, he stepped inside. Upstairs, giggles and pattering feet.

"Joselyn!" Ginny's voice. "Come back here, imp."

More giggles. *Thump thump thump.* Ginny's crutch.

"Miss Franklin, if you're not in bed in one minute," she singsonged, "you are in *biiiig* trouble."

Luke's mouth twitched. Uh-huh. Big hugs and kisses, more like. Leaving his briefcase on the coffee table, he took the stairs two at a time. Joselyn, in yellow pajamas patterned in hopping bunnies, met him at the landing's gate.

"Da*ee!*" Joy broke over her face and fell into his heart.

"Hey, tyke. What're you doing up this time of night?" Luke unhooked the gate to enter the hallway. And there was Ginny. Leaning on her crutch, smiling at him. "Hi," he said.

"Hi."

"Da." Joselyn latched happily on to his leg. "Hoe."

"Luke," Ginny rectified. "Luke."

Oddly, her correction sent a little stab into his heart.

The baby craned back her neck. "Da hoe."

"Yup, Luke's in your home, all right." Stroking the child's soft curls, he smiled at Ginny. "Where's Alexei?"

"Downstairs on the computer."

"Dog with him?"

"Yes."

"Ah. That explains no one answering my knock."

"Probably has his headset on."

Luke looked down at the little girl tugging his pant leg. "I thought Eva puts her to bed."

"She did, but Joselyn started crying the minute she left so I came up to see what was wrong and… Luke, she was standing in the crib pointing toward the washroom with one hand and holding her diaper with the other, saying, 'Jo go pot.'"

"Jo go pot?"

"Her first complete sentence." Ginny's eyes shone. "She's never said a sentence with a subject, predicate and object."

"She hasn't?" he asked stupidly.

Ginny shook her head, tears in her eyes. "Boone would be so proud."

Boone. Well, damn it, *he* was proud, too. The kid said a sentence and Ginny was sharing it with *him.* Without thinking, he bent and picked up the baby. "So," he said. "You uttered your first sentence, huh? Do you know what that means, button? It means you've joined the Land of Western Civilization and you are definitely of the species called humanoid. I'm impressed."

Ginny laughed. "You weren't this morning."

"This morning was a hundred years ago. Did she, you know—" he hitched his chin toward the washroom "—do her thing?"

"Sort of. And then she escaped."

"An escapee, too. Want her in the crib?"

"Please."

Luke walked down the hallway to the baby's room. He set her inside the crib. Expecting a fuss, he was surprised when she immediately plopped to the mattress. Tugging a worn yellow blanket to her nose, she crawled into a small ball just as two tiny fingers slipped into her mouth. A few snuffling sounds and her eyes closed.

"That's her blankie," Ginny whispered beside him. "She won't sleep without it."

Mesmerized, Luke clutched the crib's railing. A half-dozen baby scents—notably soap, oil, milk—alerted his nose. A confusion of emotions battered his heart. Out of the mix poked a star, tiny and piercing. Love. It shook him to his toes and bounced off his skin. He was a doofus around kids. Most times, their needs and behaviors were alien limbs extending from their bodies. If pressured, he'd admit he feared babies. Feared their innocence, their vulnerability. But, God help him, here he stood, dumbstruck with the pangs of first love.

"Are you all right?" Ginny asked.

He blinked. "Yeah." Cleared his throat. "She's so small."

"At birth…" Ginny spread her hands, palms up, and touched pinkies. "She was about as big as a leaf of romaine lettuce."

"Scary."

"A little, but every day it gets better."

He turned and looked at Ginny. Light from the corridor haloed her blond hair. His fingers itched to touch, to push through the soft tangle of uneven curls. To skim the length of her cheek where the light dipped, then down her neck, to the fragile collarbone in the V of her pink blouse.

Realizing where his thoughts had gone, he met her eyes. She stared back at him. Understanding clearly. But then she'd always understood him, and vice versa.

Deliberately breaking the spell, he said, "How much better did it get today?"

A slight frown curved her brows.

He said, "Eva hinted I should stop you from letting, quote, a bunch of gossip hounds ruin your chances, unquote. Care to tell me what's going on?"

Frown shifted to scowl. "Eva needs to mind her own business."

Marshaling the crutch under her arm, Ginny left the baby's room. In the hall, she headed for the stairs.

Luke reached the gate first. "Tell me."

She sighed. "Kids at school are calling Alexei ghost names."

His jaw tightened. "Let me guess. You want to cancel the preschool to ward them off."

"Only until people get used to me living here and realize there are no curses, no ghosts, *nothing*."

He drew a fast, hard breath. Much as he enjoyed his career and the languid pace of Misty River's community, some folks needed a wake-up call. Since his brother Seth had begun repairing Ginny's cottage two weeks ago, rumors whispered like fog in the night. Hell, he suspected her sanity had been questioned the moment she'd moved into the house. When she lay on the pavement, unconscious because of his car, they'd tossed comments about like a circus juggler with a batch of knives.

"Luke." Her eyes searched his face. "Do not get involved."

"Did I say I would?"

"I know that look."

"Then let me help."

"You've done enough." Balancing on one foot, she unlocked the gate. As it swung open, she straightened. "Which we need to finish here and now. It's time. Thank you for everything you've done. The kids and I are immensely grateful. But your nights on the couch are done." She gave him a sweet smile. Wrapped her warm hand around his forearm. "We'll be okay, Luke. Promise." She lifted on the toes of her good foot to kiss his jaw.

And just like that his head moved.

The corners of their mouths brushed.

Her eyes were open. Green overlaid his world for a clock tick before he pressed in closer.

Motionless, she stood while he savored. *Ginny. Ah, Ginny.*

His hand found the warm nape of her neck. He drew her closer still. And thought he'd die when her tongue touched his lips.

Years fell away. All the loneliness of the past decade vanished. She was his wife again, his lover.

His heart. His home.

He wanted to pick her up and carry her to some private place. Some place where he could simply hold her. Where he could let her see inside his soul. See the scars of her leaving that had never quite healed.

Slowly, he eased the kiss, lifted his head. Her eyes were closed and he waited a heartbeat until they fluttered open. And he saw the tears. *Aw, Ginny.*

Was she crying for him or for the father of her children?

He ran a thumb along her cheek, down her freckled nose. Nothing about her had changed, yet everything had changed.

He wanted to tell her she was beautiful. He wanted to tell her he'd be there for her, every step of the way. He wanted to ask if they could begin again.

But in the end his words lay dormant. She whispered, "Bye." Balancing her crutch, she limped to her bedroom.

He stared down the empty hallway. The house fell into a hush. Joselyn's door remained open, Ginny's closed. He almost walked back to peek in at the baby, at her sweet little face. Instead, he went down the stairs where he grabbed his briefcase off the coffee table.

Twenty feet away, in her office, Alexei sat at the computer. Luke hesitated. The kid wouldn't want his assistance anyway. A tough nut like his mother.

He walked out into the night.

* * *

Luke was ten again.

Skinny, small, dirty. Bulldozing roads with Tonkas in the backyard mucked the knees of your pants and T-shirt, and glued dirt to your palms and shoved it under your nails.

In the kitchen of his childhood home, his mother had a glass tipped to her mouth. The liquid was the color of those dried old flower stalks in that dirt patch by the front porch.

Her hard eyes held him by the back door. Her mouth curled down. "Whatcha lookin' at?"

"Nuthin', Mother." He had to call her *Mother* while his brothers called her *Mom.*

"You're filthy." *Filthy,* like it was vomit.

"I was driving bulldozers." A man's voice. How could his voice be a man's when he was only ten?

His mother came toward him, wobbling a little, the liquor in her glass doing The Wave. "Why are you always filthy?"

"I was playing," he said, and his boy's voice was back. He scuffed a toe on the mat. "I didn't mean to."

"You never mean to. Do you know how much I hate filthy kids?" Before he could answer, she went on, her tone rising. "Your brothers don't get this filthy. Your brothers play *clean.*"

"But Jon and Seth get dirty, too," he whispered.

"Dirty. Not *filthy.*" Her palm caught him across the ear and his head snapped back. "Filthy, filthy, filthy! I hate filthy!"

"I know, Mother. I won't do it again. Never. Never, Mother, *never. Never. Never.*"

Luke jerked awake, gasping air. Sweat mired his skin to the sheets. His bedroom lay silent and dark.

He looked at the digital clock on his nightstand—2:24.

When his breathing eased, he allowed himself to recall the nightmare. He hadn't had one in almost two years.

Conned yourself into thinking they'd disappeared, did you?

So what brought this one on?

Who cared?

Tossing back the sheets, he swung his feet to the floor. For a long minute, he rested, elbows on knees.

The dream scene hovered in his mind.

He rubbed his bristly cheeks.

His nightmares always held an element of his life he'd rather forget. Maxine had hated dirt; she'd made him wash his hands ten times a day when he wasn't at school.

From the time he was four until he was fourteen—when he'd finally told her to go to hell—he remembered the rough, chapped skin of his hands. *Thank God for you, Daddy, and your ever-ready jar of Noxema.*

Luke walked to the bathroom. He flipped on the light, blinked against its harshness. The echo in the mirror shocked him. Bruised eyes. Hollow cheeks.

Joke's on you, bud. You've never been a success, only a man with crappy memories.

Memories that had been barking at his heels all his life.

Don't you think it's time to put an end to it?

Trouble was, he'd only found an end with Ginny. With her at his side, he'd had no nightmares, no disquieting nights.

He filled a glass with water and drank deep. Shutting off the light, he stumbled back to bed. The sheets were cold, damp. He pulled them over his chilled body.

And hoped the dreams were finished for the night.

* * *

At ten-thirty the next morning Ginny opened the door to a tall brunette dressed in a navy business suit. She held a black briefcase. "Ginny Franklin?"

"Yes?"

The woman smiled. Her teeth advertised thousands of dollars of dental work. "My name's Rachel Brant. I'm a reporter with the *Misty River Times*. We hear you're planning a preschool." She took in the cottage. "That it over by the woods?"

"It will be when it's fixed," Ginny said carefully. "Why do you want a story on my preschool?" Did reporters write stories to promote local businesses? Tragedy, scandal, sorrow, horror. Those were the stories they chased. The juicier, the better.

Another orthodontic smile. "Yours will be the first for our little community in two years."

Okay, maybe her dream could be cited as news.

Bargain trotted onto the porch and sniffed the reporter's open-toed sandals.

"Hi, puppy," she crooned. "You're a cutie."

The dog's tail stayed down. Not one wag.

"Mama?" Joselyn clutched Ginny's casted leg and peered up at their visitor.

Rachel Brant bent to share a smile with Joselyn. "Aw, isn't she just the sweetest little thing."

Joselyn hid behind Ginny's leg.

Animals and babies don't lie. "Thank you, Ms. Brant," Ginny said. Upstairs, where Eva straightened the beds, a thump sounded. "But if I need to promote my preschool, I'll buy an ad." She moved to close the door.

The woman jumped forward, smile gone. "Mrs. Franklin,

please. I'd really like to do a story on your school. There's been talk…and I think you need all the publicity you can get."

"Talk?"

"About this place. Do you know about the legend?"

Not promotion, sensationalism. "I know about the legend."

"I can dispel it for you. Make people see another side. Bring the older generation up to the present century, so to speak." Again the megadollar smile.

Ginny regarded the woman. Tiny lines fanned her eyes. No spring chicken.

Brant's smile slipped. "Mrs. Franklin," she said softly. "I can help you."

"Why would you want to? You don't know me from Adam."

The smile disappeared. "Because I've had a lesson or two from the school of hard knocks. When my husband died a year ago, the paper was the only decent job I could get. I do their feature stories. It doesn't pay much, but then I work at the dry cleaners to compensate. So I know how hard it is to make ends meet."

"Do you have children, Ms. Brant?" If the woman had children…

"We—we weren't blessed."

Ginny's heart caved. She stepped back. "Come in, then."

Luke hauled another bunch of rotted wallboard to the Dumpster his brother had placed beside Ginny's cottage. Seth was spending the Saturday with his family and Luke needed some manual labor to get his mind off Ginny.

Right, so the best spot to do that is two-hundred feet from her house?

She wouldn't be up yet. Hell, *he* shouldn't be up yet. Not at 6:10 a.m. on a day off.

Grunting, he shoved the broken pieces over the top of the metal bin. Shoved in his mental argument, as well.

He shot another look toward the house. Ginny. Over the past two days, he'd relived their kiss a thousand times. What had she felt? Thought? Would that spine of hers turn to steel when he stepped into her space again? Kissed her again?

And he would. God help him, but he would.

A Trojan army couldn't keep him away.

Navy clouds, pregnant with rain, sheathed the morning sun. A small whirlwind scooted leaves and dust into the air as he trudged back to the cottage.

Another nightmare had visited last night. Or rather at five this morning. Two in less than three days. This one had to do with Ginny telling his eight-year-old persona to stop climbing walls. He'd never climbed walls. Mental ones, yes, but not the crash-and-knock-yourself-out kind.

The pile Seth had left on the cottage's floor was down to a few chunks of scattered wood. Luke bundled them together. Outside, a raindrop splattered on his forehead.

Terrific. He'd wanted to insert the window in the kitchenette this morning. Yesterday, Seth had brought the glass and told Luke if he wanted to work up a sweat this weekend to help himself.

Tossing the last armload into the bin, he scanned the surrounding yard for other debris. And envisioned a small playground with swings, a teeter-totter and a slide.

She wanted a fence around the building. A fence with flowery plants climbing the wood.

He'd examined her sketches on her office desk that first week when he'd wandered the main floor, unable to sleep. He should feel guilty. Snooping wasn't his style. Plain and simple? He wanted to know Ginny again. Know her dreams. Her heart.

He walked toward the rear of the cottage. Raindrops coined the dusty soil. As he came around the corner, he saw the damage.

Broken glass. Shattered windows. Graffiti.

Someone had destroyed the bathroom and bedroom windows and sprayed the newly hung vinyl siding in red paint.

Heart pumping, Luke gaped at the crooked script.

Kids and ghosts do not mix.
Put them together—beware the jinx.

He stood motionless, physically calming his lungs, his heart, the rage rocking through his veins.

In town he'd heard the gossip. From the moment she'd fallen to the pavement, the innuendoes had begun.

The rain quickened, a needle-sharp drizzle, drenching his hair and shirt. Back around the cottage he strode. Inside, he flipped open his cell phone, punched Speed Dial.

One ring. Luke checked his wristwatch—6:17. Two rings.

"Chief Tucker here," Jon said in his cop voice.

Luke thanked fate for small favors that his brother headed Misty River's police department. "It's Luke. I need you at Ginny's. Her property's been vandalized." His heart squeezed. Since the moment he'd run her down in the street with his car, one thing after another had gone wrong. Maybe *he* was the curse.

"What's been done?"

Luke imagined Jon, notepad in hand. "Broken window, graffiti to the building Seth's been fixing."

"The preschool?"

"Correct."

"Don't touch a thing. I'll send Pete over to take some shots right away."

"I want *you* here." Luke's voice rose.

"Easy, buddy. I'm on my way, but you're calling me out of bed, remember, and the camera's at the office. I don't want to waste time going there to pick it up."

"Oh." Luke's blood settled a little.

"Ginny there?"

"Still sleeping. The house is dark."

"What're you doing there?"

"Giving Seth a hand. Look, I'm sorry if I woke Rianne. I know she's up with the baby through the night."

"Cross your fingers. Travis Nicholas has been sleeping eight to ten hours for the past month."

A small intimacy his brother hadn't bothered to share during their Wednesday dawn breakfasts at Kat's Kitchen—a ritual Luke, Seth and Jon developed when Jon returned to Misty River two years ago. In the past year, Luke noticed a certain reticence in his brothers about their home lives. As if they were uncomfortable sharing their happiness with him, the remaining bachelor and eldest son. While Luke couldn't fault Jon or Seth, he often felt excluded during those moments. An outsider.

In the doorway of the cottage, he watched the farmhouse through the rain.

Your own failing. You blew your chance.

"Give them both a kiss for me," he told Jon.

"Always do. See you in a few minutes."

Luke slipped the phone into its belt holster. The house across the meadow beckoned with its warmth, its life.

If you'd let her have her wish twelve years ago...

He scrubbed a hand over his damp stubbled cheek. Hell. He had to quit wanting back the past, wanting *her.*

He walked to the bedroom, surveyed the mess of glass littering the hardwood floor. Seth, methodical and steady, had started renovations in here. Now all the room needed was paint, new wainscoting and crown molding. And, of course, a new window.

Ginny had mapped the room for her students' afternoon naps.

Luke hoped she wouldn't clobber him with her crutch when he moved a cot in tonight.

From under her umbrella, she stood staring at the jagged glass clinging to the frame of the bedroom and bathroom windows. Reread the horrible words sprayed between them.

When Luke had awoken her, she'd nearly fainted seeing him looming over her bed.

How did you get in here? she'd demanded.

You gave me an emergency key, remember?

This was the emergency.

A creep scaring her with cowardly acts.

She pressed her lips together. Swallowed down the fear. Not for herself. For her children.

What was next on the coward's list?

She watched the deputy—Pete?—kneel for a close-up

shot of a shard spiking through the grass. Through the open window she heard the bass tones of Luke and Jon. After she'd pulled on her tear-aways and a sweater, she'd roused Alexei to keep an eye on Joselyn in case she woke before Ginny returned to the house. Luke had carried her down the stairs, out the door and across the two-hundred feet of uneven terrain to the cottage.

She'd wanted to *run* to assess the damage. And Luke had known what to do. Known she needed to go immediately.

"It's not too bad, Ginny." He tried to ease her pounding heart while she was in his arms with the rain rat-a-tatting on the umbrella she held over their heads. *"It can be repaired."*

Yes, it could be repaired. But what of the fear?

Alexei had sensed her distress and asked.

She would not lie to her children.

"Ginny." Luke touched her shoulder. "Come inside the cottage. You'll get chilled."

"I won't give up. This is wrong."

He took the umbrella, slipped an arm around her waist as she shifted her crutch. "I know, honey. Jon'll track them down."

They walked around the corner of the building, toward the door, away from where Pete explained his findings to Jon.

Luke helped her onto the slippery stoop. Inside the chilly, dank room, he shook the umbrella, set it on the kitchen island.

She said, "Bargain barked up a storm last night."

His brows smacked together. "What time?"

"Two-ish. I looked out the bedroom windows, but it was too dark. The dog woke Alexei. He opened his window, but we couldn't hear anything either."

"Just so you know, I'll be moving in here tonight, Ginny. We can't take the chance they'll come back."

He was offering safety. Again. "Luke—"

"Don't argue. This is serious."

Yes. It was, damn it. Crutch thudding the hardwood, she paced the length of the room, peered into the bathroom. Glass bits and shards had fallen across the newly installed toilet and linoleum and into the claw-foot tub. Thank heaven the culprits hadn't crawled through the windows and done more damage.

Luke came up behind her. His hands were warm on her shoulders. Instinctively she leaned back against him and his arms came around her. Lifting her hand, she curled her fingers around his wrist where it pressed her rib cage.

For a dozen slow heartbeats she stood embraced in warmth and silence and a thousand emotions.

Luke.

She'd barely slept a total of twelve hours since he'd kissed her on the landing of the stairs three days ago. Endless memories circled her in the nights. Touches on her skin. Eyes darkening. The shape of his lips…

He rested his chin against her hair. Her soul absorbed his support. She whispered, "I'm glad you're here."

His arms tightened a fraction. She felt him kiss her temple.

A few more seconds she luxuriated in his strength, then she righted the crutch and shifted away. She knew what she had to say for his own well-being and safety. "I can't let you take this on as your personal crusade."

"Crusade? We're talking protection, Ginny. Yours and the kids."

She nearly faltered. "I'll hire a bodyguard."

Those silver eyes darkened. "This isn't Hollywood. It's Misty River. Population 846."

"I don't want you sleeping here," she said stubbornly.

"It won't be forever, only until the police get the guy."

"That could take months."

"Don't underestimate Jon. He's a helluva cop."

"I'm not doubting Jon. Investigations can take time. It'll be frightening enough for Alexei to see the police hanging around here today without you adding to the blend of mystery and dread by becoming our personal protector."

His head reared back. "I'd never do anything to scare Alexei."

"*You* wouldn't, but the reason behind your presence will."

"He won't be alone," Luke said quietly. "It's scaring the hell out of me, too."

For a long moment, she couldn't breathe. Luke afraid? "All right," she said finally. "You win."

He kissed her forehead. "That's my girl."

Chapter Seven

The reporter, Rachel Brant, drove out two hours later. This time she had an umbrella over her head and a camera slung over her shoulder. She told Ginny the vandalism would instill a sense of sympathy from readers if she tied it to the original story about the preschool—which she hadn't finished yet.

Cold touched Ginny's skin as she watched the woman gaze toward the rain-shrouded cottage from where they stood on the porch. The police had gone, leaving with computerized statements and a multitude of photos.

Leaving behind their yellow crime-scene tape.

As if her property should be steered clear of, like a carcass rotting in the sun.

Ginny wished for Luke, but he'd left to inform Seth about the damage. Except for her children and Eva, they were alone. "When will the story come out?" she asked the reporter.

The woman flashed a smile. "Monday's edition. Anxious?"

"I'd be a fool to say no, wouldn't I? The media has been known to—" *sensationalize* "—put a certain slant on things."

Ms. Brant's pleasantries cooled slightly. "I don't, Mrs. Franklin. I report facts."

As they are, or as you see them? Years ago both Luke and Boone had been cited incorrectly in the paper—albeit in different states and at different times. "Good. Then I look forward to reading your article." Pivoting her crutch, she moved to the door. "I'll be here all morning, if you need me."

"What does your nanny think?" the woman asked.

Ginny hesitated. "I can't answer for Mrs. Asher, but like me, she's not happy about the situation."

"Do you think it was kids acting on the nonsense talked about in their homes?"

"I don't know what's discussed in other people's homes and I'm hardly in a position to speculate."

"But certainly you've heard the gossip?"

Ginny actually laughed. "If you haven't noticed, Ms. Brant, I'm on crutches *and* I have two kids. I'm not sure where I'd have time for gossip—*if* I were one to savor it. Which I'm not."

The reporter flushed. She pushed on. "Are they worried?"

"Who?"

"Your children." A sheepish smile. "Sorry, the questions keep popping up."

Yes, and so did the insinuations about curses and ghosts. "My daughter is too young to comprehend and my son… please understand, but I can't disclose how he feels."

Rachel Brant nodded politely. "Of course. Thank you

for your time." Shouldering her umbrella, she went down the steps and across the muddy yard.

Ginny hobbled into her warm house.

The chill remained on her skin.

Luke helped Seth board the windows. The police had gathered their evidence: pictures of the broken windows, glass shards and damaged wood; paint scrapings of the slogan; statements; and fingerprint dusting. The deputy had examined the ground outside the windows for footprints, but with the rainfall any boot marks or sneaker treads had been obliterated.

An hour before supper, Luke borrowed Jon's pickup and moved a cot, blankets, a small icebox, Coleman heater, radio and a few clothes and accessories into the cottage. He hadn't seen Ginny since morning, when she'd worried about how his presence on the property would affect her children. When she'd been in his arms. And he'd closed his eyes, closed off twelve years as if they'd never happened.

But they had. And she'd have to get used to him hanging around. In his opinion, he'd rather the boy fret about the "whys" and "how comes," than have something happen to the kid.

The rain had quit, though fresh clouds hung over the trees. The bleakness besieging the day increased as evening approached.

Relishing the warmth of the heater, Luke stood at the kitchenette's counter seeking a good classical station on the radio, when Alexei opened the door.

"Hey," Luke greeted the boy.

"Mom says you're invited to supper."

"I am, huh?" His heart skipped. She hadn't written him out of her life yet. He shut off the radio.

Alexei surveyed the room. Seth had ripped rotted Sheetrock from the walls and ceiling. In a corner the kitchen's cupboards sat on the clear plastic covering the hardwood floor. Tomorrow Luke would help his brother rewire and plumb before Seth re-covered the skeletal two-by-fours with new Sheetrock.

Alexei moved across the room. "Kind of messy."

"Happens during construction."

The boy peered into the bedroom where Luke had set up the cot and a couple boxes with his clothes. "You really gonna sleep here till they catch the bad guy?"

"Does that bother you?"

A shrug. "Nah."

But Luke saw the feigned nonchalance, the unease in the boy's eyes. Softly he said, "I'm here to help, Alexei, not to make matters worse."

Small shoulders drooped. "Mom's spooked. She doesn't let on, but I know. She kept looking out the window all day." He glanced toward the intact kitchen window. "And now it's getting dark and she's, like, shutting all the drapes. We've never had the drapes shut since we moved here. Not even her bedroom ones."

Luke recalled the moonlight glossing her room the night he'd knelt beside her bed. After today, he would prefer she move into town where she'd be less vulnerable. He said, "Your mom's just being extra careful. Nothing wrong with that."

"I wish my dad were alive. He'd know what to do."

The punch hit Luke right in the gut. Cautiously, he said, "Your dad would've probably handled the situation the same way. First, he would've let the police do their job and second, he would have made sure his family was safe."

The boy scowled. "By hiring you to sleep here?"

"Your mother didn't hire me."

"Yeah, sure."

Luke jacked a hip on the counter. "It was my choice. She had nothing to do with it."

The boy's eyes narrowed. "Why are you hanging around her?"

"I'm helping her."

"She's got Eva. How come you and my mom divorced?"

So she'd told him. "That's personal."

Alexei stared at Luke. "I want to know."

"Then ask your mother."

"I'm asking you."

"You're a nosy kid, know that?"

Alexei remained mute and mulish.

Luke hiked his chin toward the door. "Dinner's getting cold."

"Are you going to hurt her again?"

"What makes you think I've ever hurt her?" But he had. With his workaholic ambitions and interim ground rules about family.

"People don't get divorced and not cry. My mom would've cried. She cried *buckets* when my dad died. She *still* cries." His eyes bore into Luke. "So are you?"

"I would never intentionally hurt your mother."

A beat passed. "That's what my dad said. But he died anyway."

Luke winced.

The boy's eyes glittered. "My dad was the best."

"I'm sure he was."

"You're not like him at all."

Luke barely breathed. "I don't want to be," he said gently.

"I loved my dad. I loved him more than anyone in the whole world." Alexei swiped his right eye. "Except my mom."

"I understand." And Luke did. When Travis Tucker had been home from a long hauling trip, he'd stood as the buffer between Luke and his mother. Luke had loved his big, strong-shouldered dad with a singular mind-set. Beyond words. Beyond comprehension.

More than anyone. Until he had met Ginny.

The boy backed toward the door. His lip quivered. "No one will ever be as good as my dad. Nobody."

"Alexei." Luke stepped forward.

"Don't come to supper. I don't want you there." The boy fled, slamming out the door into the night.

Wind shook the boarded windows. Rain muttered in the eaves.

Luke set his hands on his hips and bowed his head.

Ah, kid, he thought. *You're more like me than I realized.*

"Is Luke coming to supper?" His mom asked when he entered the kitchen. She had changed into a flowery skirt and red sweater and was setting the table left-handed, crutch under her right arm. Joselyn, in a pair of purple jeans, arranged her toy teacup on a chair.

"He's, um, not hungry." Face warm, Alexei bent to pet a wriggling Bargain.

"He must have eaten in town then," Eva remarked from the stove where she mashed the potatoes.

"Yeah." Alexei let the puppy lick his neck. "At that restaurant." His mom gave him a funny look, like she didn't believe him, so he added, "You know the one across the street but a ways down from the library?"

"Kat's?" Mom asked.

"I think so." Alexei hated lying.

He hated the idea of Luke sitting at their table more.

Guilt squeezed his stomach. Luke wasn't a bad guy. And Joselyn liked him a lot. That had to mean something. Alexei had read somewhere that babies had the instinct of animals. They could tell if a person was good or not through some sort of sixth sense. Alexei just felt sad for his dad, that was all. *He* should be the one Joselyn ran to every time he came into the house. *He* should be the one concerned about his mom.

Most of all, he didn't like the way his mom looked at Luke. The way she had once looked at his dad.

But his dad was dead.

He would never be in this house, no matter what he said in the stupid will on that stupid TV.

He'd never see how long Joselyn's hair had grown. Never see how much Alexei had improved in his handwriting with Mrs. Chollas's tutoring. Never see Mom's leg getting better.

And he'd never come into this kitchen for supper.

That's why Alexei didn't want Luke eating at their table, sitting where his dad should be sitting, talking to Mama, calling Joselyn button—

A knock sounded.

"Was that the door?" Eva asked.

"I'll get it," Alexei said.

"That's okay." His mom crutched her way toward the living room. "Go wash your hands. We're eating in five minutes."

He started down the hall just as his mom opened the door. Rain-scented air breezed into the house.

"Hi," he heard Luke murmur.

"Hi," his mom answered. Her voice sounded soft and dreamy. "Everything okay?"

"Everything's fine. Alexei here?"

"Yes. I'll get him."

"No," Luke said as Alexei pressed back into the shadow of the hallway. "I just wanted to make sure he got home."

"Oh, well." Quietly. A smile in her voice. "Thanks for worrying."

"Daee?" Joselyn stood in the doorway of the kitchen. She rushed forward. "Daeeee!"

"It's Luke, sweet pea," his mom corrected.

"Hey, tyke," Luke said. A soft grunt. Alexei knew Luke had picked up his sister. "How you doing, huh?"

"Mam. Da. Go, Ep-say."

"Alexei's washing his hands, punkin. And we have to eat." There was a moment's hesitation. "Alexei said you've already had supper, but you're welcome to a fresh cup of coffee."

Alexei nearly died on the spot. The silence drifted forever. "Alexei's right, except I have a couple of things to finish before it gets too late. Thanks anyway. Be good now, button nose. See you."

"Daee, um!"

"Luke has to go, Josie."

"No bye... No bye! Daee, no bye!"

"Joselyn."

"No bye, Mam. Daee, no bye!" His sister began to wail. "Da-tee, no byyyeeee."

"Oh, sweetheart..."

"Take it easy, tyke."

Joselyn cried harder. Tears slurred words.

"I hate to ask—" his mother's voice rose above the howls "—but could you stay until she goes to bed?"

Alexei slunk into the washroom and quietly closed the door.

He didn't dare look in the mirror.

They made it through the meal without further incident.

Ginny set aside her fork and knife; glanced across the table at Luke. The kitchen's lighting winked in his pecan-colored hair.

Sometime throughout the day, he'd changed his attire. Jeans and a fresh shirt of soft gray cotton that matched his eyes.

She looked into them now. And saw a lifetime of history, *their* history. Of happiness and sorrow. Of love and tears.

His mouth held another history. One so recent and full of emotion she wanted to rush around the table, feel its liveness again. And his hands. She needed his hands on her skin, in her hair, *everywhere.*

Shame washed across her heart. What kind of wife was she to be mooning about Luke instead of grieving over Boone?

But Boone's dead!

But not forgotten. She was in love with Boone. Wasn't she?

Yes! She'd *loved* Boone.

Past tense, Ginny.

And now?

Now, Luke embraced her with his eyes and her heart stuttered.

Would little Robby have looked through those same gray irises?

Ginny stared at her plate. She would have to tell Luke about his son soon. But not until the situation between Alexei and Luke was settled, not until whatever was going on between *her* and Luke had run its course or had found some sense of peace.

"Can I be excused?" Alexei asked.

Ginny jerked her attention left. Alexei. Through the entire meal he hadn't said a word. "Everything okay, honey?"

"Yeah."

"All right. Rinse your dishes in the sink."

He pushed back his chair.

Eva rose, stacking plates. "I'll clear the pots." When Ginny reached for her crutch, the older woman set a hand on her shoulder. "Sit and enjoy your tea."

In her high chair between Luke and Ginny, Joselyn fussed to get down. Before Ginny could push herself to stand, Luke lifted the baby out and stood her on the floor. Joselyn trotted to the cloth doll sprawled next to the wicker planter on the dining table. Her little fingers clutched a black-shoed toe and pulled the doll down.

"Bay," she said, bringing the doll to Luke. "Da, bay."

"She wants you to take her baby," Ginny told him.

He darted her a look. "What am I supposed to do with it?"

"Cuddle it, sing to it, pretend to kiss it." She smiled. "It's called make-believe."

He stared at the doll Joselyn had laid on his knee. "I don't know how to play make-believe."

Eva ran the tap in the sink. Pots and dishes clattered.

Softly, Ginny said, "Remember when you played with toys and fantasized?"

His eyes burned. "I try to forget those days."

Because of his mother. *Oh, Luke,* she thought. *Will you ever get past your childhood?*

Joselyn pushed the doll against his stomach. "Bay," she said again, and Ginny's heart spilled love at the sight of her little girl's sweet grin.

"Take it, Luke," she whispered.

Slowly, he picked up the doll. "Baby," he told Joselyn. "You have a pretty baby." His lips moved into a smile. "But you're a prettier baby." He lifted the doll, snuggled it into his neck. "Pretty baby," he crooned.

Joselyn clapped her hands, bounced on her toes. She patted his knee. "Bay, Daee."

"You got it, kiddo. It's a baby." He laid the doll on his knee.

"Up," Joselyn tugged his leg.

Luke lifted the baby and nestled her and the doll in his arms. Ginny's eyes blurred. *Do you realize Joselyn loves you?* What did it matter that her daughter, in her innocence, had transferred her affection from Boone to Luke? What mattered was the sight of man and child together in this warm kitchen, with leftovers congealing in dishes and the sound of Eva busy at the sink.

Ten years ago, Luke might have sat like this with their own son—if Robby had lived. Another watershed of shame spread through Ginny. She should have phoned Luke when she'd discovered her pregnancy upon arrival in Charleston.

But she'd been scared.

Eight years of marriage hadn't tamed his determination and drive for glory. He'd been close to making partner in one of the most prestigious law firms in Seattle. Children, he'd said, could come later. When his career reached that top plateau. When they were financially secure.

When his fear of failure crept off, tail between its legs.

How much later? she'd asked him. Desperate with her own fear of never becoming a mother.

Soon, honey, he'd replied. *Next year.*

But next year had come and gone and still he used his condoms; insisted she remain on birth control. *Just a little while longer.*

She was nearing thirty.

A little while longer loomed like an eternity.

So she walked out. One day simply decided to call it quits. Packed a suitcase, left a note and walked through the door of their luxury home one final time.

Two months later, on a rainy night, she opened the door of her rented apartment and there he stood. Tears in his eyes. A red rose in his hand.

Her heart broke all over again at the memory. They cried. He begged. Pleaded.

Is it so easy to stop loving, Ginny? he'd asked.

And she crumpled. As long as she lived she would never stop loving him. The night ended in a heartbreak of lovemaking.

But it wasn't enough. The next morning she made arrangements to move to West Virginia and her sister.

Ginny sent the divorce papers through another lawyer.

Two days after receiving the documents—signed by Luke—the doctor confirmed her suspicions. She was pregnant. Pregnant with the child Luke had feared would repress his road to glory.

Still…she would have contacted him the day Robby slipped from her womb. *If* that day and the ten others that followed hadn't spun her into a horrific vacuum of fright and angst while her son battled for his tiny life.

Bargain woofed. The pup rushed from the hallway where Alexei had disappeared, to the front door.

Luke rose from his chair, Joselyn and doll tucked in one arm. He came around the table to set the baby in Ginny's lap.

"Hold on, Eva," he said to the woman toweling her hands and heading for the door. "Let me get it."

Ginny caught the wariness on his face. He didn't trust that their visitor was friendly. Her stomach clenched.

Damn it. This was not New York. This was Misty River, Oregon. People didn't come to the door armed for war.

Or did they?

Someone sprayed hate on the walls of your preschool and smashed windows.

She set Joselyn down. Reaching for the ever-ready crutch, Ginny shoved to her feet. This was her house. She would meet whoever was standing on her porch.

Luke opened the door to the rainy night just as she came into the foyer. A cool gust brought in the scent of wet earth and grass. Bargain rushed out to sniff the damp cuffs of the tall, black-haired man who had once been her brother-in-law.

"J.T.," Luke said. "Got news?"

Joselyn played a solemn peekaboo around Luke's legs; Alexei peered from the hallway.

Dressed in a yellow slicker, Jon Tucker ran a hand over his rain-sprinkled hair. "Luke." A question hovered in the police chief's eyes as he looked from his brother to her. "Ginny."

He held out a clear plastic Ziploc bag. Inside was a button. "We found this in the mud behind your cottage. Either of you recognize it?"

Ginny took the bag. The muddy button, about the size of a quarter, was crudely carved from wood in the shape of an eagle's head and painted red. Thread holes were the bird's eyes; a piece of half-inch-long black string twined within them.

"I've never seen a button like this." Ginny offered back the bag. "It looks homemade."

Jon nodded. "We're thinking the same."

"I've seen it before," Luke said. "But damned if I can remember where. Did you ask Seth? Maybe one of his crew lost it."

"Already checked. Dead end." Jon tucked the bag into the pocket of his yellow rain jacket. "We've contacted the dry cleaners and Betty's Alterations, in case someone requires stitch work over the next week."

Luke said, "I doubt that's been sewn by a seamstress."

"Agreed. But if the button was torn from the clothing for one reason or another, the cloth might need some crafty sewing. Hey, Eva," Jon greeted the housekeeper as she came up behind Ginny. "Didn't know you were still here." He pulled out the bag. "This look familiar to you?"

Eva studied the button; shook her head. "Looks antisocial, if you ask me." She made a shivering sound.

"Can I see it?" a small voice behind the group asked.

Alexei looked from Ginny to Luke to Jon.

"You bet, son." Jon nodded to Eva.

Alexei took the bag. He explored both sides for several lengthy seconds. "I think one of the kids at the high school has a jacket with buttons like this."

"Know which one?"

Alexei shook his head. His blue eyes zeroed on Jon. "I only saw him once when we first moved here."

"Where?" Luke asked.

"When I was coming out of the library. He was walking

past with another kid. They were smoking and laughing. I had to walk behind them a little ways to where Mama was parked."

"Can you guess how old they were, honey?" Ginny asked.

Alexei shrugged. "I dunno. Maybe tenth grade."

Jon cached the bag in his pocket. "Can you describe them?"

Her son shook his head. "I…I just remember these buttons on the back of one guy's jacket. I think it was a blue jean jacket. He had a bunch of the buttons, like a *T*. That's all I remember."

Jon stepped forward and patted Alexei's shoulder. "Thank you, son. This'll be a huge help."

"Really?"

"You bet."

"See." Joselyn pulled at Ginny's skirt. "Ma, see!"

"No, angel." Ginny stroked her daughter's silky wheat-ripened curls. "It's not a toy. You can't play with it."

"See." The baby patted Ginny's cast. "Mama, see." She turned to Luke, her little hands slapping his thigh. "Da, see!" Tears amplified her green eyes.

"Hey, there, half-pint." Jon hunkered down to Joselyn's level. "What's all the fuss about?"

Suddenly shy, the baby moved behind Luke and, clutching his right leg, peeked at Jon.

"Give me the bag," he said to Jon.

Ginny watched as Luke squatted in the doorway with his brother and showed the bagged button to her daughter.

Two big men. One tiny baby.

Luke's arm came around Joselyn as he held the plastic bag for her to investigate. "It's just a piece of old wood," he told the baby, his voice deep and low and soothing.

"Nothing special. Just a useless piece of old wood some-one made into an eagle button. Look, it's all muddy and dirty—" he made a face "—and stinky." He held his nose.

Jon stared at his brother. Ginny understood the man's puzzlement. Luke and children didn't mesh. At least they hadn't in the past.

Joselyn pulled her finger from her mouth and touched the bag. "Bah?"

"Yup, all stinky and dirty," Luke agreed as if he talked baby gibberish every day. "Very bad."

Ginny's respect for him jumped ten miles.

"It's Jon's," he said. "Not mine or yours or Mama's." He shook his head. "Not Eva's, not Alexei's."

"Ep-say?" Joselyn turned to her brother and Jon hid the bag in his jacket.

"Nope, not even Alexei's." Luke lifted the baby into his arms and stood.

Eyes full of amusement, Jon rose as well. "You always were good at sweet-talking the ladies, little brother."

Luke shot a look at Ginny. "Not always."

Her throat tightened. She looked away. "Would you like a coffee, Jon?"

"No, thanks. I should be getting home." He backed away. "If you have any questions or remember anything, give me a shout."

"We will," Ginny said. She turned to Joselyn in Luke's arms. "It's time for your bath, little mite."

The baby went willingly with Eva. Luke closed the door.

Alexei asked, "Mama, why would those kids want to wreck our cottage?"

"We don't know if it was them, son."

"But that kid lost a button off his coat."

"*Someone* lost that button. That doesn't necessarily mean it was the boy you saw walking down the street."

"Was it because of the ghosts?"

Warily, Ginny looked at Luke. "There are no ghosts here, Alexei. Now, I need you to help Eva with your sister while I talk to Luke for a minute."

The boy hesitated, then walked to the stairs. When he was gone, Ginny said to Luke, "Thank you for what you did with Joselyn."

He stepped forward, leaned in and set his mouth on hers.

Electricity. It sprang through her body. Blazed over her skin. She gripped her crutch in her right hand, found his bristly cheek with her left.

His fingers, burning through the hair at her nape.

Down her spine.

Pulling her closer.

Body pressing body.

The foyer wall at her back.

She recognized his arousal. His desire. It fed her own.

"Luke." She canted her head against the wall as he kissed her cheeks, chin, throat.

She'd dreamed of this, of him in those slumberous hours before sleep and again before dawn.

He kissed as no other, touched as no other. She knew that now. Eleven years. Eleven years with a man she'd come to love deeply had not shed Luke from her soul.

"Ginny." His voice, intoxicating her every nerve.

Yes, she thought. *Take me away from my memories. Please hold me and never let go.*

But he had. He had let go. When she'd most needed his empathy, he'd signed the papers she'd served, severed their marriage because he hadn't believed in her—or himself.

She eased back and looked into his sober eyes. "You need to go. The kids and Eva are right around the corner."

He set a palm on her chest where her heart flailed like a wounded bird. "Feel that, Ginny?" he asked quietly. "It's still there between us. Can you deny it?"

She couldn't. "A few kisses doesn't eliminate the fact I have a completely different life now. My family comes first. I told you." She stepped out of his arms, unlocked the door.

He moved to the threshold. A shadow slipped over his left shoulder. "Give us a chance, Gin. Give *me* a chance. I haven't stopped thinking about you since that day in the street. Every day, I've wished I'd given you what you'd wanted back then." His knuckles grazed her cheek. "It's my greatest failing."

He turned and strode into the wet night.

Ginny shut the door. Leaning against it, she fought back the crushing sense of loss. When would Luke stop using the yardstick of success and failure to measure his life?

Chapter Eight

"Look at this." Luke's secretary laid the *Misty River Times* on his desk. "Seems our new resident is in for a battle."

Luke glanced away from the deposition under his fingers to the forty-page tabloid. Ginny's preschool honored the front page.

His heart jounced. Vandals Or Ghosts Torment Preschool? What the hell kind of title was that?

Two color photos ran with the story. The largest picture was of the cottage's smashed windows and spray-painted slogan. Beneath the picture the caption read: "Vandals damage preschool under construction at Franklin's Mill site." The second smaller photo revealed Ginny sitting on her sofa with Joselyn tucked under her arm. Ginny wore a half smile; Joselyn, finger in her mouth, stared wide-eyed at the camera. "Ms. Ginny Franklin and her toddler hope for the best."

Luke frowned. *Hope for the best?* First off, Joselyn was too young to understand the concept of hope. Second, hadn't Ginny said the reporter—he read the byline—Rachel Brant wanted the interview the day before the vandalism?

"Son of a bitch," he muttered as he began reading.

Have the ghosts of Franklin's Mill been stirred to anger? Or was it a prank by locals? Those are the questions facing new owner, Ginny Franklin, of Franklin's old mill site this morning after Friday night's destruction of her newly renovated cottage, which she had hoped to turn into a preschool next September.

Luke skimmed the next few paragraphs about Ginny's return to Oregon with her children and her enthusiasm about living in her childhood town. His eye caught on the next paragraph.

The spooky legend of Franklin's Mill wends back to August 8, 1964 when nineteen-year-old Maggie Stuart drowned in the Misty River. Three months later Deke Franklin, distraught over the loss of his business and financial security, shot himself in the basement of his home. Deke Franklin was also Ginny Franklin's father-in-law. Is it any wonder his spirit is restless with the river flowing not a hundred feet from the door of a proposed preschool where children will play?

Luke's blood thumped in his ears. "First of all, you damn idiot," he grumbled to the absent reporter. "It isn't a hundred feet, but three hundred *yards*. That's over an eighth of a mile. And it wasn't suicide. Franklin was cleaning his rifle when it went off accidentally."

However, Franklin insists parents shouldn't worry. "The preschool will be fenced and the children will be within my sight at all times," she said. "I'll never allow them near the river." Still, over the years, other incidents have warranted the legend concerning the spirits walking the property. In 1971 Binder Frazier was fishing nearby when a mother bear mauled him, leaving him unconscious before a buddy shot the animal. Ten years later, twelfth-graders celebrating prom night along the river were chased through the woods by eerie lights and howlings. But it seems the curse of the land may stem back to ancient times. In the nineties, four children found an ancient Indian skull and fragments of a skeleton near the mill site. Archaeologists and anthropologists scoured the area, but found no evidence of a village. They concluded the tribal man had died alone due to a broken neck. Then last year, two local men earned jail time for growing marijuana—

Luke threw the bi-weekly in the trash. Pure drivel. Grabbing his suit coat off the hook behind his door, he stalked from his office. "Alice, close up. I'm going home."

In the back parking lot, the late-afternoon sun radiated heat. Luke wolfed the distance to his car.

Ginny was all he could think. Ten minutes, and the story would land in her roadside mailbox, courtesy of the rural-route delivery.

Maxine Tucker walked up the weed-encroached drive-way leading to her ramshackle house. She'd worked a full afternoon at the library, shelving books, re-covering worn, tattered ones.

Her feet hurt and her shoulders ached more than usual as she climbed the steps of her broken-down porch. One of these days she would hire someone to repair her steps. Maybe she could ask Seth.

She smiled a little, thinking of her thirty-eight-year-old son with his gentle pregnant wife and sweet teenaged daughter. Seth and his construction company, his strong arms, could fix her porch in a couple hours. No, she wouldn't ask. He owed her nothing. None of her boys owed her a blessed second of their time.

Long ago, she had held them in her arms and they had offered their toothless grins.

She hadn't yet become an alcoholic then. Only a woman desperate for the attention of her husband. *Ah, Travis. Why couldn't you have loved me just a little? I wasn't Maggie, but I was her twin. And I did love you.*

The newspaper stuck out of her mailbox. She carried it along with the day's bills past the century-old grandfather clock into her kitchen where she set the pile on her scarred table. On evenings when the paper arrived, she ate her supper while catching up on the local news.

Squeaky meowed around her ankles.

Pouring fresh water into a small dish, Maxine stroked the feline's soft fur. "Miss me, sweetie?" The cat purred and butted her head against Maxine's shin. "I missed you, too."

Jon's children presented her with the cat last year. A gift for no reason other than to make her happy.

Her grandbabies. *If you could see them now, Travis. Your sons would make you proud.*

As always her mind strayed to Luke. Eldest, but so aloof, so driven. So *wounded*. Because of her. Dishonor had her hands trembling. They would never be close, she and Luke. But he needed her. She felt it deep in her heart.

Travis. Help me. Help me find absolution with your son before I die.

She was so tired. Of life, of forty years of heartache.

While rifling through her mail, she began unbuttoning her coat. Her stomach growled. Time to toss a bit of food together.

The paper's bold title snagged her attention.

"Oh, no." Maxine exhaled a soft gust of air and slumped onto a chair, coat and supper forgotten.

Five minutes later, she lifted her head, but remained seated while the grandfather clock ticktocked its way down the hour.

Maggie, she thought. *Travis.*

Boone.

All gone. Only she was left.

Exhaustion pulled from a dozen directions. The agony and heartache, the loss of things that would never be again and the chances she'd thrown away.

She pressed arthritic fingers against her eyes where the tears burned and guilt flared into a headache.

Driving into the lowering sun, Luke had no idea what he would say to Ginny. He mulled over retaliation against the paper and the reporter. Suing for libel.

Rachel Brant had done her homework.

Every "event" cited in her story once serviced the *Misty River Times* as news. And Ginny's quotes—while true to her vision—were interwoven to fit the reporter's ghostly theme.

Eva opened the door. The smell of some curried concoction reminded Luke of his missed lunch.

"Where is she?" he asked.

"Upstairs with the baby. Something wrong?"

He stepped inside, handing over the news tabloid he'd found in Ginny's mailbox. "Read this and let me know." Without waiting, he took the stairs.

He found her in Joselyn's room, changing the child's shirt.

Standing in her crib, Joselyn clapped her hands. "Daee!" Her cheery little face warmed his heart.

Ginny's head turned. Sunny curls fell across harried eyes. He stepped forward. "What can I do?"

Her fingers flew over the five buttons of the baby's pink shirt. "Almost done. We spilled some grape juice."

"Ah." He noted a tiny stained T-shirt at her feet. "Eva can't climb the stairs anymore?" He didn't like the thought of Ginny lugging her casted leg to the second floor more than necessary. That was why he'd hired a nanny.

Ginny picked up the soiled shirt. "Eva was busy mopping up the mess." With one hand she retrieved her crutch leaning against the crib; with the other she lifted Joselyn.

"Here." Luke took the baby. She smelled of sweetness and…home. Before he could analyze that last thought, he plucked at the toddler's clean shirt. "Hey, Miss Josie-Lyn. Have a tough day, did you?"

"Stubborn is more like it." The fatigue eased from Ginny's eyes as she regarded her child. "She didn't nap this afternoon. Wanted to go outside every two minutes. Poor Eva. She's been double-timing since she got here this morning."

"Jo, dow." Joselyn squirmed to be released.

Luke raised his brows. "Is that right? Maybe I don't want to put you down," he teased. "Ever think of that?"

"Da, dow!" Joselyn slapped his cheek. Luke blinked at the mosquito sting.

"Joselyn! No!" Ginny snatched the baby's hand. "That is *not* nice. You say sorry. Right now."

"Easy, Mom." Luke watched two fat tears well in the baby's eyes. His heart caved. "It's no big deal."

"It's a huge deal," she argued. "I do not want her slapping to get her way. Josie, say sorry."

The child's bottom lip pouted. The next instant, she hid her warm, damp face in Luke's neck.

"Put her in the crib. She needs to say she's sorry before we leave this room."

"Ginny—"

"Luke, please do as I ask."

You know nothing about raising children. The inference hung between them like a wet diaper. He set Joselyn in the crib. The little girl whimpered and rubbed a hand across her nose.

"I knew it. She's so tired. Oh, angel." Ginny palmed her daughter's back. Joselyn curled into a ball, thumb in her mouth. "If you sleep now, we'll never get to bed tonight."

"Why not let her catnap? Fifteen minutes."

Ginny sighed. Leaning down, she kissed Joselyn's cheek. "Fifteen minutes then," she whispered, pulling up the railing.

Side by side, they watched the baby. Luke freed his imagination. This baby. Him. Ginny. "Where's Alexei?" he asked. Alexei, crucial to Ginny's package.

"Working on homework in the office."

He kept watch on Joselyn. "The story ran today."

Ginny turned. Her breath fanned his neck. "You've read it?"

He nodded, trying to ignore the heated space between their arms on the railing.

"And?"

"I brought the paper. Eva's reading it at the moment."

Her eyes searched his. "Should *I* read it?"

He wouldn't lie. "If you do, you won't sleep tonight. She made it sound as if your land's been haunted for a millennium." He went on to summarize what he'd read.

Ginny's mouth drew cursor straight. "Damn it. I should've listened to my instincts. I knew that woman was trouble from the second I opened the door. Eva warned me. But, no. I was so anxious to show this community my grand plan for their kids. After what happened in town with the posters, I wanted to prove their hocus-pocus legend only lived in the minds of a few. That it wasn't the vote of the majority." Ginny snorted softly. "I'll be lucky not to get spit upon next time I go to town." Her eyes rounded. "Alexei. Oh, God."

Crutch in hand, she turned for the door.

Luke caught her hand. "What is it?"

"Last week kids were calling him names at school. Casper and ghostbuster and who knows what else." Her eyes went a little wild. "This woman doesn't know what she's unleashed, Luke."

She found her son on the sofa, reading the story. At his feet, the pup gnawed the sneaker. In the kitchen, Eva rattled pots on the stove. Alexei raised his head as Ginny hobbled off the last stair. Distress clouded his dear face.

"Mama, I thought the article was going to be about the

preschool and stuff. Why's it got all this ghost junk in it? Why's it say Dad's land is haunted?"

She lowered herself beside Alexei. Nearby, Luke stood watching them.

"I'm not sure, honey." Ginny stroked back the flip of blond hair on his smooth, young forehead. "I haven't read it," she admitted. "But from what Luke's told me, a lot of it has been blown out of proportion."

Luke tugged at the legs of his charcoal trousers before squatting to Alexei's level. "Sometimes reporters and newspapers dredge up information and twist it around to make it more intriguing. In other words, more attractive for their customers to buy copies."

"You mean this—" Alexei slapped the paper "—isn't true?"

"Some of the previous incidents did happen. But then people started adding to them. When I was in first grade, we used to play a game called telephone. A bunch of us would sit in a circle and somebody would whisper something in one kid's ear, then that kid would tell it to the next kid, but with his own spin on the tale. By the time the story got around to the originator, it had altered completely from the way it started." Luke nodded to the paper. "In real life we call it gossip or hogwash."

The gentleness in Luke's eyes stopped Ginny's breath. Across the coffee table, she wanted to grab his hands. Hang on.

"Can't we sue?" Alexei asked.

Luke shook his head slowly. "Not unless it's a defamation of character. In other words, the story slanders your mom in a way that tarnishes her reputation and personality."

"I don't get it." Her son stared at the paper. "Why would

anyone want to make stuff up about us and…and wreck our cottage? We never did anything to them." Bewilderment filled his delft eyes.

"Sometimes, son, things which are unfamiliar or scary make people behave in ways they wouldn't normally behave."

Alexei looked at Ginny. "Did I act like that when you brought me to America? I was really scared then."

She couldn't resist. She kissed his hair. "No, baby. You were a very brave boy." Remembering the withdrawn two-year-old he had been, she wished he'd stamped his feet or thrown a tantrum. Instead, he'd remained in his room most days, playing with the few toys the Russian orphanage had allowed him to take along.

A year of love and encouragement brought you from your silent cave, Alexei. But not once did you rebel or blame us for bringing you into strange territory.

She studied the thin curve of his nape. "You're still very courageous, going to a new school, making new friends. It makes me so very proud, son, because I know how hard it was for you to leave your friends in Charleston." He'd cried into his pillow for a week, she knew. "But you did it because I asked."

"It's what Dad wanted, too."

"Yes. It was. But I wanted it more."

"You did?"

"I've always wanted to come back to my childhood home." She caught Luke's watchful eyes. "I missed it. Your dad knew that."

"But your parents are dead and Auntie Eryn is in West Virginia. What's here?"

"Auntie Eryn also wants to move back, honey."

Joy lit his face. Eryn's son was Alexei's age. "She does? When?"

"Not for another year."

Disappointment wilted his shoulders.

Ginny said, "But we'll survive on our own. We're family, Alexei, and nothing is stronger than family." She glanced at Luke. "Always remember that. We've weathered a lot worse."

"Like when Dad died, right?"

"Yes." Dishes clinked in the kitchen.

"Do you think he's a ghost now?"

"I like to think of him as a very gentle spirit."

"Would he be here? With us?"

"Maybe."

Alexei's lips pressed together. "He'd never hurt us. He wouldn't do what that reporter said."

"No, honey, he wouldn't. Now, I need you to go upstairs and wake your sister."

The boy shifted his gaze toward Luke crouched two feet away. "Can I talk to you after?"

Luke didn't hesitate. "Anytime."

"Okay." Three seconds later, singsonging his sister's name, Alexei disappeared up the stairs, the pup climbing after him.

Ginny faced Luke. He remained crouched, bare forearms resting on trouser-clad thighs, silver-splashed tie slightly askew. Their eyes locked. She drew a steady breath. "Thank you for being here."

He came around the coffee table. His palm was warm under her elbow as he helped her from the couch. "We're in this together, Ginny. Just so you know." His eyes dared her defiance. "You and I, we were family once. And as you said, family comes first." Turning, he walked to the door. "Tell Alexei I'll be back in a couple hours."

Then he was gone.

The flashlight guided Alexei across the bumpy meadow. His mom wouldn't let him go until he'd finished helping with the dishes and completed his homework. Bargain ran from one bush clump to the next, sniffing, tongue lolling.

Alexei loved school, but he hated how long it took to get his thoughts down on paper. Mrs. Chollas, his teacher, was showing him ways to recognize the shape of letters during their private sessions after school. He liked Mrs. Chollas best of all his teachers. She understood how embarrassed he felt most of the time. She never rushed him, never made him feel stupid. Not the way other teachers had.

Not the way Luke had that one night.

Tonight, though, Luke had surprised Alexei. He'd seen something in the man's eyes. Something that thawed Alexei's feelings. Luke understood fear. Alexei saw it when the guy looked at his mother. Luke was worried about what this dumb ghost stuff would do to Alexei's mom. And that scared Alexei more than any campfire ghost story he'd ever heard.

The beam caught the windshield of Luke's car. Alexei caught a whiff of exhaust on the night air. Less than five minutes ago Luke had driven past their house. Probably back from supper in town. Alexei wondered why his mom hadn't invited the guy to eat with them.

He climbed the steps, knocked on the cottage door. Through the big side window, Alexei saw Luke leave the bedroom and cross to the front door; it swung open.

Alexei stood staring at the tall, silver-eyed man his mom

had once married. He'd changed clothes. Jeans and a black pullover. He looked tough, like a gangster.

Everything Alexei had wanted to say jammed in his throat.

"Hey, Alexei." Luke smiled. "Been expecting you."

Alexei shut off the flashlight and stepped inside. Luke closed the door. He motioned to the kitchen counter and one of those store pies Alexei's mom sometimes bought. Luke's boots thudded on the wooden floor.

"I was just about to have some apple pie with ice cream," Luke said. "Want to join me?"

"Sure."

"Great." Luke dished up a slice for Alexei; dug out a huge scoop of ice cream—way huger than his mom would have given. He handed Alexei the plate. Jutting his chin toward a stack of lumber, he said, "Have a seat."

They sat and for several minutes ate their pie. Luke set his plate on the floor between his booted feet. "You want to talk about the newspaper story."

"Yeah," Alexei said. "I want to hire you as my lawyer."

Luke's eyebrows shot up.

"I get five dollars a week allowance for helping around the house. I got seventy-five bucks saved in the bank, not counting interest. I know it isn't as much as you'd charge, but I'll be getting more this summer when Mama fixes up the yard. And then for my birthday—"

Luke raised a hand. "Hold on. Let's see what you want me to do first, then we'll talk price. Okay?"

Alexei sighed, relieved. Luke wouldn't bug him about not having to pay. This was real. Not some kid's game.

"I want you to talk to that reporter and tell her to write an apology to my mom in the paper. And if she doesn't write an apology you're going sue her *and* the paper."

"Alexei, as I said—"

"I know. You said that to sue, she had to write things that would hurt my mom's reputation. Maybe what she wrote wasn't *that* bad. But it *is* going to hurt my mom's future job. What that reporter did was make it so no one will bring their kid to her preschool. And that means she won't get any money. Which means she won't be able to feed us kids. I don't care about me, but I care about Josie. She needs milk and clothes and diapers and stuff for babies."

Luke's eyes held admiration. Alexei drove on. "Tonight Mama got a call from a guy who'd wanted to send his kid to the preschool. But when he read the story, he cancelled the registration."

Luke's brows crumpled.

"See, that's what I mean. Nobody is going to sign up." Tears were pushing up his throat. He swallowed them back. "And I bet—" his voice squeaked "—no one will hire her in town now, either."

Luke leaned forward, elbows on his knees. He pushed both hands through his hair and held them there. For a long silent moment he sat motionless. Alexei thought he looked like one of those tigers on *Discovery*. Crouched to spring.

Finally, Luke sat back. "I'll talk to the reporter for you. But on one condition."

Alexei waited, breathless.

"I want you to tell me—not your mother—if kids at the school give you any flak because of this."

Alexei frowned. "Mama's got enough to worry about."

"Good. So you'll tell me?"

"Why do you want to know? I can fight my own battles."

"I'm sure you can." Luke's eyes drilled him. "Take it or leave it, Alexei."

"What are you going to do—if I tell you?"

"Leave that to me."

Suddenly Alexei imagined Luke storming into class, yanking Brett Otts out of his desk and shaking him so hard his teeth banged. Alexei almost grinned. Until he pictured Brett's friends ganging up on him later. "I don't want you coming to the school," he blurted. "Or going to their houses."

Luke's eyes softened. "I won't embarrass you, Alexei. Trust me on that, okay?"

Alexei breathed easier. "Okay. But I still want to, you know, pay you."

"That's okay. I'll do it pro bono." Luke held out a hand. "Deal for deal. Fair enough?"

Alexei nodded. They shook on it.

"Does this mean you're officially my lawyer now?"

"I'm officially your lawyer."

"You can't tell Mama or anyone anything I tell you?"

Luke's eyes narrowed. "What you tell me is confidential."

Alexei liked the sound of that. So he dared. "I think you still love my mom."

Luke sat still as a cat watching a bird. "That a fact?"

"Uh-huh. And I think you'd marry her if she'd let you. Know what else I think?"

"Can't wait to hear."

"I think I can trust you not to ask her."

Luke stood, all casualness gone. "Meddling with people's feelings is not part of our deal, Alexei." He picked up the plates. "I'll let you know tomorrow how it goes with the paper. Good night."

"I can trust you not to ask her."

Luke lay on his cot in the cottage and let Alexei's words sink into his bones.

Boy was a pistol. He'd sighted Luke's intentions on day one—even if Luke himself hadn't yet realized what he wanted. Seeing Ginny again had spun his world on an unbalanced axis. But every day gone by righted the axis a fraction.

And today, reading that story, set it all into perspective.

Ginny, in pain. Her family, at risk. Because of the blind ambition of one reporter.

Blind, like he'd been a dozen years ago.

He wasn't blind anymore. He had a career, an office, a community. He might not be top dog at a prestigious Seattle firm, but he was needed here just the same. Making a difference in people's lives—the ordinary citizen, the blue-collar joe. People needing help via pro bono.

His satisfaction. His success.

He'd succeed with Ginny. And Alexei.

Trust. Such a precarious factor when it came to the heart.

"I can trust you not to ask her."

The boy's heart had bled with those words. Luke saw it in those serious blue eyes, the bend of that soft, childish mouth.

Outside the naked window, the day's low-lying clouds blanketed the stars. A wind strummed a branch of the old maple along the roof.

"Not to ask her."

Four words, four powerhouse words knocking the breath from his lungs, kicking his world off center. Again. Had he promised Alexei, Luke would've had to stand by his word.

But he hadn't promised.

He couldn't.

He scrubbed his hands over his whiskers. His digital wristwatch read 12:53. A month she'd been in Misty River. A month where he slept less than four hours each night.

Luke tossed back the covers. Cool air chilled his naked

legs; he yanked on his boots. He'd catch up on the court briefs he had lugged home. Flashlight in hand, he walked into the central room.

Outside a cat meowed.

Ginny didn't have a cat.

Luke walked to the door. The night wind sighed over the grass, whispered through the budding leaves.

No cat. He closed the door.

About to settle in bed with his files, he heard it again. Soft and faint. A cat's wail.

"Damn it." Determined to find the animal and fix its problem, he hauled on his jeans. Grabbing the flashlight again, he decided to do a tour around the building.

On the cottage stoop, he listened. Nothing. The wind continued to serenade the meadow. Stepping off the stoop, he headed around to the back of the building. Still nothing. "Kitty," he called softly. "Here, kitty."

The flashlight etched the trees around the property.

Then he heard it…sobbing.

Luke stood stone still.

Yes, there, in the wind, someone sobbed.

Careful of the workmen's debris and uneven terrain, he walked around to the front of the cottage facing the river. And listened.

Silence.

He waited. Seconds. Minutes.

His heart clouted his rib cage. His throat wheezed air.

There. Crying. Indistinct and watery. The sound flung away and back again, across the river to the house, above the trees. Echoing and chasing along the night wind.

Luke rounded the cottage. Ginny's place loomed over the jagged treeline, a dark behemoth with glowing eyes.

He shook his head. Eyes? *Windows.* The living room was ablaze with light. Now he heard it. Not a cat.

Joselyn.

Crying her little heart out.

Chapter Nine

Luke strode across the field; leaped the porch steps. The door flung open as he reached it.

Disheveled hair haloed by the sofa lamp, Ginny stood in a wrinkled cotton nightgown. The teary, red-faced baby clung to her neck. Before he could take another step, Ginny held up her hand. "Have you ever had chicken pox?"

"Chicken pox?" Luke flicked a look at the crying baby, then at a pajama-clad Alexei. "I had it when I was five."

Relief dropped over Ginny's face. "Thank God. So have we." She hobbled aside so he could enter. "I gave her some baby aspirin but her temp's still at a hundred. I think we should go to the hospital." Whimpering, Joselyn pressed her forehead into Ginny's neck. "It's okay, sweetheart." She stroked the baby's back. "Mommy's going to take away the pain."

"Here," Luke said. "Let me hold her." He took the baby. "Alexei, go up and get dressed, then bring your mom her tear-away pants and a top so she doesn't have to climb the stairs. Go sit," he told Ginny. "I'll walk with her for a minute."

Joselyn didn't want Luke. She wanted Ginny. Fussing and squirming in his arms, the baby reached around his neck for her mother. Her eyes were glazed, her skin flushed and damp under her Winnie-the-Pooh T-shirt and diapered underpants. She felt good in his arms. "Easy, tyke. Give your mom a rest, okay?"

Joselyn worked up a good howl. Ginny hurried back to Luke.

"I'm here, angel," she said. She gripped his arm while soothing her child. "I'm right here."

"Mamaaaa." The baby wrapped her arms around Ginny's neck.

Luke let her go. And felt oddly abandoned. Until now, Joselyn had followed him the way Bargain followed Alexei.

"Don't take it personal," Ginny said as if reading the ache in his heart. "At times she'd forsake Boone."

But he wasn't Boone.

And this was *his* moment, *his* Joselyn. The baby he'd come to know and care about.

Hell. What was he thinking? These were Ginny's children. Not his. He had made his choices—years ago.

He stared at the crying baby, at Ginny rocking her.

And deep in his soul he understood.

He'd always be on the outside looking in. A pathetic man wishing on stars that had burned out long ago.

As they neared the hospital, Ginny pressed her lips to Joselyn's forehead. Still hot. But she'd slept for the first time since Alexei had awakened her for supper. Poor baby.

The sight of the red Emergency sign pushed a cold sweat from Ginny's skin. Another hospital. And her precious baby sick, again. *Oh, Robby!* His peewee face loomed, a specter in her mind's eye. Concave chest struggling to grasp lifesaving oxygen. Ginny clutched Joselyn. The baby whimpered. "Shh, angel. Mama's got you." *Josie isn't Robby. She's healthy. She's strong.*

Every year, thousands of children—babies included— contracted chicken pox. Rarely did the disease claim a life.

Comforting facts she gripped as they sped through the night.

Humming to ease her mind as much as her child, she glanced over her shoulder. Alexei sat curled under a blanket in the corner of the car, out like a light. She hated the thought of waking him in a few minutes.

Her eyes wove to Luke. The dash lights inscribed the lean lines of his cheeks and nose. Both hands held the wheel—as though he competed in the Indy 500.

This was the Luke she recognized.

Intense.

Desperate.

He hadn't said a word since starting her station wagon and guiding its headlights through the dark.

Frantic is what she'd been, opening that front door tonight. Wondering how she would manage her burdensome leg pressing a gas pedal and Joselyn wailing in her car seat.

So, why *had* he stood on her porch at one in the morning? Couldn't he sleep? Had he been checking the premises and heard Joselyn's cry?

Ginny had witnessed the hurt in his eyes when her daughter slapped his cheek today. Then again tonight when she'd preferred Ginny's arms to Luke's. How did you tell a man who'd never had children, never wanted them, that those children's moods swung left and right, the same as an adult's? That things weren't funny and sweet and loving all the time? That this race to the hospital was real-time family?

At the front entrance, Luke stopped the car. Joselyn began to fuss the instant the motor died.

Ginny let Luke bundle her daughter in the blanket they had brought along, then carry her into the building.

Managing her crutches, she followed. Under the cast, her skin itched. Two hundred mosquito bites fueled by the car's warmth. Behind her, Alexei whined about the cold and being tired. Tomorrow she'd let him stay home from school.

The hospital slept. In the small waiting room to the left, a table lamp glowed. The corridors leading left and right were dark except for several subdued lights along the way.

Ahead, a nurse sat at the station talking to Luke. Joselyn, mouthing her thumb, whimpered on his shoulder.

Ginny told Alexei to curl up on the sofa in the waiting room, then swung her crutches toward the check-in desk.

"Doctor's on his way," Luke told Ginny.

Joselyn watched her with red, fatigued eyes. Her sweet baby. She wanted to take on the sickness, wanted to take on the confusion, the pain, so her child did not suffer.

Luke's hand found the nape of her neck. He pulled her close, kissing her brow. "She's all right, honey," he whispered.

For a moment, she leaned into him, all her strength gone. His chest was strong and broad, his cotton T-shirt soft and warm. He smelled wonderfully male. Ah, but this— *this* she missed most. Sharing life's ups and downs with someone. Knowing he would be there to pick up the slack, offer a shoulder, protect her children. Always sharing.

When Boone had become sick two years before, when he complained of exhaustion and headaches, Ginny had shouldered much of their daily routine. Running Alexei to school and friends and activities, dentists and doctors, bringing home the groceries, keeping up the house, walking Joselyn through teething nights. An endless string of to-dos that at one time Boone had shared.

Until he began losing weight and could no longer walk the distances they once had in the evenings.

Go see Mitch, she'd told him. Countless times.

What's he going to find? I'm overworked, that's all.

Then one morning he'd fainted and she'd driven him in to see his doctor friend. Two days later, Mitch phoned with the prognosis. An inoperable tumor deep in the brain.

Luke's thumb caressed her temple. Face buried against him, she familiarized herself with his scent. *Luke-scent* she once called it. Enough to make her high.

"Here's Doc Stearns," he murmured against her ear.

The same doctor who had tended her broken leg. He greeted them quietly before they followed him into a cubicle where he examined a fussy Joselyn on a sheeted gurney. Clusters of red spots covered the baby's back and tummy. A few flecked her legs. Under the bright fluorescent lighting, Ginny spotted one in the crown of her daughter's hair.

"Chicken pox, all right," the doctor said, dressing Joselyn with gentle hands. "Keep her nails short for the itch. Baby aspirin every four hours and bathe her three times a day with warm water and a couple teaspoons of baking soda." He smiled at Ginny. "In a day or two the spots will blister and crust, and by the end of the week it'll be all over. If not, see me."

He handed Joselyn to Luke. "Take your family home. And try not to worry."

"He's not fam—" Ginny said, but the doctor had strode from the cubicle.

She glimpsed Luke rubbing Joselyn's back as the baby snuffled against his shoulder. "Don't be afraid, Ginny," he said softly, and a small tremor chased her spine.

"Of course I'm afraid. My daughter's sick—"

His eyes anchored her. "I'm not talking about Joselyn."

She snatched her purse off the chair. "My child is all *I'm* talking about and I need to put her to bed." Crutches in motion, she hobbled from the examining room.

Joselyn sleeping against her chest, Ginny glanced at Luke through the darkness in the car. She'd known what he meant, pure and clear. Don't be afraid of believing they could be a family.

Don't be afraid of commitment.

Except, she'd tried commitment twice. Once with Luke, once with Boone, and look where it had taken her.

"I'm moving the cot into the house," he said, as if he knew what she was thinking.

Too tired to respond, she stared down the tunnel of headlights. But her heart eased its crazed pace.

At dawn, Luke left a voice mail for Alice to reschedule his appointments to next week. Then he took the day off.

In case Ginny needed him.

He found coffee beans in the kitchen cupboard and brewed a pot. Outside, sitting on the porch steps in a T-shirt, jeans and bare feet, he watched the sun brighten the world. *Will you ever forgive me, Ginny? Will you ever see beyond the past?*

Through the screen door ten minutes later, he heard Joselyn's call and Ginny's scramble to get to her room.

Luke took the stairs two at a time. Ginny stood at the crib in a sleeveless cotton nightie undressing the baby, crooning to her, checking the extent of the chicken pox.

"Da-tee." Joselyn smiled, forgiving him for whatever wrongs he'd done yesterday.

"Hey, snookums. How you feeling this morning?"

She patted her tummy where red spots now blistered. "Owie."

"I believe it." His hand found Ginny's shoulder, massaged. She hadn't awarded him a glance, a word. *Look at me, Ginny. I'm here for you.* "How's Mom?"

"Wishing for about a week of sleep." She pulled the sheets from the crib, tossed them onto the hamper in the corner. The nightie's large armholes dipped. His groin acknowledged the full swell of bare breast.

"Then go catch a few hours more."

"Right. And how do you suppose I do that? In another hour Alexei will be up and this one will be at high speed. Things change when you have a family, Luke."

"So you keep telling me." He picked up the baby, settled her soft, warm weight in his arms. "Go on. I'll look after Miss Jo."

"She needs an oatmeal bath first and calamine lotion and her nails clipped and a clean diaper and—" Ginny pushed the hair from her eyes "—that's *before* breakfast."

"We'll manage." Come hell or high water, he'd prove his worth. Carrying the baby, he walked out of the room, down the hall to the bathroom. Quietly, he shut the door.

"Miss Josie-Lyn," he whispered. "You and I are going to do this bathing thing right this time. No squealing. No sloshing water all over. No running through the house naked. And absolutely no waking Mommy. Got it?"

Joselyn gave him a sloppy kiss on his bristly chin.

Ginny had Luke park her boat of a car in front of the *Misty River Times,* a two-storied, gray clapboard building on Main that had been witness to the decade before the Second World War.

Now that she was here, all the anger of last night rushed back. Because of Rachel Brant and her insinuations, her embellished inaccuracies, Small Wonders Preschool had died a quick death. The cancellation of her one client proved it.

Ginny checked her watch. Half hour before lunch. Staff, including reporters, should still be at their desks. Unless something urgent developed, morning, according to Rachel Brant, was when most of the writing, editing and layouts were completed.

After catching up on sleep this morning, Alexei had been anxious for school; they had dropped him off fifteen minutes ago, the principal understanding the reason for her son's lateness. Two other cases of chicken pox had called in that morning.

At home, Ginny hadn't wanted to leave Joselyn with Eva, but the older woman shooed them out the door with a "Don't let that reporter get away with this nonsense."

Nonsense was right.

Luke came around to help Ginny onto the sidewalk. She let him haul out the crutches, open the door to the building. Inside, she said, "Let me do the talking." At his lifted brows, she went on, "It's me she bad-mouthed."

At the front desk, she asked to see Ms. Brant.

"Do you have an appointment?" the receptionist asked. She clicked a button on a multilit switchboard.

"No, but I'd like to talk to her about a story she wrote about me in yesterday's paper."

The woman wrote something on a slip of paper. "Which story?"

"The one blotting up the whole front page."

The receptionist's head snapped up. "*You're* Ginny Franklin?"

"If I say yes, are *you* running for cover?"

Beside her Luke snorted.

The woman's gaze flicked his way. "Of course not." She rose. "Let me see if Ms. Brant has a moment."

"Make it five," Ginny told her. To Luke she muttered, "Is that enough time to scratch her eyes out?"

His hand on her shoulder was warm, supportive. "Count to ten, honey. Going in with both barrels will only get you another headline, not a head start."

Her anger dissipated. "You're right." Their eyes held. "I'm glad you're here," she whispered. And meant it.

The receptionist returned. "She can see you in fifteen minutes. If you'd like to wait…" She gestured to a sofa and chair near the front window. "Can I get you a coffee?"

Rachel Brant hadn't waited. Not when it came to ruining Ginny's dreams.

"No thanks." Swinging her crutches around, she made her way through an archway to the left where five cubicles housed desks and computers. Four were empty.

"Just a minute—" the receptionist said. "Mrs. Franklin!"

"Stay where you are—Elsie, is it?" Luke said behind Ginny. "This won't take long."

Twenty feet into the room, and she found Rachel Brant typing furiously on a computer keyboard.

"Ms. Brant. We are talking right *now*."

The woman jerked around. "Mrs. Franklin. I thought I told Elsie I'd see you in fifteen minutes."

"I passed on your message, Rachel." Face flushed, the receptionist pushed her way between Ginny and Luke.

Luke deftly swung an arm around the woman's waist and headed her back to the front. "She knows that, Elsie, but you see Mrs. Franklin's busy, and with her broken leg and all…" His voice ebbed with distance.

Vaguely aware of Luke guiding Elsie from the newsroom, Ginny stared at Rachel Brant. "You wrote trash."

The woman's eyes narrowed. "I wrote news."

"I thought you were a woman of honor. A woman who had the guts to tell the truth without glorification. But you're no better than the slime who write for those disgusting tabloids you see at checkout counters."

The reporter's nostrils flared. "I'll have you know, Mrs. Franklin, I did a lot of research for that story."

"What you did, Ms. Brant, was cowardly. You hide behind your so-called research and ruin people's lives. You smear innocent folk through the printed word and call it news." Anger stung her cheeks. "You didn't want a family story, a *feel-good* story, as you called it. You wanted self-importance."

"The phone's been ringing like crazy this morning." The woman pushed back her chair and stood, looming over Ginny. "Everyone's sympathizing with you!"

Ginny nearly choked. "And what good will that do me? Will it put food in my children's stomachs? Will it pay the electric bill? The heat in winter? Will it give my son new shoes when he grows out of his old ones? Ms. Brant, you have succinctly destroyed my livelihood with your *news*." She inhaled a composed breath. "Not one of those sympathizing families will register their children in my preschool." She stepped back. "Your ridiculous ghost resurrection nipped that in the bud." Tears burned her throat. "Have a nice day."

"It's not ridiculous," the woman called after her.

Ginny limped from the room.

Luke met her at the reception desk. Hard lines contoured his face. Concern and something soul deep darkened his eyes.

She steered her crutches for the door. "I need to go home."

Luke was conscious of every shift Ginny made, sitting in the passenger seat, looking out the side window.

They didn't talk.

He understood her need to confront the reporter.

He would go back and deal with the woman himself. Keep his promise to Alexei. But first, Ginny.

"You okay?" he asked finally.

"I'm fine."

He reached across the console, took her hand. Her fingers had always been slim, delicate. "It'll work out, honey."

A shrug.

"You have to believe it, Gin. People aren't stupid. Not everyone will buy into this poppycock."

She turned her head, and for an instant he saw her eyes—those dark, heartache eyes—before he attended to the road again.

"Okay," he said. "We need to change their minds."

"How?"

"Write a letter to the editor to start. Every nutcase in the woodwork will be writing, why not you?"

A small smile. "I'm a nutcase now?"

"You know what I mean."

"I do. I just don't think it would do any good. People's minds were made up long before she wrote the story. My posters proved that."

They did. He had found two ripped, foot-printed halves littering the sidewalk near his office last Friday. He squeezed her hand.

Suddenly she grinned. "All right. I'll do it. I'll write one this afternoon and take it back before they close their doors for the night."

At four o'clock Luke took the letter to the paper. Elsie greeted him with a frown. Not asking if Ms. Brant was in, he strode through the newsroom to Bruce Kirk's office. He and Bruce had known each other since grade school. Their relationship had never been cozy. Kirk had been one of those kids no one liked. Rail thin, he'd had the personality of a weasel in high school. Neither his physique or likability had changed. Moreover, Bruce hadn't worked for his position, he'd fallen into it when his father, a kind, decent man, died two years ago.

Luke slapped the letter on Kirk's desk. "I want you to print this in the next edition."

The managing editor/publisher boosted a thin, black eyebrow. "Gotta be local, entertaining and current."

"It's all that and more. Read it."

The man plucked a toothpick from between his lips; tossed the letter next to a pile. "After those." He smirked. "They came in this morning. First come, first served."

Luke placed his hands on the desk. "After what you had that reporter write, you'll run this one first."

"That a threat, Tucker?"

"Did you hear an 'or else'?"

"No, but that means nothing." Kirk glanced at the letter. "Yours or hers?"

"If you mean Mrs. Franklin, yes. She wrote it."

"You representing her?"

Only for the legalese of her property, but I've just extended those services. "I am."

Another glance at the letter.

"Pick it up," Luke advised. "You might discover something truthful."

Kirk snorted, but he took up the letter, scanned the print. Ginny had written three to-the-point paragraphs. Kirk frowned at the last one. Luke smiled, remembering the words:

If the community believes all it reads, then we are no better than the those poor propagandized folk in countries where extremists dictate the order of life.

"Going a little far, isn't she, comparing the *Times* to fanatics?"

Luke offered the grin of a Cheshire cat and pushed off the desk. "My point exactly. Next time think twice before goading the community. Repercussions are unpredictable."

Kirk tossed the page aside with a who-cares shrug. "Tell her it's too controversial."

Luke gave a snort. "You always were a wuss when it came to the hard-nosed truth."

"This paper prints *only* the truth."

"You don't run that letter, Bruce? We'll talk again. In

court. Take care now, hear?" Luke almost whistled as he left the office, but he had one more stop. For Alexei.

Rachel Brant stood in her cubicle shoving notebooks and a tape recorder into a briefcase.

"Ms. Brant?"

Her head swung up. "What do you want?"

Luke leaned against the edge of her cubicle. "Not much. Just an apology. On the front page."

"Get real." She tossed a PalmPilot into the briefcase.

Luke pushed off the partition. "Next edition, Wednesday. Have an apology or a retraction on the front page."

She closed the briefcase; straightened. She stood a few inches shorter than his six-two. "I wrote nothing wrong."

"Only in your mind. Write the apology, Ms. Brant." *If you want your next paycheck.*

As if considering, she bent her head, released a sigh. "Sometimes, Mr. Tucker—" she looked him in the eye "—you've got to do what you got to do. I'm no different than Mrs. Franklin. I got bills, too. A boy at home." The hard look eased. "I need the work, *good* work." Her voice lowered. "Recognition will get me out of this town and through the right door of another."

Cold fingers keyed Luke's skin. "Recognition on the backs of others. You're a hell of a piece of work, Ms. Brant. I hope your son is proud to call you mom—*if* you even have a son."

Air hissed through her teeth. "You bastard. How dare you? You know nothing of my life."

Luke didn't waver. Blood pounded his ears. Quietly he said, "I don't give a rat's ass about your life. The only people who matter to me are Ginny Franklin and her kids. Write that retraction and you'll never see me again. Don't, and you and your boss in there—" he jerked his head "—will be visiting with me daily." He turned, then stopped. "Tell your son hi for me."

"Go to hell."

"Hard to do with you blocking the path."

Saturday morning Alexei peddled his bike down the road for town. This was his first trip on his bike. He'd left a note to his mom on the kitchen table while she was upstairs with Eva and Josie. He didn't want to ask permission because he knew his mom's answer. Better to pretend he didn't know.

Thing was, he did know. His dad had practically written the rules on his forehead. *Never, ever go anywhere without asking us first. Better to be safe than sorry.*

Today was different. He needed to do this without his mom hanging around like she had the last couple Saturdays. Before the accident she used to drop him off at the library. Now with her broken leg, she was stuck there with him.

He peddled down the highway. It wasn't far to town. Only about a mile. In the car it took about a minute.

A truck passed by, its draft swaying his bike.

Okay, maybe this wasn't such a good idea.

Alexei pushed on. He wasn't letting a bit of wind stop him. Just like he hadn't let those stupid kids at school make him cry with their stupid name-calling. That reporter's story was the talk of the whole school. Even the teachers—not Mrs. Chollas, but others at recess—were talking.

His dad would've called it gossip. Like Luke.

Hogwash. Alexei liked that word better. He pictured a stinky, muddy puddle where hogs lay to get out of the sun.

And then when they got up, all this dirty water would slosh down their backs and sides, leaving mud covering them like a coat.

The news story had smeared Alexei and his family. Covered them in a dirty brown coat of hogwash.

Sweat beaded his upper lip as he reached the town limits. He turned down Main, flipped his bike onto the sidewalk then peddled like crazy for the next block to the library.

Rolling his bike into the bike stand, he hopped off.

Inside, the building was cool and dim and quiet. He loved its smell. Old wood. Old books. And peace.

Mrs. Tucker sat in her reading corner. She looked over and smiled when he walked past to the computer he always used. She was telling one of her stories and the kids sat with their mouths open, like always.

He booted up the computer. Soon Google was ready for him to do his search and he typed in Misty River OR. Behind him, Mrs. Tucker finished her story about an old shoe. The kids were clamoring for more, but apparently she'd already told three. Alexei was sorry he'd missed them. Her own tales were the best. Not for the first time, he wondered if she wrote them down.

He clicked on the town's URL. Nothing about legends. He searched further, looking through their history page. He clicked on Logging Era—and read about his dad's grand-father starting a logging business around 1922. The article was short and said nothing about his dad's father, Deke, except that he'd tried to develop a resort on the old mill site before he died in 1964.

"Looking for the legend?"

Alexei jumped. Mrs. Tucker stood behind him, a

gentle smile on her wrinkled face. In some ways—especially the nose and eyes—she looked like Luke. But she wasn't tall and she was shaped like a grandmother. Soft and a little saggy.

"You won't find it there," she said. "Come with me."

She took him to a door that opened to the basement. Slowly, they made their way down the stairs. At the bottom, she flicked another light and he saw shelves upon shelves of discarded books.

"Wow," he exclaimed. "Why don't you recycle these?"

"We've been meaning to, but it seems there's never any time." She led him to a wall of cardboard boxes, all labeled by year. She pointed to 1964, June–December. "That's the first one you'll want."

Alexei grabbed a wooden stepladder nearby and set about hauling down the box. It was heavy. And dusty.

Tearing open the flaps, he saw a yellowed stack of the *Misty River Times*. From his pocket he took out the small Dictaphone recorder Luke had given him. If there was anything here the reporter had missed or twisted around, Alexei wanted to find it to help his mom get out of this mess.

"They should be in chronological order," Maxine said. "Look for June 9."

He found it within minutes. "What am I looking for?"

"The day the legend began."

He stared at her. "Then there really is a legend?"

Her eyes were sad. "Yes, son. There is."

"Do you believe it?"

"I should, shouldn't I, since it's about my twin sister."

"Holy cow! Are you kidding?" He stared at the newspapers with their yellowed, tattered edges. "You mean…"

His throat felt dry. "You mean it was Luke's aunt who drowned and started this whole thing?"

A funny look crossed Mrs. Tucker's face. Like she was going to cry or something. "Right. Luke's aunt."

"Sorry, Mrs. Tucker." Alexei patted her arm. "I shouldn't have gotten all excited. I mean, she's your... I know what it's like when somebody you love dies."

"I heard about your daddy."

"Yeah." He hung his head. "Guess with this ghost thing everyone has by now. They're probably thinking the curse killed him, too, because he's a Franklin. Well, it didn't." Alexei hated when his voice cracked. "Cancer killed him."

Mrs. Tucker set an arm around his shoulder. This close, she smelled nice. Like flowers. She said, "As long as *you* know it wasn't a curse or a legend, that's all that matters."

Footsteps thudded down the stairs. Alexei looked up to see Luke on the bottom step, one hand balanced against a ceiling beam. He stared straight at Mrs. Tucker. "What're you doing with Ginny's son?" he asked coldly.

Chapter Ten

"Hello, Luke," Maxine said. She swallowed back her nerves. Luke could have her in a knot with just a look. "Alexei was doing some research and I was showing him where to find it."

He came off the basement steps and walked toward them. His eyes switched to the boy at her side, and gentled. "Your mom wants you home, Alexei. She's very worried."

"But I left her a note on the table."

"It's you riding your bike into town that has her upset. The highway is a dangerous place for a ten-year-old boy."

Maxine had never seen the gentle smile he offered the child. Certainly, he hadn't learned it from her example.

Luke set a hand on Alexei's shoulder and looked at the box by their feet. "What're you researching?"

"The legend." Alexei picked up the paper he'd found.

"This is when it started. Lookit here. It tells about this guy who was fishing in the river on our property and he saw Mrs. Tucker's sister, I mean your mom's sister, even though she wasn't really there. He saw her ghost walking toward him and she—"

"Alexei." Luke extracted the paper gently from the boy's hands and dropped it on the pile. "There's an old saying that goes like this… Believe half of what you see, some of what you hear and none of what you read. In other words, be cautious with how you approach things. Sometimes they're not what they appear."

"Like hogwash?"

Another of those rare smiles. "Yeah, like hogwash."

"But your aunt drowned."

"A long time ago, Alexei." Luke's face reflected only calm. "Let's leave her to peace. Dragging up all this old news as if she's to blame isn't fair to her."

"Guess not." The boy shot Maxine a look of worry. Her heart kicked. Like Luke at that age, Alexei wanted only to please. But unlike Luke, the boy received kind-hearted guidance. She had never been kind-hearted with Luke.

He said, "Your mom's waiting in the car. Why don't you go reassure her you're all right? I'll be up in a few minutes."

"Okay." The boy bounded for the stairs.

Luke watched him go. He turned to Maxine, mouth hard. "Stay away from him."

Maxine's heart fluttered. "Alexei came to me. I didn't seek him out."

"Then tell him you're busy. Hell, you've always had a million excuses. Use one."

Like she had with him, years ago.

"Get Paul's dad to drive you to soccer. I got a headache."

"*Borrow a notebook from your friend. I don't have time to buy one.*"

"*Make your own lunch. I'm tired.*"

Mostly she'd been drunk.

"I'm sorry," she whispered. But he didn't hear. Already, he was striding for the stairs.

Maxine stared at the musty papers with their ghostly tales. *Oh, Maggie. You would disown me if you knew what I've done.*

Ginny watched her son trip down the library steps and come toward Luke's Mustang. She turned on the ignition to roll down the window. "Get your bike, son, and we'll put it in the trunk."

"Are you really mad?"

"I'm not happy with what you did, Alexei. If you wanted to come to the library, you could have waited until Eva was free or asked Luke to bring you."

"Am I grounded?"

She'd thought about this all the way into town. "I think two days off the computer and no library trip next Saturday is fair."

He kicked his toe at the sidewalk. "I guess."

She almost gave in to his woebegone face. "Son—"

"Ginny Franklin?"

Turning in her seat, Ginny saw a tall, spindly woman approach the car from the rear. She wore an outdated peasant dress that reached the rim of dirty high-top sneakers. A tan shawl draped her shoulders and twin silver barrettes winked in her frizzy white hair.

"You still planning to run a preschool out at Franklin's mill site?"

Ginny hesitated. Supporter or protestor? "I am."

The woman studied her for a moment. "Sell the property, move to another town. You bring bad luck here."

"Excuse me?"

"You picked the wrong place to live. Leave Misty River before it's too late."

"Alexei," Ginny called. "Get in the car."

"No, no." The woman clamped long fingers over the edge of the window. "He needs to hear, too. The safety of your family is at stake. What happened to you with your broken leg was a warning. The vandalism of that cottage is the second sign. A third warning and it will be too late."

Joselyn's chicken pox was not a third warning.

Alexei dropped the bike to the sidewalk. He scrambled into the car, slammed the door.

"Listen for the sake of your children." The woman's eyes were bright flames.

"Leave us alone." Ginny tried to dislodge the woman's hands, but she had the grip of an arm wrestler.

"You'll be sorry," she singsonged, "living on plagued land."

"Get away." Desperately, Ginny pressed the window button. The glass whirred up, but the woman hung on, spilling her oracles, until Ginny was forced to stop the automatic glass before pinching fingers. "Listen. For your own good."

Luke, where are you?

He strode through the library doors.

"There's Luke!" Two-worded relief in Alexei's voice.

Seeing Luke's tall, big-shouldered frame, his stern, dark features, Ginny released an audible breath. In that moment, she knew. She loved him. Perhaps she'd never stopped, not really, *if* she were to analyze her heart.

"Mazey Markam," he called. "You move along now. The library is no place for preaching."

"Mr. Lawyer." Pale eyes drilled Luke. "Tell this woman she must leave our community. The curse hangs over her head."

Luke took the woman's arm. "Now, Mazey. You want me to call Barbara?"

A strong name that had fear crossing Mazey's eyes. "Barbara? No, Mr. Lawyer. I will leave now. Do not call my daughter. Please. Thank you." Mazey hurried down the sidewalk, shawl and skirt fluttering like tiny flags in her wake.

Luke picked up Alexei's bike. Unlocking the trunk, he lifted the bike inside.

"That woman's crazy." Alexei glanced through the rear window as Luke anchored the bike.

"Alexei." Whether or not Mazey had frightened them, Ginny recognized the woman's real mental dysfunction.

Luke slammed shut the trunk. Two seconds later, he climbed behind the wheel. "You okay?" His eyes fixed on Ginny.

Now that you're here, yes. She nodded.

He swung into the street. "You just met Crazy Mazey. She's been institutionalized a few times over the past ten years, but for the last three she showed enough progress that her daughter allowed her to live in a group home in town. Every so often, though, she scares the hell out of folks." He shot a look across the cab. "Don't take her words to heart, Gin."

"She said my home is plagued."

He reached, squeezed her icy hand. Her heart tumbled. "Mazey says that to everyone. She's not stable."

"But people will believe her because of the paper and the vandalism. According to her, three strikes and I'm out. It'll take a miracle before anyone, besides you, Eva, Seth and Jon, will set foot on my property."

Luke wrapped both hands around the wheel. "Then we'll find one, damn it."

Luke pulled up to his mother's house at four-thirty.

Had his former home always looked this small? This drab? The clapboard shouted for a coat of paint. Someone had put on a new roof recently. Seth? Jon?

His brothers, the handymen.

The wood had nearly rotted through the bottom step to the porch. He pictured his mother clinging to the silvered handrail as she descended. *Fix the steps for her, Luke. You know the right end of a hammer and a nail. Daddy taught you that. Don't you think it's time to stop the badass son routine?*

He was here, wasn't he?

First time in…twenty years? He couldn't recall his last visit or its reason. Definitely wouldn't have been for chitchat.

Today he was here for Ginny. Only for Ginny.

Her green eyes had propelled him to this house. Alexei's worry about his mother had propelled him to this house. Innocent Josie-Lyn, with her winsome smile and sweet laugh, had propelled him to this house.

Family.

Family not of his own making, but the making of a woman he'd once cherished as no other—and threw over for success. And that choice had been because of the woman inside *this* house. For those reasons alone, he should hate her more. But he couldn't.

As Luke stood on the porch of his childhood home, an

ease entered his heart. His mother was human. She'd made mistakes, just as he had. He couldn't blame their estrangement all on Maxine Tucker. At some point the responsibility was his own.

He raised his hand, knocked.

Next to a small wind chime in a corner of the porch, a spider spun its web. A chill ran over Luke. Once he'd felt like a bug in an inescapable web.

The door opened. His mother stood staring at him. She wore the same clothes as she had this morning: black slacks, a flower-dotted blouse. Pale green slippers housed her feet. A cat peered around her ankle, but didn't venture farther.

At eleven this morning in the dimly lit basement of the library, he hadn't paid attention to his mother's face. Now, in the light of the afternoon, he saw deep creases around eyes, lips and neck. He saw her small attempt at makeup: pink lipstick that had worn off over the hours but still remained in several lip pleats. Those colored pleats made her mortal in a way he'd never imagined.

"Hello, Mother."

She blinked as if hearing his voice made him real and not a phantom of the past. "Luke."

"I came to ask you something. Do you have a minute?"

She stepped back. "Of course. Would you like some tea?"

"Sure." He could do that for an old woman.

She led him to the back, to the kitchen where already a pot steeped. As though she'd been expecting him. From a tub-bellied jar on the counter, she laid out several cookies. "I bake cookies for my grandchildren," she said. And he knew it was true. The house smelled of baking. "This week it's sugar cookies. They're Hallie's favorites. Jon's son loves the chocolate-chip variety and his girls Brittany and

Emily love peanut-butter crunch." She offered him the plate. "You used to love these, as well."

He had. But she'd seldom let him eat one before a meal and definitely not before bed. *"All that sugar makes you hyper."*

He wondered if she remembered that as he took a cookie.

She poured two mugs of tea, strong the way he liked, then hauled out the cream. "Sugar?"

"No, just that." He nodded at the tiny pitcher she set out.

"Me, too." She picked up the cat and sat at the table with the creature purring in her lap. His mother's hands were knobby with arthritis, but they were gentle on the feline's head.

He sat across the table. Jon once told him their mother liked John Philip Sousa. Luke had noted the state-of-the-art entertainment center in the living room. Today the house was silent. He dipped the cookie into his tea. "Are you still in touch with your people?"

Her "people" were Nez Percé. Maxine was an eighth Native American on her father's side. She seldom talked about the fact and only once had taken her sons to the reservation an hour south, where some long-distance relatives, cousins and elders lived. Luke suspected that he, Seth and Jon had all inherited their easy-to-tan skin and straight dark hair from their bygone horseman ancestors, though his nose resembled Maxine's straight one from her English side.

"I see my aunt sometimes," she said. "Why?"

His great-aunt lived on the reservation. An old woman Luke hadn't seen in over twenty years. "What can you find out about getting land blessed?"

Maxine's gray eyes, so like his own, were steady. "Ginny Franklin's land," she said softly.

Luke ate the second half of the cookie. "I want people to believe in her and the preschool. They won't as long as this town thinks that property is haunted." *And I need to prove to Ginny I'm in this with her for the long haul.*

The thought had him sloshing his tea when he set it down. "Sorry." Hurriedly, he swiped at the spill with his hand, almost expecting Maxine to slap his fingers.

"Don't worry." She continued stroking the cat. "It's an old table. Seen a lot of wear and tear. What makes you think the town will accept a blessing from a Native American?"

"If he or she is an elder with some prominence they'll accept it."

"The elder won't come unless there's Native American relevance."

"What about that thousand-year-old tribal skeleton found ten years ago? Maybe it's time to put him to rest."

She nodded. "I'll see what I can do."

He rose, shoved in his chair. "Thanks. And for the cookies and tea. They hit the spot."

She pushed the cat from her lap; stood, too. "Take a batch home for the boy."

Home for the boy. As if Luke lived there. As if Alexei, Ginny and Joselyn were his family. A warmth spread through his chest. Until he remembered. Ginny. She still didn't believe in him. Ignoring the sting, he took his mother's offer: a tall plastic container brimming with treats.

"They were for Hallie, but I'll bake a new batch tonight."

"Thanks. Alexei will love them." He walked to the front door.

Maxine followed. "I won't let you down, Luke."

Not like before. For a second he hesitated, wanting to touch her arm. Hug her like a son would.

"Call me when you know."

He trotted down the rickety porch steps.

Maybe next weekend he and Alexei could fix them.

Ginny glanced toward the hallway leading to the computer room where Alexei played a video game. Upstairs, Eva encouraged Joselyn to go potty.

Ginny and Luke stood side by side at the kitchen counter while he told her about visiting his mother, and she placed the cookies he'd brought back into a ceramic jar shaped like a tubby cat.

"You want to have the land *blessed?*" she asked in a voice meant only for his ears. "Wouldn't that be confessing there really *are* ghosts running around here?"

"Honey, that's what people believe anyway." His dark brows rose. "Right? Give them a dose of their own medicine, as they say. Bring a shaman or an elder out here, along with some high-ranking personalities, get them to chant to the wind, beat a few drums and, voilà, your spirit problems are laid to rest."

She set the cookies aside. "How can you be so glib about your own heritage?"

"If I were glib—" He leaned a hip to the counter, turned her chin his way. "I wouldn't have asked my mother."

Ginny knew he spoke the truth.

She felt his eyes touch her soul, his breath on her lips. She wanted him to kiss her. Hold her. Tell her everything was in its right place. She said, "I won't let this be turned into a carnival, Luke."

"From what I remember, my mother's ancestors are not entertainment seekers. If they come, it'll be because the sacredness of the occasion brought them. Don't forget, centuries ago *their* ancestors lived and died right where we stand. Long before there ever was a Franklin's mill or a Misty River populace. Or a reporter called Rachel Brant. If they come it'll be because they believe in granting those spirits peace."

"It's not your mom's people I worry about. It's the town and its gawkers, its Crazy Mazeys, its Rachel Brants and whoever damaged my preschool. I don't want any of them sneering at my family, thinking we're a bunch of—"

He turned her so they faced each other. "Ginny. Trust me on this, okay? I won't let anything hurt you or the kids. I'll be with you every step of the way. I promise."

Some hint of doubt must have lurked in her eyes. After all, for eight years she had trusted his promises, had expected him to be *with her.* In the end, his words had flown on the meekest breeze and her faith in him had died. Replacing that faith was a skepticism so huge she hadn't dared tell him about her pregnancy after their divorce. Hadn't dared because even then, *even then* he might not have cared enough—and rejected their baby. And that, surely, would have killed her.

What about these past six weeks? She could not deny he had been at her side. *Every step of the way.* By hiring Eva, checking with Jon on the vandalism, supporting her at the newspaper, driving Joselyn to the hospital.

Small, quick remedies. But not like this.

Securing a Native American shaman to put her land at peace was a massive undertaking. Sticking by someone meant commitment. *The long haul.* Would he be there this time?

A discarded yellow crayon and a sheet of loose-leaf paper with Joselyn's scribbles lay on the counter. Ginny flipped the page. With the crayon, she drew a large heart.

"What are you doing?" Luke asked.

Inside the heart she set three of Maxine's cookies. "These are me and the kids." She chose a fourth cookie, placed it outside the heart. "This is where I see you."

"Meaning?"

"It's where you've always chosen to be, Luke. Separate from family. This thing you're proposing could backfire. It could have dire consequences for your career. And if so, then what? Where does that leave you and me?"

He stepped back. "I suppose I deserve that," he said. When she opened her mouth to soothe what she'd said, he put a finger to her lips. "It's all right. One day you'll see I've changed." His mouth tugged into a rueful smile and a soft beam of light fell into her heart.

The next minute she stood with the murmurings of Eva and Joselyn drifting down the stairs.

She was alone.

Luke had left. Again.

After dusk crept over the trees and Joselyn was settled in her crib with her blankie, Ginny told Alexei she needed to talk to Luke. Leaving the boy watching a TV sitcom, she hobbled down the porch steps with Bargain and headed for the cottage. Eva had left moments before; only Luke's Mustang sat beside her car. He hadn't left. And she'd heard hammering after supper, though Seth had gone home around five-thirty.

On Monday the cast would come off. She couldn't wait to walk on her own two feet again. Under the plaster the skin had quit itching with the regrowth of hair.

But tonight, it wasn't her leg that made her restless. It was Luke.

She'd hurt him with her doubts. *Just like he'd hurt you twelve years ago with his lies.* Not really lies. Bleak promises.

But he's different now. He cares more.

Was that it? Was the self-centeredness truly gone? What he proposed hovered in the back of her mind. Such an undertaking. What if it didn't work? What if people laughed at her, at the tribal members? What if the illusion of spirits and ghosts mushroomed into something she and her family never lived down?

Would Luke be there for them then?

Bargain, sniffing the grass, woofed and turned toward the river. Her tail windmilled as she ran.

"Where are you off to, mutt?" Ginny called. "Bargain, come!"

She glanced back at the house, then at the cottage. Should she tell Eva or Luke? Dangit, by the time she returned to the house or reached the cottage, the dog could be in a rough current.

Ginny swung off the cottage path and headed for the spot where the animal disappeared in the willows along the bank.

"Bargain!"

Hummocks, brambles and long grass slowed Ginny's progress. By the time she reached the tree line, the pup had vanished. A narrow, willow-shrouded path led down the embankment to a margin of sand and rock. Beyond them flowed Misty River's dark waters.

Choosing her route gingerly, Ginny started toward the sand.

Halfway down, a deep voice jerked her from focus. "What the hell are you doing?" Luke climbed the path in four long strides. Bargain, tongue lolling in glee, romped at his heels.

"Looking for my dog." God, had he always looked the part of a dark avenging angel?

Stern eyes bore into hers. Slipping an arm around her waist, he took her left crutch in hand. "Jeez, Ginny. Have you no sense? You could have fallen on these rocks."

"I was careful." But her hand slipped across his back for balance and caught his shoulder. He was warm and strong and smelled of river and night.

"Come on. Let's get you back up to a safer level."

"No, I want to see the water."

He looked at her. Their faces were close. She could see the double rows of lashes hemming those silver eyes, the black whiskery beginnings of the day's beard. She imagined what he was thinking. This very spot had been his since he was a small boy, when he sought to escape Maxine. He would come here on his bicycle to skip stones. To think. To cry.

He would come here and talk to *her*.

The mother he'd never known. Maggie. The legendary ghost he scoffed as an adult, but in which he had believed with all his child's heart.

Until this moment, Ginny had forgotten about those memories he harbored. Forgotten the truth behind his arduous fight to make something of himself. He'd done it for Maggie. Because his father had once told him that she was a woman of heart and spirit, of quality and merit. A woman Travis Tucker had never forgotten.

The man's words had sunk deep into Luke. And with Maxine's abuse, they had twisted and tangled in his mind, until all he'd been able to do was run for the top of the lofty peak where Maggie stood in his mind.

Why hadn't she remembered that? Ginny wondered. "Were you skipping stones?" she asked softly.

He shrugged. "A couple."

Because of her? "Take me to the water, Luke. I haven't been there since we moved into the house."

He nodded and they picked their way down the last ten feet to level ground. Luke's arm tightened as Ginny navigated the few yards of river rock before they reached the smooth, hard-packed shore sand.

Bargain ran to the water's edge and lapped her pink tongue into the clear current. She ran to a small stick of driftwood, dropped down and began gnawing its end like a bone.

A cuticle moon strewn with winking stars hung over the copse of fir on the opposite bank. River water, moss and damp earth suffused the cool evening air. Ginny breathed deep. Luke's arm remained around her waist; her fingers gripped his shoulder. If they turned inward, their bodies would press. She didn't let go.

"I loved West Virginia," she said. "But I missed the ruggedness of Oregon."

"I missed you."

"Luke…"

"After the divorce and I moved back, I'd jog at five-thirty every morning. I spent a lot of dawns right here where we're standing, thinking about us, thinking about what I could have done differently. About two years later, I met a woman. A very decent person. It lasted fourteen months. She got tired of hearing your name in our conversations. After her, there was Jenny. I called her Ginny in bed once."

"You don't need to tell me this."

"Yeah, I do." He laid the crutches on the sand.

Standing in front of her, he tugged her close. "I never stopped skipping stones on my morning jogs," he said. "Not until you moved back." His fingers trembled as he tucked a wayward curl behind her ear. "How could you marry him?"

She heard the frustration and hurt in his voice, and suspected they evolved from a long-buried grievance with himself. That skewed tunnel-visioned ambition, which had cost him their marriage. She chose her words with care. "Boone was like a father at first. My heart—" her throat tightened "—my heart was in shreds. Boone gave me hope."

"I'm glad. I'm glad because I couldn't bear the thought of you hurting, Ginny. And I'd hurt you so damned bad."

She placed a palm against his heart. "We hurt each other." *I'll hurt you again when I explain Robby.* "Luke, there's something you need to know."

"Can it wait? I need to kiss you right now. I've been needing to for days. Hell, for years."

The river sang with his words. She struggled out of their lull. "This is important."

"So is this." He bent his head, settled his mouth on hers, and took her to a place where only he existed.

Chapter Eleven

Taste, scent, touch.

Each struck her separately, yet surrounded like a warm blanket. Had she ever forgotten him? In the back of her mind, she knew the truth. Luke was ingrained on her soul, like a mystery she carried with her but could never completely resolve.

Her arms wrapped around his neck, holding him in place.

Her blood chanted his name.

The night, the river, the wildness of tongues.

She was drunk. On him.

Beneath her sweater, he touched—and her skin flashed heat. *Never leave. Please, never leave.* The words streamed across her mind, her heart.

She needed him closer. Her noncasted foot climbed his calf, and he groaned. "Ginny, Ginny. Here, honey. Now."

Yes! Now.

His lips anchored her. He struggled from his jacket, stripped off her sweater.

"Luke, I'm not—"

She fell into his hands, his warm, strong hands. "You kill me," he muttered and bent to kiss her naked breasts. "You absolutely kill me."

"I'm not the same." *My breasts are pear-shaped. My stomach's still paunchy from the baby. I have—*

"No," he whispered on her skin. Voiding her hesitation. "You're more beautiful than ever. Ginny, feel me."

He didn't wait for her to reach, but took her hand, pushed it between them where he pressed her belly.

Memories floated up. Of him rising above her for the first time. Of him walking naked and damp from the shower.

She knew the texture of him. The musk, the salt.

And yearned for all. Again.

"Luke, I can't think." *We need to talk about Robby.*

"I don't want you to think, honey. Just feel. Feel, Ginny. Me. You." His hands ran over her back, caught under her knees. Careful of her cast—of her—he laid her on his coat spread out on the sand. "Feel," he whispered. "Feel us."

Lyrics to serenade her heart.

He hoisted her skirt, worked his jeans, worked a condom from a pocket. Starlight spilled across his smile. "I'd hoped."

She reached to help. "I'm glad." But she wasn't. She wanted him, not latex. She wanted him as she'd had him that last night. When Robby was conceived. "Luke, we need to…" *Talk. I need to tell you about your son.*

"I'm safe," he said against her hair. Misreading her frayed intention. "I had myself tested last year. I haven't been with anyone since."

Tears. Welling from a pit of regret. For them both. "I've only been with Boone. But in the past two years with his illness…"

Luke touched her face gently. Set his forehead to hers. "Before we do this, Ginny, I want to say only one thing. I love you. I've never stopped loving you."

"Luke, I can't say the same…"

"I know. You loved him."

"But differently from you."

"Doesn't matter. I'm glad there was someone for you. You're a nurturer, Gin. You need family."

Tears filled her throat. *You were my family once.*

Then he pressed into her, strong and secure, as if he'd always been a part of her, and she remembered Robby who was his family, too. She closed her eyes and held Luke to her heart.

He let the night air chill his skin as he waited for the ripples to cease. His jacket had worked away from Ginny's head; his forehead pressed into the sand. The mustiness of the river stormed his nose. *This,* he thought, *is heaven.*

Lying in Ginny's arms.

His body, at rest, but still one with her.

The river burbling twenty feet away.

Night cloaking them in stars and peace.

He raised his head and saw her dark, lovely eyes. A sheen covered her cheeks. Her tears. He'd felt them come in the aftermath. Quietly ripping his soul.

Soft kisses, tender kisses. His heart beat a slow march. Ginny. His Ginny. Always and forever.

He touched her hair, pushed a strand from her forehead where the moon laid its light. "Give us another chance,

Ginny." *I'll be there for you. I'll be there for your children.* The words scrambled in his throat.

She stayed beneath him, quiet, still. Mesmerizing his eyes.

"Nickel for your thoughts?" he whispered. To ease the mood, to ease the heartbreak he felt weighing her down.

A tiny smile. "Not a penny?"

"Nickels are worth more."

"I was thinking about us."

"Good start." He offered his own smile.

Hers faded. "About how much…we've…missed."

"Twelve years."

"More."

He waited. Her sorrow leaked around him. His heart scurried between his ribs. She regretted this, regretted him. He pushed up, reached for her sweater. Helped her into it.

Shaking out his coat, he said, "I'm not sorry, Gin. Not for one damned second. I'd do it again, in a heartbeat. And every heartbeat after that."

Assisting her to her feet, he picked up the crutches.

Tail-happy, Bargain trotted over from the driftwood stick as if she'd just remembered her human friends.

Ginny regarded the pup for a moment. "I'm not sorry, either." Her eyes riveted on him. "I've never been sorry about this part of our relationship, Luke."

Something in him died, the way she said *this part.* As if all the other parts left gaps and further choices. He knew they had once. Maybe they still did.

Angling her crutches, she stepped closer. Until her face was beneath his. "Nine months after I left Seattle I had a baby. Robby. That's what I wanted to tell you before…before we…you and I…"

The river altered, bubbling to blasting. What was she

saying? She'd had *his* baby? He shot back a step. "You—you were pregnant when…?"

"When I moved to West Virginia. But I didn't know for another two months and—"

"You had *my baby?* And never *told me?*" His heart rammed his throat. Beat his brain. What had she called it? Robby. "Jeez, Ginny. Why? Why didn't you tell me?" He glanced toward the path that led to her house. To where another boy played with his sister. Alexei. Not…*Robby.* "Where is he? Where's my son?"

Her mouth crimped. Her eyes glistened. He couldn't reach out. Couldn't touch her.

"He died," she murmured. He barely heard the words with the thundering river, the roaring of his blood. "His lungs were underdeveloped. He… For eleven days he struggled so hard to live." A tear fell down her cheek. "So very hard. It broke my heart."

Yes, he could see that. "And you never once thought to contact me." Had he been such an ogre?

"I *wanted* to." Her eyes turned desperate. "Every day, after I found out about my pregnancy, I wanted to phone you."

"Then why didn't you?" Anger. Burning his lungs.

"Because I was afraid. Afraid you'd—you'd—"

And suddenly he knew. *Knew.* His shoulders slumped under a boulder of agony. "Afraid I'd reject the baby." How could she have believed it?

Because you'd told her enough times, fool. In a thousand ways. *"Next year. We'll start a family next year… Let's just be the two us for a while… Do we really need kids? We have each other. Isn't that enough?"*

Not for her. *Not for her.* Ginny, his earth woman.

She stood in the moonlight, fingers pressed to her mouth, crutch shivering under her arm. Eyes, pools of torment.

Luke stepped forward. "Ginny." He wrapped her against his chest, where the ache for his lost son stabbed like ten thousand knives. A son he'd never known, never seen. Would never see. A tiny bundle created from him and her.

Shame and guilt wounded his eyes. He pressed his face into her hair. So *many* lost years. Right from the day they married he'd got it all wrong.

They stood for long minutes in a bond of grief. At last, she bussed her face against his coat and stepped away. "I need to go. Alexei will be wondering where I've gone to."

Luke nodded and helped her across the rocks to the path. The pup scrambled ahead, bent on home, but Luke made Ginny climb slowly, taking care of her casted leg. Once she slipped and he caught her easily against his side. They didn't speak, intent on the house across the meadow.

On the porch, she stopped. "Luke, I know it's too soon to ask, but I hope you'll be able to forgive me one day."

"It's not you who needs forgiving, Ginny." Blindly he turned and headed for the cottage. Behind him, he heard her speak to the pup, then the door opened and closed.

As Sunday's sunrise nudged over the treetops, Luke got in his car and drove to his condo in town. His skin felt taut as a trampoline canvas. Beard stubble covered his cheeks and jaw. His bones smarted as if he'd slept on rocky ground, without bedding.

He needed a shower. He needed to wash *her* from his body. From his mind. Betrayal ate through his heart, a gnawing fiend sporting vampire fangs.

Twelve years she'd bridled the existence of their son.

Six weeks he'd been in her house, in her life, in her kids' lives. And not a word. Not a single word when he'd held the door open a hundred times. *"Can we be friends? Let's start again."*

A tornado of utterances and memories keeping his mind alive all night. Whirling, twisting, surging. Round and round and round. A never-ending cycle led by one name, one five-lettered, faceless name. *Robby.*

He'd had a son.

In a single unguarded moment he'd given Ginny what Boone Franklin couldn't in eight years—until it was too late.

Except Luke's blood had died, and Franklin's lived. Fate or irony? Either way, Luke had lost. Lost his wife. Lost his son. Lost every goddamned thing that mattered.

Hindsight, such a crafty-clawed vixen. Had he tried harder to believe in Ginny, in her hopes, her dreams, rather than allow his self-doubts to drive him, where would it have taken them?

Home.

Not his condo, not Boone Franklin's heritage, but some place in the country, nonetheless. Some place where trees sheltered a house and flowers colored the porch. Where a couple of kids, possibly a boy with her eyes, a girl with his coloring, rushed through the door to greet him when day was done.

His street lay empty as a shell in the quiet morning. A cat slunk under a hedge as he pulled into the short driveway of his condo and shut off the motor. He sat listening to it tick in cadence with his heart. So, what now? She wanted forgiveness.

It's not you who needs forgiving, Ginny, he'd told her. But the ache in his chest spoke differently.

He sat until the sun heated his neck through the side window. Still he didn't move. *Ginny. Robby.* The names dive-bombed his heart. He wanted her. In his bed, in his life. He wanted her kids in his life. He wanted a home with them all.

But not without Robby.

Without what she'd done rising like deadwood between them.

At lunchtime on Monday, Maxine and Seth rode out to Ginny Franklin's in his truck. Seth. Maxine's youngest. A good boy. Quiet, steady. She was overjoyed that he'd found Breena last year. And now Seth was expecting his second child, and a first for Breena. One more grandchild for Maxine. These days she had to pinch herself to make sure it was true, this happiness she felt.

She hadn't liked the woman Seth first married seventeen years ago. But Breena was different. Another quiet one, calm and sweet. Hallie laughed a lot these days, and she and her friends always made time to stop by the library after school on Maxine's workdays.

Like Jon's girls. A pair of peas in a pod, those two. Brittany and Emily. Always full of pep and giggles. Fussing like little mothers over their baby brother, Travis Nicholas. Pestering their older brother, Sam, who took it as well as could be expected for a lad of fifteen.

Jon's wife was another jewel. Rianne had known her share of grief, but Jon had healed her. They'd healed each other. Just like Breena and Seth. Love did that. Maxine's heart ached a little at the thought. If only her Travis had been able to love her…

Well, no matter. She knew her boys loved their wives with all their hearts.

Maxine wished for the thousandth time Luke would find someone, too. She knew about his marriage to Ginny years ago. But then something happened and they divorced. Maxine wasn't sure what caused the split, but she'd mourned the loss for his sake. Luke didn't know that, of course.

She had always liked Ginny Keegan. That was the name she knew her by when her boys were in school.

Ginny, of the sparkling blond hair and lovely green eyes. Anchoring Maxine's restless Luke.

Seth turned into Ginny's lane. The sun was sharp over the trees and Maxine blinked against the glare. A hot afternoon in store. In her lap rested another batch of cookies. Chocolate chip, macadamia nut, peanut butter and a few teething biscuits for the baby.

"You're gonna make us all fat with those cookies," Seth teased, halting the truck in front of Ginny's porch.

"They're low-fat. I use minimal light margarine."

Seth chuckled. "Like that makes a difference." He climbed down and came around to assist her from the truck, then held her elbow as she climbed the porch steps.

"You'd think I was an old crone," she grumbled.

Again the soft chuckle. "You're hardly a crone, Ma."

"Just old, huh?"

He winked and she saw Luke in his eyes. "Call my cell when you're ready."

Taking a deep breath, she walked to the door and knocked.

A boisterous bark sounded inside. She'd forgotten about the dog and hoped it wouldn't jump up to snatch the cookies.

The door opened and there stood a slightly older version of the high school girl Maxine remembered, dressed in pink shorts and a white cotton top. A big gold clip captured most of her flaxen hair, though she blew away a few unruly curls from her eyes as she bent to tug back the black, wriggling puppy sniffing Maxine's shoes.

She said, "Hello, Ginny. Remember me?"

The woman's eyes widened. "Maxine?"

"It's me. Been a long time, hasn't it?"

"Yes, but what a nice surprise. Come on in." She stepped back, careful not to push aside the toddler clutching her legs.

"Bug, he-ah," the tiny girl said pointing at the puppy.

"Bargain, here," Ginny repeated, helping the child. The puppy obeyed happily. "Please, excuse the mess. I had my cast removed this morning and was catching a few therapy exercises."

Maxine surveyed the "mess": a jumble of storybooks on the sofa, a trio of dolls cuddled in a red towel under the coffee table tented with a blue blanket and an exercise mat on the floor.

A family home full of welcome.

Her intuition had been right to come, to see this woman who had Luke entering his boyhood home—*Maxine's* home—for the first time in twenty-five years.

Clutching her purse, Maxine said, "I didn't mean to interrupt."

Ginny waved off the worry. "Not at all. I was finishing off my cooldown exercise. Would you like lunch? I'm about to fix a bowl of soup for Josie."

"Maybe a cup of tea."

"Coming right up."

Maxine followed woman, child and puppy into a spacious kitchen where new maple cupboards gleamed and red roses burst from a tall vase in the center of the table. "How lovely," she murmured, bending to the bouquet. An envelope enclosed the attached card.

"Luke," Ginny answered Maxine's curiosity. "He had them delivered an hour ago."

Maxine studied the woman busy at the counter with kettle, cups and soup. Her arms were slender and white, her body small, with the lushness of motherhood in the right spots. Travis would've called her legs "long's a country mile." Against the Santa Fe–patterned vinyl, her bare feet paralleled her limbs: pale, slim, elegant. Yet, there flowed around her an earthiness.

"My son is a good man," she said, hoping this woman would recognize Maxine's intent.

Ginny glanced over her shoulder. Her eyes were kind. "Sit down and rest, why don't you? The tea will be ready in a minute."

Maxine sat. And watched Ginny Franklin's smooth, deft motions as she set the child in the high chair, then worked around the stove. At last she brought the lunch—tea, sugar, cream, soup, crackers and a chicken-salad sandwich—to the table. Maxine poured a little cream into her tea. "How long did you have your cast?"

"Six weeks." Ginny slipped part of the sandwich onto a bread plate and set it before Maxine. "And my leg itched for five and a half of them."

They smiled at each other.

Maxine said, "Once I fell and broke my elbow." She'd been drunk and missed the bottom basement step. Luke had found her and she'd snarled at him to leave her alone. He'd sat in a corner waiting, in case she fainted or passed out. "I was shoving knitting needles up that cast by the third day." And bellyaching to Travis. Those weeks had been hell, especially on Luke who caught the brunt of her tirades.

She set down her tea. Her hand shook and a little liquid spilled over the side of the cup.

"Ginny." Hiding nothing, she looked into the younger woman's eyes. "I want to have this land blessed not only for you, but also for my son. I need to do this for him. That's why I've come here today. To ask that you'll accept the offer and not be afraid. My people understand the land better than anyone in this country. It was their mother for many millenniums. They won't harm your property."

"Did Luke tell you I was afraid?"

"No. But these kinds of things make people nervous and I wanted to assure you the ceremony will be handled with the deepest respect."

"Because of your sister?"

"Especially because of my sister."

"And Luke? How does he fit into this?"

Maxine didn't hesitate. "You mean everything to him. I saw that the day he came to ask me the favor. He wants to set things right again with you."

"Did he say that?"

"It was there. In his eyes."

Ginny wiped the baby's face with a damp cloth. "I've already told him it's okay. For the blessing, I mean."

"Thank you. Not to seem bold, but I've already contacted the elders."

"When will they come?"

"In ten days."

"Should I do anything to prepare?"

"They'll do everything. It won't be a long ceremony. Maybe an hour at the most."

Ginny blew a deep breath. "It seems surreal, all this... this legend stuff. I don't remember much of it when I was growing up. Guess that's the beauty of being young. Your biggest worry is the zit on your chin. Luke calls the stories hogwash."

Her smile lit Maxine's heart. "I agree with him. My sister never would have appeared to that old goat, Basil Dunham. But because he was mayor of Misty River at the time, everyone believed him. All that man ever did was listen to himself talk. Especially about his fishing trips."

Ginny grunted softly. "Well, he certainly started a whopper fish story with this one."

"That he did."

The baby wanted down. Ginny cleaned her little face and hands before lifting her free. Immediately Joselyn headed for Maxine.

"Hey, there, sweet pea," she crooned. "Tummy all full?"

"Tum." Joselyn patted her little belly. She stretched out her arms. "Up."

"No, Josie." Ginny settled the baby on her lap. "Maxine doesn't need your grimy little fingers all over her nice clothes."

"I don't mind."

Joselyn squirmed.

"You sure?" Ginny held her tight; the baby wriggled harder.

"Absolutely." She offered her arms. Within seconds, the baby climbed into Maxine's lap, popped her thumb into her mouth and settled against the older woman. "She's a cuddly little thing."

Ginny smiled. "Depends on the person."

A knock sounded.

Yipping, the pup scrambled from the kitchen. Ginny followed the dog, shushing her en route. The door opened and Maxine heard Luke's deep voice. Immediately, Joselyn snapped awake. "Daee?"

"Luke," Maxine whispered.

"Daee!" The baby slipped from Maxine's lap and rushed out of the kitchen. "Da hoe! Da hoe, Mammy!"

"No, Luke's not home, Josie," Maxine heard Ginny say. "He has to go back to work."

"Hey, there, button. Whatcha doing with your bib on backward?"

Maxine sat motionless. Luke's voice was Travis's forty years ago, when Luke was a toddler hungry for his daddy's smile.

"The leg looks good," Luke said to Ginny.

"Feels good, too."

"Did you get the roses?"

"Yes, thank you. They're gorgeous."

"They're red." His voice had deepened, softened.

"Very."

"Know what red roses mean?" A quiet question.

"I do," Ginny said.

Maxine did, as well. She couldn't breathe. Secreted in the kitchen twenty feet away, she was hearing her son woo his ex-wife. She closed her eyes.

Red roses. For love. *Make it happen, Travis.*

Luke said, "What you explained the other night—"

"Your mother's here."

"My mother? What for?" Surprise along with annoyance.

"She's visiting."

Maxine could well imagine Luke's expression: dark

and suspicious as he stared at the woman keeping him in the entranceway.

Ginny pressed on. "Alexei and Maxine have become friends at the library." When still he said nothing, she added in a lower voice, "She's changed, Luke. And I'm welcoming her into my home."

"All right." Acceptance. "We need to talk, Ginny."

"Yes. Later."

A ringing silence, and then he stated, "We're not finished with this."

"We'll never be finished with it, Luke."

Finished with what? Maxine wondered. Their past?

"I gotta go," Luke said. "Be good to Mommy, button."

"Da hoe. No bye-bye."

"Yes, bye-bye, tyke." A pause. "I'll see you later." He meant Ginny.

The door closed. "Come on, peachy-pie. Let's go talk to Maxine."

"Ma-tee."

"*Right.* Maxine." Ginny walked into the kitchen. "Sorry about that. He would've come in, except he was in a bit of a rush."

Maxine understood. Luke did not wish to talk to her any more than needed. That was okay, too. She had come to see this woman he cared about. And found her answer. Rising, she gathered up her purse. "Thank you for the tea. It was very nice."

"You're welcome. Thank *you* for the cookies."

Maxine nodded and walked to the door. Ginny carried the baby on her hip, the puppy gamboling alongside. Stepping into the heat of the afternoon, Maxine paused. Carefully, she searched for the words to express the emotion in her heart. "You have a sweet family and a good home." Her eyes held those grass-green ones. "For the first time in a long while you've made my son feel."

She turned and walked into the glaring sun.

That afternoon Ginny put Joselyn in her crib for a nap. Baby monitor in hand, she went downstairs intent on painting the kitchen with the lovely mint-green paint she bought the day she had walked into Luke's car.

He had sent her roses.

Red roses for passion, for love.

He had come to see if she was okay after the cast.

"It's not you who needs forgiving." His eyes, scored with anguish, shattered in guilt. First because of their divorce and now Robby. The memory of their tiny son lifeless in her arms, her horrible, wracking sobs, slashed her insides all over again. During those final moments she had needed Luke more than air. More than the beat of her heart.

Had he felt it that night after he left her on the porch? Had he gone to the cottage, lain awake thinking, grieving, hurting, as she had in those hideous days and nights after Robby's death?

"You've made my son feel."

Oh, yes. An hour ago, at the door, his eyes told her exactly how much she had made him feel. She had broken his heart. Because she had not trusted him.

Because her faith in him had not measured up to the love she expressed in their marriage.

Scattering plastic sheets over the floor, she set about readying the kitchen, pushing open the windows, moving table and chairs, barring out the dog. But as she bent over the tin to stir the paint with its thin wooden stick, her eyes burned. Oh, God, she had meant to hurt him as she'd been hurt, to cleave a chunk of his very soul.

His mother had implied Ginny was a good person.

Hurting someone intentionally was not good.

Chapter Twelve

Six Nez Percé band members checked into the Sleep Inn motel late Thursday afternoon. As Ginny grated cheese on a spinach lasagna, Maxine called with the news.

"They want to see your property after supper," Luke's mother said. "To get a sense or feel for it. Will that be okay?"

Seth and his two helpers would be done their work for the day. "Yes, that's fine." A sketch of nerves traced Ginny's skin. This was it. No matter the outcome, the ceremony would leave lasting effects. "Will you be coming with them, Maxine?"

"Yes."

And Luke? Will he be here? She hadn't seen him since last Monday. Since he'd stood in her doorway and asked if she was okay and told her they weren't finished. God help her, but she hoped they'd never be "finished" again. This past week she'd barely slept. She missed his voice, his laugh, his teasing Joselyn. She missed the long looks. The kissing. Specifically the kissing. And the touching. *Don't go there!*

Most of all, she missed *him*. Missed the man she'd come to love again, who was part of her past and present—and her future. If he could forgive her.

"Luke will be there, too," Maxine said, reading Ginny's angst over the line.

She closed her eyes briefly, let her heart settle. "Who's the elder or the shaman?"

"Thomas Many Moons." A soft chuckle. "He comes by his name honestly at 102. Except for his wrinkles, you'd never guess his age. No cane, no glasses and in the summer he still sleeps outdoors."

"Wow. Sounds like the real McCoy."

"He is. And Ginny?"

"Yes?"

"He'll get this done for you."

She didn't doubt it. But would the community believe him?

Walking between his mom and Luke, Alexei shivered with excitement. They were following three of the six tribal leaders across the rough terrain of the meadow. Alexei glanced back at the remaining three Native Americans— Luke's great-uncle Abel, a half-blind medicine woman and her grown daughter. They sat in Adirondack chairs on the porch with Mrs. Tucker. Joselyn flit amidst the group, laying dolls and teddy bears in their laps.

Mr. Many Moons, the shaman, was a tall man with shoulders angled like one of those oxen's yokes Alexei saw in pioneer pictures. He led the way toward the old mill site that Alexei's mom had forbid him to go near. George and Clara, the band's elders, walked slightly behind him.

"Where are they going?" Alexei whispered up at Luke.

"To where the ancient bones were found ten years ago."

"But I thought they were supposed to be going to the river where Mrs. Tucker's sister drowned."

His mother rubbed Alexei's shoulder. "They will, son. But first they want to see the location of *their* ancestors."

"You mean that old skeleton was their relative? How would they know that?" He'd researched a lot about the Nez Percé on the Net, but he hadn't come across anything like what would be happening on their land tomorrow.

His mom said, "A thousand years ago, he might have been related to almost any and all the tribes in the U.S., which makes him a relative of the Nez Percé."

"Then why didn't they put him at rest when those kids found the bones? Why now?"

"Because," Luke said, "the land wasn't Native American land, so they had no claim to the bones. Your mom is the first to allow them to come and send their ancestor to a better place."

"That right, Mama?"

"Yes, honey."

The men stopped a short distance from the broken-down mill site. In the dusk, the building crowded against a tangle of brambles, bushes and weeds with purple flowers. Giant spruce trees rose like jagged black witches' hats behind the mill.

Thomas Many Moons threw back his head and raised his arms as if he were stamping his tall body against the orange evening sky.

Alexei sidled against Luke. "What's he doing?" he whispered.

In a clear voice, the old shaman said, "I am asking my brother's spirit to wait for us here in the morning." He turned and smiled at Alexei. "You must always ask the spirits for permission to speak to them."

"Why?"

"It is polite."

"But what if he doesn't listen?" Then his mom's land would be cursed forever.

Mr. Many Moons nodded as if sensing Alexei's worry. His black eyes were kind. "Then we will wait until he does."

How will you know? Alexei wanted to ask, but his mom would think he was rude.

The old man put a hand to his heart. "I will know in here."

Alexei's jaw dropped. The old guy could read minds? This was *way* cool!

The shaman turned his attention on Luke. "Show me where the white woman, your mother, drowned."

Luke pointed to the opening in the trees, which would take them down to the water. "There."

Nodding, the Native American trio headed toward the path.

Alexei's brow knotted. He stared up at Luke. "He's confused," he whispered. "Your mama's on the porch."

"He's not confused," Luke said. "I was adopted by her."

"Adopted? You mean…?" He looked to where the adults sat among the flickering bug candles. Mrs. Tucker had Joselyn on her lap. Their heads were bent together.

Luke turned Alexei toward the shaman. "I'll explain later."

"Just tell me this." Alexei glanced at Luke. "Do you ever miss, you know, your…your first mom?"

"Always."

"Okay," Alexei said. That's how he felt about his dad. He missed him every day. He jogged ahead to catch up. Over his shoulder he saw his mom take Luke's hand. And he remembered how he had felt when she'd taken his hand for the first time in that Russian orphanage. As though he'd found home.

The old shaman stopped at the top of the riverbank, and again raised his hands to the night.

Alexei thought of the stories he had read in the library and on the Internet about Chief Joseph of the Nez Percé. Of his dying of a broken heart in 1904 over the fact his people couldn't go home. Alexei couldn't imagine grieving so hard for your family that you'd die. He couldn't even remember his family in Russia. They'd been taken from him when he was a baby. But he might have grieved if the Franklins hadn't found him when they did.

Watching Thomas Many Moons, he thought of the mother drowning, and of her struggle to live in that fast-moving water. Had she called out to Luke? Alexei shivered. A hundred nights he had cried in that orphanage. Cried for his mother—*any* mother. And then she had come.

"Soon," Alexei whispered to the night, to the spirits he imagined were listening. "Soon everything will be okay and you'll get to go home, too."

At eight the next morning, Ginny opened the door to the reporter Rachel Brant.

"I heard you're having some kind of Native American ceremony on your property," the woman said, "to get rid of the ghosts?"

Ginny took a long breath. "There are no ghosts, Ms.

Brant, except those living in your mind. If you'll excuse me, I have work to do." She moved to close the door. The reporter slapped a hand against the wood. Ginny lifted her chin. "Maybe I didn't make myself clear the first time. Please leave."

"Look, I'm sorry about the story. Let me make it up to you."

Ginny laughed. "You must be kidding."

"What do you know about the singer/songwriter Kitty Rae Davis?"

"Nothing I'd share with you."

"Did you know she's been asked to attend?"

"Then why aren't you questioning her instead of ruining my day? Goodbye, Ms. Brant." Ginny closed the door, threw the lock. Waiting a moment, she listened for receding footsteps. When they came, and a motor started up, she sank against the wood. Kitty Rae Davis? Coming to the ceremony?

Last night neither Maxine nor the tribal elders had mentioned a word about the singer. Was the reporter flapping her gums?

"Who's Kitty Rae?" Alexei stood in the kitchen doorway.

"A Native American singer."

"Is she famous?"

"She was very popular once, yes."

"Why is she coming here?"

"She's not, Alexei. Eat your breakfast and get ready. The shaman will be here in a half hour."

Joselyn ran between her brother and the dog. "Mama! Me go pot!"

Thank God for normality. "Okay, peach." Ginny caught up her baby with a quick kiss. "Let's hurry."

* * *

Thomas Many Moons and his entourage didn't arrive until ten past ten. By then the graded area in front of Ginny's house looked like a parking lot. She counted twenty-three cars. Alexei, who had been vigilant by the window, tore through the house. "Mama, they're here! They're here!"

Carrying Joselyn, Ginny went down the porch steps to greet the old shaman climbing from Luke's car. Rain clouds scraped the western hills. A cool wind trifled with the old man's long salt-and-pepper hair and rippled the deerskin tassels of his sleeves. Around his neck, his medicine bag caught the light in a helix of blue, red, apple-green and orange.

The morning almost over, Ginny felt as if she'd battled a ground war with the kids skipping from room to room like Luke's stones across water since seven o'clock. She did not appreciate Thomas Many Moons' sense of schedule.

She saw Luke's smile and her day balanced itself.

"Good morning," she said to the shaman. Shame pulsed across her skin. He had a right to be late. A century of years lay in his face, in his bones.

"Good morning," he murmured.

Joselyn reached for Luke. "Daee."

Ginny didn't correct her daughter as Luke lifted Joselyn, bundled against the day in her yellow jacket, from Ginny's arms. "Hey, button. Ready for the big event?" He settled the baby on his shoulders. Her tiny fingers latched on to his dark hair.

Soap-bubble giggles. They floated from the child's rosy mouth and into Ginny's heart.

Thomas Many Moons studied Luke and the baby for a moment, then looked at the people crowding the two cars that had brought the guests. A third car stopped behind Luke's. A man and woman got out. The woman reached into the rear seat and retrieved a guitar. Behind them, Ginny heard the murmur of the crowd fall to a hush. Hoisting her guitar over one shoulder, Kitty Rae Davis, her lovely face bright with friendliness, walked to where Ginny stood with Alexei, Luke and Thomas.

The singer nodded to the shaman. "Mr. Many Moons," she said reverently. "I am honored to meet you."

His head moved ever so slightly. "Ms. Davis. This day I will not forget."

They smiled at each other. Kitty held out her free hand to Ginny. "I'm Kitty Rae Davis."

Ginny's mouth hung open. "I didn't realize— Goodness… This is a surprise. A wonderful surprise. *Welcome.*"

She glanced at Luke. *No one told me* his silver eyes relayed. But his lips twitched.

Thomas said, "We will begin now." Tall and straight, his deerskin jacket natural to his frame, his moccasins leaving barely a print in the dirt, he headed for the mill site, parting townsfolk like a new-millennium Moses.

The ceremony lasted thirty minutes. From his medicine bag, Thomas Many Moons scattered bits of Mother Earth—an eagle's feather, dried berries, seeds, a tiny stone, flowers of the camas root and chunks of cedar wood—to the rising wind.

Luke listened to the old man's voice, intoning prayers in the Nez Percé tongue. Soothing the most restive soul. Alexei stood beside Ginny. Her slim hand lay on the boy's shoulder. Protective, yet encouraging. Several times, her serious eyes wove to Luke's, and he remembered her words of the night before at Alexei's astonishment over his adoption.

"You've become a different man to Alexei."

"In what way?" he'd asked.

"Respect. For not making light of the matter. And for understanding."

She had taken Luke's hand then. A lifeline in an emotional abyss.

He scanned the sky. Pregnant clouds hung low. A few raindrops wet his face. Thomas Many Moons' voice waved with the wind. Up, down, up, down. Kitty strummed her guitar softly. The elders chanted a chorus, pacifying the ancient spirits of the land.

The shaman moved to the path that led down the riverbank. Some of the townsfolk waited at the top of the path, some descended. Ahead, the water churned and flowed, its currents strong beneath the surface. The wind sighed long and loud in the heavy, baronial branches. Upstream, a misty rain approached. Through it, a lone woman carrying a baby walked over the sand toward them. Her long coppery hair whipped with the gusty breeze. A latecomer?

Joselyn began to fret. Luke slipped her down into his arms. "Hey, snookums," he whispered. "Getting a tad breezy up there?"

"Da." Patting his cheek, she planted a sloppy kiss on his mouth. His chest hurt. He suspected the pain was love.

Reaching over, Ginny adjusted the baby's yellow hat. Luke met her eyes. Had they been alone, he would've snagged her closer, kissed her parted lips, but she stepped back and once more her attention riveted on Thomas Many Moons.

Luke smiled to himself. Ginny hadn't been able to disguise her desire. He focused on the shoreline, idly search-ing for the woman. Taller than most, he browsed the crowd. No coppery head. Where had she gone? Had she gone up the bank? No, he wouldn't have missed that fiery hair. He surveyed the river's line, north and south. A shiver skimmed his arms. The woman had vanished—as if she'd never been there at all.

Not three minutes after the singer climbed inside her vehicle and left and the crowd dispersed, the sky unloaded its rainy burden. From under an umbrella, Rachel Brant snapped photographs of Ginny on her porch as she spoke with Thomas Many Moons. Luke had warned the reporter she was not to take any photographs during the ceremony. He had assigned Jon the job of ensuring it wouldn't hap-pen. Now she snapped two more pictures.

Luke stepped in front of the camera. Rain ran down his collar and dripped from his nose. "Enough," he said softly. "Show's over."

In the shadow of the umbrella, her eyes flashed. "Is that what it was? A show?"

"In your mind I don't doubt it."

She clutched the Canon close to her breast. "You don't have a clue what's in my mind."

"Thank mercy for small favors." He pointed with his chin. "Now get out of here. Go write your filth. Just re-member sixty other people were here today and those sixty shook that man's hand back there."

She let out a half laugh. "Oh, please. They only did it because he knows the singer and she'd already left."

Luke tucked his hands in the pockets of his fast-damp-ening chinos. He didn't trust himself not to shove the woman into her car and slam the door. Instead, he stepped back. "Say hi to your editor for us."

When the reporter had gone, he climbed the porch steps, swiping rain from his eyes.

Thomas said, "You do not like the reporter."

"I don't trust her," Luke conceded.

The old man pursed his lips. "She will come around."

Luke glanced at Ginny. "We can only hope. Thank you for coming today."

"The spirits will rest now." Thomas turned to Ginny. "It is good you are the caretaker. You will bring happiness here." His soulful eyes held Luke's. "But you will need to change issues in here." He tapped his chest. "When you do, this house will find peace. You will find peace." He touched Luke's shoulder, Ginny's elbow. "Together you will do this. Then you will be free."

He walked down the steps, through the rain and climbed into the last waiting car, a big Buick. As the vehicle disappeared from the meadow, the downpour beat the porch roof, gurgled in the eaves. Thunder drummed over the hills.

Luke said, "I need to go home and change out of these wet clothes."

She came beside him, looking as he did at the wet day. "Will you be back?"

Turning his head, he asked, "Do you want me back, Ginny?" and saw she understood. Back as the man in her life.

"Yes. Very much."

The gray day shadowed her eyes. He wanted, more than anything, to warm his skin with her. Forgetting his vow to keep at a distance, he bent his head. The kiss lasted a long moment.

"Tonight," he said, "we need to talk." *About Robby.*

"I know."

He stroked her cheek and then, as Thomas Many Moons had done, walked into the rain and drove away.

The phone began ringing within thirty minutes of the shaman's departure.

Within ninety minutes, Ginny's registration list for the preschool maxed out. And still the phone rang. She began a waiting list.

How good it felt to say, "I'm sorry, but I'm booked for September."

To ensure a spot, two mothers had written checks before leaving the ceremony; she deposited the money in the bank after dropping Alexei at school for the afternoon.

She wasn't naive enough to believe it had been Thomas Many Moons and the Nez Percé elders lulling the spirits into submission. It was the appearance of a celebrity.

In a complete reversal, people were clamoring to share some of her notoriety.

"Are you related to Kitty Rae Davis?" one man had asked before driving off her property.

"How long have you known her?" the second woman to write a check inquired.

"This is so *exciting* to have a *neighbor* who's friends with someone *famous,*" a third woman exclaimed over the phone.

To those people she longed to say, *go to hell.* Instead, she clamped off the thought and said pleasantly, "Ms. Davis is an associate of Mr. Many Moons. She and I never met before today." After the fourth explanation, Ginny realized no matter what she said, people were going to believe what they wanted. Just as they had not twenty-four hours ago when they still believed a curse lay on her land.

After she finished her banking, she drove with Joselyn across the old railway tracks to Maxine's house.

Luke's mother greeted her at the door dressed in a green fisherman's hat and an army coat. "You've caught me about to repot my fig tree," she said as though she were expecting Ginny.

"I didn't mean to interrupt."

"You'll never do that, honey. Come in. I've got something for that little cutie." She smiled at Joselyn, who grinned in return. Back in the kitchen, Maxine selected a book from a small shelf and handed it to Joselyn. "It's all about puppies and kittens."

"Bug?" Joselyn queried. "Kee?"

"Say thank you," Ginny coaxed.

"Tah."

Maxine laughed. "You're welcome, darlin'."

Beyond the screen door a three-foot fig bush in a root-bound ball sat on the stone patio under a tattered umbrella. An empty plastic pot and a bag of prepared soil stood ready. The day's rain had slackened to a fine mist. The kitchen smelled of damp earth and grass.

"Can I help?" she asked, as Maxine went out into the wet day.

"Keep me company through the screen?"

Ginny pulled up a chair. She watched Luke's mother work the soil into the new pot, then scrape away leached soil from the plant. "Why didn't you come to the ceremony this morning?"

The woman's lumpy fingers worked as she spoke. "It was better I stay away."

"But if it wasn't for you, I wouldn't be opening a pre-school in the fall."

Maxine's head lifted. "They changed their minds, did they?"

"So far twenty-two families."

Maxine grunted. Ginny wasn't sure if the sound came from transferring the fig into its new home or acknowledgment.

"Was Luke there?" Maxine asked.

"All three of your sons were there." *They asked for you.*

"Luke needs their support."

"I'm not sure he believed the stories."

Maxine tamped the black earth around the plant. "No, he wouldn't. It's too close to the heart." She stared at the fig. "I was not a good mother."

He still loves you. "It's not too late," Ginny said quietly.

Maxine eased onto a plastic chair and brushed away the gray strands in her eyes. "It's been forty years too late." Rain tapped the umbrella and caught a portion of the fig's leaves. "Travis once told me, 'if you can't love my boy, then at least like him.' I'm afraid I didn't even do that. My nephew, who became my son." She shook her head. "I was so jealous of him."

Why? Ginny wanted to ask. *How could you as a mother be jealous of a little boy?*

"He had my husband's unconditional love," Maxine whispered, regarding the fig absently. "Because Luke was my sister's son and Travis had loved her." Her lips quivered. She covered her face with soil-stained hands. "I wish I could undo my life."

Ginny pushed open the screen door. Gently, she urged the weeping woman from the chair. "Come. I'll make us some tea."

* * *

Lying on her side, Joselyn rubbed her blankie against her cheek and slid two fingers into her mouth. Ginny leaned over the crib, awash with love for her daughter. These moments before her children fell asleep held a peace she could not name.

"I wish I could undo my life."

Oh, Luke. Her heart ached for the unhappiness of an innocent little boy desperate for a mother's love. Until today, Ginny had not comprehended, *honestly* comprehended, all he'd endured.

Yes, she knew about his childhood.

She knew of Maxine's alcoholism.

She knew about the abuse.

But she had never stood in Luke's shoes until today, until Maxine Tucker had cried in her arms and wildly begged forgiveness over and over again.

Tearing the mother's heart in Ginny.

Her hand shook as she stroked her baby's soft hair. Leaning in, she set a dream kiss on Joselyn's sweet-smelling temple. *I love you so much, angel-mine.*

Had Maggie whispered the words to Luke once? Before the water took her?

Yes! Ginny thought, and her heart ached harder. How different life would have been for him had Maggie lived.

She should have encouraged counseling when she and Luke were married. Ah, but she had her share to atone.

Starting with Robby.

Robby who would've had his daddy's dark hair. Standing tall at twelve, like his daddy. Robby, the signature of *their* love. For in the moment of the baby's conception, they truly had loved each other. Beyond compare.

Shutting off the night lamp, Ginny glanced once more at her sleeping child. *Sweet lullabies, pookie.*

Downstairs she found Alexei at the kitchen table, catching up on the schoolwork he'd missed that morning.

Over his shoulder, she scanned the pages spread across the table. "Almost done?"

"Everything but English."

His most dreaded subject. And most beloved. "Mrs. Chollas's tutoring helping?"

"Sorta. Luke's Dictaphone works better."

A small trill hummed through her body. "I wish we'd thought of it before."

"Me, too." He looked dejectedly at the notebook where he'd written a number of sentences Ginny assumed had been with Mrs. Chollas's assistance. Above them, little rectangles were drawn around a list of singular words.

Word shapes.

An old concept, but new for her son.

She kissed his hair. "Use whatever works, baby. The end result is all that matters."

"Yeah, but sometimes it really sucks."

"Think so? I'm seeing a huge improvement." Which was true. Letters were more distinct, words more level to the line.

"Is Luke coming over tonight?"

Ginny checked the stove clock—8:14. "He said he'd be here by eight-thirty."

"I want to show him this." From under his binder, Alexei pulled out a sheet he'd finished. The writing was meticulous and correct; the sentences structured and complete.

Pride swelled her chest. She stroked a hand over her son's thin neck. "That'll make him happy, honey."

"I think he was sad today."

"I think so, too."

A knock sounded. Ginny went to the door. Luke stood in the dying light of day, potent and big shouldered in denim, his gray eyes intent on her face.

"Hey," she said on a wispy breath.

"Hey."

"Luke!" Alexei came through the kitchen, worksheet in hand. "Guess what?"

Luke closed the door behind him. "What, tiger?"

"Lookit this. That tape recorder you gave me really works."

Luke examined the page. "You are one clever kid, know that?"

"Yeah?" A beaming grin.

"Oh, yeah. Wanna be a lawyer one day?" He winked.

Alexei shrugged. "Maybe. Did you read what I wrote?"

A closer scan of the sheet. Alexei darted a look at Ginny. He hadn't shown her this page. That he shared it with Luke first spoke volumes.

Long seconds later, Luke lifted his head. "Powerful stuff, buddy."

"It's for this English project. We're supposed to do a three-minute oral presentation next Friday on anything we want long's it's not bad or slanderous. We're gonna be marked for content and stuff."

"You'll ace it, hands down."

"Can you help me do some research on your computer? We don't have high-speed Internet so it takes forever to use the search engines."

"You bet. Monday after school a good time?"

"All right!" Alexei spun back to the kitchen. "Gotta finish my other junk now."

"What was that all about?" Ginny whispered.

"Adoptions. His own mostly. Didn't you read it?"

A little puzzled, she shook her head. "Usually he tells me about anything major like this."

"He thinks we share a common link because of what I said last night."

She pressed her lips, kept back the tears. "You do, Luke. He's a good kid and he won't talk, especially if you ask him to keep anything personal close to his chest."

"You know," he said, rubbing his neck. "I've been racking my mind for a way to connect with him and here it falls into my lap. Boom. If I was into New Age nonsense, I'd call it fate."

"Maybe it is."

"Yeah, maybe." His eyes were charcoal. And he hadn't touched her yet. "Where is Robby's grave, Ginny?"

"In Charleston, West Virginia."

"I'm flying out to see it."

"Luke."

"I have the right to see his grave. Do you have a picture of him?"

"Yes." Her ribs hurt from the boxing of her heart. "I have a whole album of him." *Please, touch me. Touch my arm or my hand before I fall apart.* "I'll get it."

"Thank you."

Formal. Stoic. She walked to the stairs, went up to her bedroom, pulled the love-weary leather album from her night table. Would he look at it here? Or take it home?

Downstairs she handed over the photo book and he tucked it under his arm. "I'll bring it back Monday."

"Keep it as long as you need." *He's your son.* "Each picture has a date and description, but if something doesn't make sense or you have a question…"

"I'll call. Thanks," he said again.

"Luke," she said as he walked out onto the night-shrouded porch. *I want to sit with you, side by side, and explain every picture. I want to tell you how much I loved our baby. Still love our baby.* "Safe flight."

Moments later, she stood alone, staring at the stars. "Boone," she murmured. "If you're up there, help us."

Chapter Thirteen

At his kitchen table, Luke sat staring down at the brown leather photo album. The harsh lighting caught the embossed ridges of mountains and trees across the cover. A thousand thoughts plying his mind, he traced the grooves.

He'd been a father. For almost two weeks, he had been a daddy. His son had breathed while he breathed, opened his eyes upon waking as Luke did, yawned, cried.

And he had never known.

He blinked to ward off the tears and opened the album to the first page. Robby, she had written in her long, elegant writing. Stickers of hearts and balloons and flowers floated around the name. In a corner, she'd written "Our son, born on April 20, 1995—Tuesday's child, full of grace."

Was that why you couldn't live, little man? Heaven needed you?

He turned to the next page. And there was his son, looking up from an eight-by-ten photo in blazing, life-hued color.

A hard knot beat in Luke's throat. *Robby.*

His eyes were the navy blue of babies, not yet true, but still painfully beautiful. Spun thread, his dark lashes curled up in peewee fans. His mouth, smaller than a rose petal, was the only feature the baby had claimed from Ginny.

With a small shock, Luke saw himself.

In the shape of the baby's nose.

In those almond-formed eyes with their slightly turned down outer edges—a Nez Percé remnant all Tucker men inherited.

In the long, black hair touching ears no bigger than a thumbnail.

In the dark, linear lines that one day would evolve as straight, black brows.

Had he lived.

"Ah, little man." Tears blurred Luke's vision. He touched the tube trailing from Robby's nose and followed it off the page. "Wish I'd known you."

Bowing over the page, he leaned his forehead against his fists. Ginny wasn't at fault. She'd followed his will. He hadn't wanted a family. Hadn't wanted kids.

She had made this album. For them.

Our son, she'd written on that first page. She had included him. After everything, she'd included him.

But she hadn't contacted him. Would she have if Robby had lived?

Shaken, he looked through the book. Page by painful page. He saw her with Robby. Feeding him at her breast and later with a bottle and then leaning over the bassinet as only tubes fed into his minimouth.

He saw her rocking Robby in a chair. Holding him near her cheek with her eyes closed. As if dreaming of days to come. Or praying for his life.

Photo after photo.

Nurses with Robby.

Boone Franklin in his doctor's white lab coat, pens in his left breast pocket.

Robby crying. Robby receiving a clean diaper.

Robby discolored, fighting for a wisp of air.

And last of all, Robby's tiny headstone. The only tangible part of his son Luke would ever see.

Folding his arms over the page, he burrowed his face and let the tears come.

Alexei bounded up the steps of the Misty River Library. His mom was getting groceries with Joselyn so he had about an hour before she picked him up.

He hoped Mrs. Tucker had finished her storytelling. This Saturday, the day after the Nez Percé ceremony, he wasn't in the mood for storytelling. What he needed was Mrs. Tucker's help.

She was putting away the storybooks in the children's section.

"Mrs. Tucker?"

"Yes?" She turned around. "Oh, hello, Alexei. You just missed story time."

His face warmed. "We didn't get to town until now," he said. Which was the truth. He didn't add that he'd delayed his mom by telling her he wanted to complete his Google research on adoptions for his presentation.

"No matter," she said, smiling. "There's next week."

"Sure. Mrs. Tucker—" He stepped closer, looked around. "Can I talk to you privately?"

Her eyebrows pulled together. "Come with me." She led him into a small, book-cluttered office behind the checkout counter. Shutting the door, she asked, "What is it?"

"Does the legend, you know the one everyone was scared of, does it have anything to do with baby graves?"

Behind her glasses, Mrs. Tucker eyes narrowed. "Where did you hear such a thing, Alexei?"

"Does it?" he persisted.

"I've never heard of it. Is that a rumor going around at school? If it is, I'll talk to the principal myself and—"

"My mom and Luke were talking about it last night."

Mrs. Tucker blinked and for about five seconds stared at him. "What on earth for?"

Alexei released a breath. He thought the old woman might storm out of the office and never speak to him again. Luke was her son after all. Her adopted son, but still her son.

He said, "Luke asked my mom where Robby's grave was when I was in the kitchen. And she said in Charleston. And then he said something about flying out there today. I couldn't hear the rest. Then she went upstairs and got this photo album I've never seen." Mrs. Tucker's face was stone-gray. "Do you think the legend started there, in West Virginia?" Alexei frowned. "You okay, Mrs. Tucker?"

Her chin jerked, her eyelids blinked rapidly. "I'm fine." She went to the door, curled her fingers around the handle. "Alexei, do me a favor and tell Mrs. Stephens at the counter I won't be able to work for a few days."

"What? Where you going?"

"Home. I don't feel well."

"Mrs. Tucker?" He dogged her out of the library. "Want me to call my mom? She's at Safeway and can drive you…" But the old woman was hurrying down the sidewalk, acting as if she couldn't hear him. As if he'd made her sick with his question.

Late Saturday morning, Luke caught a flight out of Portland bound for Charleston. The night before he'd slept three hours—once he dragged himself to bed. And then he dreamed fitful, restless dreams about Maxine and Robby and Ginny. Dreams that woke him in a sweat and funneled an ache through his bones.

Sitting in the window seat of first class, he pushed an airline pillow under his head, closed his eyes and hoped the four-and-a-half hour flight granted him some rest. It didn't.

He thought of Ginny. Not as his wife or as the woman she was today, but as the high school girl he'd fallen in love with.

He remembered the moment he'd noticed her, *really* noticed her. He'd been twenty-one and finishing his first year of college; she was seventeen and finishing high school. Four years he'd known her as the kid from West Virginia, whose divorced dad had bought the house on the corner of their street.

But that May, weeks before her graduation, he'd come home after his college exams and there she was walking home one rainy afternoon with her knapsack over one shoulder and her bright hair doing sexy things down her back under a black umbrella.

He'd been sitting on the porch steps, debating whether to leave the next day, head back to Seattle, look for a decent-paying summer job, or give Bill Sr. at the Garage Center a call. Throughout high school, Luke had worked for the old man and the job was still there, waiting for him. If he could stand living with his mother one last summer.

Then he saw Ginny of the goddess hair. Of the woman's shape. Of the sweet and serious face. And he had called her name.

Instantly, she stopped, looked straight at him. At thirty feet, he hadn't discerned the color of her eyes.

"How's school these days?" he'd asked.

"Same as always. Some days boring, others interesting."

Not a tittering teen, but a wise woman. Intrigued, he coaxed, *"And today?"*

"We learned about Le Chatelier's principle."

He had stood then and walked down the pitted driveway to the sidewalk where she waited. At an arm's length, he slipped the heavy knapsack from her shoulder onto his own. She had green eyes with dark flecks. Dark as some river stones he skipped. And that quickly, he'd fallen in love. *"Tell me about Le Chatelier's principle while we walk to your house."*

Two days later on a moonless night he kissed her.

Two weeks later by the river's edge he made love to her.

Two months later in his old truck he asked her to marry him.

Now, twenty-three years later, he was flying two thousand miles to see the grave of their son.

At ten o'clock on Sunday Ginny picked up the kitchen phone on its second ring.

"Hi, Ginny," a deep voice said. *Luke?* "It's Jon Tucker." The air left her lungs. "Hey, Jon."

She hadn't heard from Luke since Friday night. Had he flown out to see their son's resting place?

"Just wanted to let you know we got the guys who damaged your preschool."

"You did?" She caught Alexei's gaze as he piggybacked Joselyn into the kitchen, Bargain on his heels.

"Yep, so you can tell your son his button theory was dead-on. It was the perp's jacket that lost it."

"He'll be thrilled to know that. Who were they?"

"The brother of a kid we sent to youth rehabilitation last summer for car theft and a dozen other crimes. Family's been in trouble before. Father rips off welfare, mother works as a cocktail waitress. Kids pretty much run wild."

The taunts Alexei had endured killed her sympathy. "What was their excuse this time?"

"They claim it was a prank to stir up the community. My hunch? To get back at Luke and me for putting the brother in detention. This kid knew Luke was helping you and that Seth was rebuilding the cottage. They were the link to me."

Her heart went out to him. "I'm glad you're chief here."

"That's what Rianne keeps saying."

Rianne, his wife. "I'd love to meet her one day."

"She says the same about you. So does Breena, Seth's wife. When Luke gets back we'll have a Tucker family barbecue at our house."

"Thanks. The kids will love it."

"It's a deal then."

She debated. "Jon? Is Luke…?"

"He's in West Virginia."

"Oh. I…um, didn't know he'd go so soon. I'm just…I'm worried about him." She felt foolish baring her heart to Jon.

"I know. If it's any consolation, he said he'll be back."

She pinched the bridge of her nose. Barred the swell of emotion. "I hope so," she whispered.

When she hung up, Alexei stood in front of her. "Mama?"

"Sit down, son. There's something you need to know."

Sunday morning, Luke drove from the hotel to the cemetery, which Ginny had written under the photo of the headstone. He parked the rental car on the street, then began walking the rows. A map attached to the album page had marked Robby's row and site number. He pictured Ginny unfolding and refolding the map a thousand times over the years, fraying its edges, thinning its creases. He imagined her returning one faraway day, in her twilight age. Her heart would have its sorrow yet, but her eyes would be dry. She might smile, remembering the sweetness of her baby's skin.

Will you let me come along, Ginny, and hold your hand?

A wind toyed with the tall oaks scattered across the hillside and assembled white clouds into horsetails. Overhead, the sun hailed its heat onto the granite and stone markers so in the distance they swayed, sails on water.

The next row was Robby's. Luke slowed his pace. His heart drummed in his chest, his palms sweated.

Thirty-two, thirty-three…

Thirty-five.

He stared at the tiny rectangular stone at home in the well-kept grass—then let his gaze weave slowly to the inscription.

Robert Luke Tucker

April 20, 1995–May 1, 1995

Beloved baby son of Luke and Ginny

At the foot of the stone she'd put "Robby, Angel of our hearts."

Over and over he read the words. Baby son. Angel of our hearts. Robby. Beloved. *Son.*

He crouched down, traced the coarse edges of cut stone where the words lay forever.

His boy. Flesh and bone of his body.

And Ginny's.

Ginny, carrying his baby for nine months.

Feeling Robby's first movements.

Crying in the pain of birth.

Suffering at the inexplicable end.

Alone and afraid. Because of him. Because of his arrogance and self-importance. So apprehensive that when Robby died, she couldn't explain their lung-damaged son to a man who scorned family.

Luke couldn't breathe. Couldn't stop the crazed race of his pulse. His chest hurt. He pressed a hand against the pain. *Robby! Ginny!* He believed he might die, right there, on the warm grass of his child's eternal home.

"I'm s-sorry, Ginny. So sorry."

He huddled over the stone, covered his face, waited for his heart to slow. *One thousand, two thousand, three thousand…*

Under his nose, the acrid odor of granite was sharp, the metal plate hot. When he realized he could analyze his surroundings, he sat back and mopped his face with his forearm.

For a minute, Luke listened to the birds in the trees. His heart and breathing settled. Stretching his right leg, he dug into his jeans pocket for his gift.

White with a thin track of amber through its center, the stone was one he'd found on Ginny's property. He turned the flat, round disc over in his palm. On the night before the Nez Percé ceremony, he'd taken a fine permanent marker and printed on one side: *"To Robby—Love, Dad."*

Carefully, he set the stone on the marker, beside the plate with its inscription.

"We would've skipped stones together, son," Luke murmured, then rose and retraced his steps through the maple-shaded lane.

He saw the cab parked a small distance behind his car before his mother came through the cemetery's entrance gate.

Luke stopped midstride. What the hell…?

He watched her approach, slow and steady, her feet in the no-nonsense black shoes of those with arthritis, a beige shawl wrapping her shoulders over a blue dress patterned in tiny white flowers. Her eyes regarded him behind her thick-rimmed glasses.

"Mother," he greeted when she stopped three feet away.

"Hello, Luke."

"What are you doing here?"

"Hoping to see you. Seems I timed my flight right."

Irritation nudged. She had helped with Ginny's land and now she figured she was back in his life? "Who told you I was here?" he demanded.

"Jon. He drove me to the Portland airport." Eyes searching, she looked down the lane. "You saw…?"

"Yes."

She took a step forward and he noticed her gray eyes were red. Weeping red. "Would you show me?"

Why? My son has nothing to do with you. But he moved aside and let her take his arm and they began the slow climb up the slope.

"Alexei was worried after he heard you and Ginny talking the other night," she said. "He came to me at the library, thinking this had to do with the legend."

"Have you told anyone?" Robby was no one's business but Ginny's and his own.

"Not even Jon."

Luke grunted. Neither had he told his brother the reason for the trip when he asked Jon to keep an eye on Ginny and the kids.

They walked in silence until he stood again at the little rectangular headstone. His rock gleamed with sunlight.

Maxine's fingers trembled on his arm, but she continued her hold. "After Maggie died, I was so afraid something would happen to you."

"I was with my father."

"Yes, but your daddy was only nineteen years old. Barely a man. And he…he was so lost without her."

Luke looked down at the woman clutching his arm. Her face turned to him. She went on, "You were Maggie's son. I was her twin. Our blood was the same, but you came from her. You had her eyes, her nose, her smile."

"You have the same. You were identical twins."

She shook her head, looked to the crest of the hill. "She was an innocent with a heart big as the moon. We'd known Travis since we were six. But he loved her, only her. When she died, he… He would've died too if not for you." Maxine gazed at the wispy clouds in the sky. "I told him I would look after you. I told him it didn't matter that he didn't love me. As long as we loved you. But I hoped—" she pressed her chest "—in here, that he would forget her one day, that he would come to love me, as well."

Luke stood motionless. His mind churned through the events of his life. His father's love. Maxine's dislike.

She continued. "At first, I understood. We were both grieving. But he never stopped and no matter what I said or did, he couldn't forget her. Because you had her face, her sweet smile. And I…" She looked at Luke. A tear dropped to the softness of her aged cheek. "I wish with all my heart I could make them better, those years. Turn back the clock, have another chance to be the mother you needed."

Forgive me. Her eyes pleaded. And for the first time, he recognized the torment in her soul. Twelve years he'd carried the same anguish. They had come full circle, he and Maxine. The risks she'd taken in marrying his father weren't unlike the risks Ginny would take in accepting him back into her life.

Alexei would stand in Luke's childhood shoes, a boy between parents. Joselyn was the baby Luke had been, handed from the spirit of one parent to the living replica of another.

God help him, but Luke did not want the past repeated. Not with the kids, Ginny or himself.

Here, he thought. *Here is where I leave it behind.* The past, the sorrows. Here, with his angel son.

He turned to the woman he'd known as his mother for over forty years and drew her into his arms. Against her gray hair, he murmured, "Let's go home, Ma."

From where she was painting a serene blue on the wall behind the bathroom door, Ginny heard the radio shut off in the cottage's front area. She stepped off the stool, laid down her brush. Around the door, she saw Luke walk toward her.

Her blood slowed at the sight of him in a black polo and gray chinos. His hair was crisp and dark and his eyes, oh, his eyes never let her go.

He stopped within reach. "I called but the radio was pretty loud."

A million thoughts mazed her mind. She couldn't track one except that he'd come back. To her.

His hand lifted, touched her chin. "You got a little here."

She brushed at the spot. "Gone?"

He stepped closer, rubbed gently with his thumb. "Gone." Then, pushing off her tea-towel bandanna, his hands were in her hair. "Ginny," he said and kissed her.

Afterward, he wrapped her against him and she couldn't find the energy to tell him that her big, old red shirt was covered in blue paint flecks and her ratty jeans streaked in plaster dust and that she would dirty his clean clothes.

"I saw Eva's car." His voice trembled against her ear. "She with Joselyn?"

"Yes. Until I finish painting."

"I'll help."

But he didn't let go. Against the scent of him she said, "The bathroom's all that's left."

He looked down at her. "How's Alexei?"

"He knows about Robby."

"How'd he take it?"

"With the questions of a ten-year-old. He's sad. And very excited to know more." She searched his eyes. "Jon told me you went to Charleston."

"I needed to see, Ginny. I needed..." He slipped his arms away, tucked his hands into his pockets. "Something."

Of their son. "Did you find it?"

His eyes, so serious. "I found I can't take the risk."

Of course. She'd always known, hadn't she? Still, his rejection tore the scars on her heart. She hugged her middle, held her bleeding self together. "I'm sorry for you, Luke."

"No," he said, tugging her across the room. "Come with me to the river. I want to show you something."

Under a cloudy sky that looked as bleak as she felt, he led her across the clearing, to the riverbank. They went down the path, over the rocky strip, to the sandy shoreline and the spot where they had loved ten days ago.

The river laughed its way to the Columbia. On tall skinny legs, a white-throated killdeer ran the sand, snapping bugs.

Luke picked up a small branch of driftwood. Hunkering on the sand, he drew a large heart. A second smaller one he carved inside. Within the center of this last heart, he clustered three white stones. A darker stone he set directly above them.

She watched intently. "What are you doing?"

He held out a hand and drew her down beside him. "When you were seventeen we came here one night and made love for the first time. Remember?"

"I've never forgotten," she said, hypnotized by his gray, gray eyes.

"Last week we made love for the first time since our divorce. Right here. And Thomas Many Moons celebrated the spirit of my mother here. Did you know I saw her walking along the shore that morning? She carried a baby in her arms."

Ginny pushed the lock of dark hair from his forehead. "Oh, Luke." Her heart hurt with love.

"You don't have to believe me. I didn't want to believe it either. But it was her. I looked up an old picture my dad had in a box he gave me when I was a kid. She was there. In the same dress, with her red hair blowing in the wind. Me in her arms. She was laughing into the camera. I stared at the photo for an hour. *An hour.* And knew."

"I believe you." And she did. A mother's heart never abandons her children.

His mouth curved a tiny smile. "Then I went out to Charleston. I read your words about Robby. *Angel of our hearts.* He's in good care, Ginny. He's with his grandmother. *I saw it.*"

Holding back tears, Ginny bit her bottom lip.

"So you see," he said, "the risk I couldn't take was losing you and Alexei and Joselyn. I love those kids like they're my own. And *you.* Ah, babe…"

"Luke…"

Pointing to the smaller heart, he explained, "That's you holding the kids. This is me—" he traced the line of the larger heart "—holding all of us." He touched her cheek where a tear fell. "I never stopped loving you, Ginny," he whispered. "Never."

Lyrics, serenading her heart. Rushing through each cell of her body. Healing her soul.

Kneeling there on the sand, she held his dear face in her paint-splattered hands, and kissed him.

Tasted the salt of their tears.

"I love you, Luke. With every beat of my heart. Will you marry me again? Will you raise my children, and any others should we be so lucky, together with me? Will you grow old with me this time?"

He laughed, caught her to him and brought her to the cool, damp sand. She felt only the warmth of him, the peace in him. "Ah, Ginny. I'll marry you today, tomorrow, whenever you wish."

Her grin was full of wonder and joy. "Let's tell Alexei tonight and let him choose the date."

A flicker of worry. "Will he be okay with…us?"

She smoothed two fingers across his brow. "He said we've come full circle."

"Kid's smart as a whip."

"He is."

Above them, the clouds broke apart and the sun lit the trees and banks and twinkled on the water. But in his eyes, her heart shone like fire.

* * * * *

Look for Rachel's story coming in December 2006.

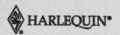

HARLEQUIN®

American ROMANCE®

IS THRILLED TO BRING YOU A
HEARTWARMING MINISERIES BY
BESTSELLING AUTHOR

Judy Christenberry

Separated during childhood, five siblings from the
Lone Star state are destined to rediscover one another,
find true love and a build a Texas-sized family legacy
they can call their own....

You won't want to miss the fifth and
final installment of this beloved family saga!

VANESSA'S MATCH
On sale June 2006 (HAR#1117)

Also look for:

REBECCA'S LITTLE SECRET
On sale September 2004 (HAR#1033)

RACHEL'S COWBOY
On sale March 2005 (HAR#1058)

A SOLDIER'S RETURN
On sale July 2005 (HAR#1073)

A TEXAS FAMILY REUNION
On sale January 2006 (HAR #1097)

HOTEL MARCHAND

Four sisters.
A family legacy.
And someone is out to destroy it.

A captivating new limited continuity, launching June 2006

The most beautiful hotel in New Orleans,
and someone is out to destroy it. But mystery,
danger and some surprising family revelations
and discoveries won't stop the Marchand sisters
from protecting their birthright...
and finding love along the way.

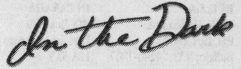

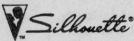

COMING NEXT MONTH